The Forge
and
the Forest

The Forge
and
the Forest

BETTY UNDERWOOD

1975

Houghton Mifflin Company Boston

Special thanks to Marilyn Burns McCullough

C – 1
6.95
12-80

Library of Congress Cataloging in Publication Data

Underwood, Betty.
    The forge and the forest.

    SUMMARY: An orphaned French girl's life becomes
a turmoil of conflicting emotions toward the iron-
willed pastor who is her guardian, the growing abolitionist movement, and the role of women in her society.
    [1. New England — Social life and customs — Fiction.
2. Abolitionists — Fiction] I. Title.
PZ7.U419Fo   [Fic]   74-29448
ISBN 0-395-20492-5

To Ray
from
Mea
who would
sometimes
have felt
alone
in this world
but
for him

The Forge
and
the Forest

1

November 1834

The coach door slammed, choking off the sound of the baby's wail.

The driver shouted. The cavernous wood body of the Concord coach bounced in its crude leather straps, the running gear quivered, then to the beat of hoofs and jangle of harness they rumbled into the road.

Bernadette craned around Robb McIves to catch a last glimpse of her Canterbury cousins, especially mother Hester jiggling baby Rachel.

Suddenly Bernadette burst from her seat, crouched by the door, waving frantically.

Hester, David, Paul, Rachel . . . and behind them the high-roofed schoolhouse of Prudence Crandall, a few marching windows still flashing in the morning sun, those that weren't boarded up.

"Sit down," Pastor Robb McIves commanded.

She turned from the window, squeezed in between Pastor and another large fellow. What kept her from sobbing was needing not to bump people with her elbows and knees; in the last year they'd grown to be such an aggravation to her.

"That's better," Robb McIves declared. "Let's not waste good learning time caterwauling, Bernadette. You know why I'm taking you home with me; I've promised your great-uncle to mold you into a pious Christian female."

Knee to knee across from her, two mittened old ladies bent with startled raptness to the young minister's brisk words.

First overcome by farewell emotion, now by embarrassment, Bernadette ducked her chin into her cloak.

"God has a plan for the world and we're bound fast by it, child. Doubtless in Montreal some priest taught you God's mercy could be bought."

"Our old priest," Bernadette stammered, "never sold me anything."

Scowling under his Russian fur hat, Pastor McIves chose to ignore her remark. "Well, the truth is, you can't buy your way, no, nor pray your way into heaven . . ."

All of a sudden the coach fell into an enormous turnpike pothole.

The elderly maiden ladies flew off their seats into the air, came down blinking like reproachful owls. Smothering panic, Bernadette fought off heavy bodies pressing against her.

"What's the matter with that driver?" a passenger growled, poked his head out the window, shouted, "Easy! Can't you see?"

"Easy yourself!" the distant derisive reply floated back. "Keep your nose in and let me drive."

"Fie!" one of the maiden ladies gasped.

"He's a surly sort, that one," the passenger declared. "Complained my package was too big for the baggage boat and threw it up on top."

Impatiently, Robb McIves leaned toward Bernadette. "Never mind them. Pay attention, Bernadette. Ever since

2

Eve led Adam to sin, two great systems have underlain Christianity. If there's original sin in man because of Eve, with God's help there's also free will to choose good."

"Yes, sir," she murmured, very glad at his mention of free will. Ever since she'd come out of Canada she'd heard a marvelous lot about sinning; sinning didn't suit her. But fast travel and rough road were making it hard to concentrate on Pastor's weighty words.

Without warning, they bounced into three potholes in a row; grumbling passengers were just resettling themselves when the coach swooped downhill. Involuntarily Bernadette shut her eyes to block out woods which weren't autumn brown and gold anymore but a streak of amber. The thud of the horses' hoofs beat an excited tattoo under them.

"God have mercy," Pastor McIves breathed in her ear. "What *is* wrong with that fellow?"

When they finally leveled into a long running stretch, the man who'd shouted out the window spoke up grimly, "I'll tell you what's wrong with our coachman. He's under the influence."

Influence? Bernadette turned wondering brown eyes up to Pastor McIves.

"Drunk," Robb said in disgust.

"Oh, dear!" the old ladies gasped.

But even though it was hard to hang on, Pastor wouldn't give up. "It makes an enormous problem, Bernadette," he recommenced intently. "If God ordains man's fate, the struggle to be saved for heaven seems useless. In Connecticut, New Lights shout man *can* perfect himself; Old Lights shout back original sin makes man powerless."

Picturesque phrases, *New Lights, Old Lights,* quarrelsome phrases which caught her unwilling fancy. "Are you Old or New Light?" she asked.

"Both," he replied after a pause. "My minister father

3

taught me man doesn't freely choose to love his Lord better than himself — that's depravity. Yet my temperament makes me side with the new evangelism — we *can* turn from selfishness to good works . . ."

She was about to exclaim she was glad he was more of a New Light when there was a stunning crash and the coach tipped crazily. "Wheel hit a stump," Robb breathed, raising his head from its ducked position.

"Look!" she pointed.

"Baggage!" someone shouted. "It's falling off!"

"My carpetbag!" the man at the window roared, waving his fist. "Pick that stuff up, you fool!"

But they rushed on, wheels grinding; and no reply from the coachman — instead, a sudden loud singing:

> *I'll hide behind a bunch of thistle*
> *And shoot ye dead with a great hoss pistol . . .*

Abruptly, young Pastor McIves pulled Bernadette over to him, put both hands over her ears, mashing her bonnet. When he let her go, the singing up above had subsided into an indistinct roar.

In a loud, determined voice Pastor declared, "Clergymen are the ones who present the salvation experience in all its rapturous release from despair." Her new guardian laid down the gauntlet severely: "Under my roof you're to make spiritual progress. You must examine yourself daily for error, confide in me what sin you find. When you're converted you'll take membership in my church."

She came to life with a start. "Belong to *your* church?" she exclaimed, thinking in twelve-year-old horror of the Iron Gods she'd discovered in Ohio and Canterbury. "I like Catholics better; I liked going to Mass when I was little. In Canada, God loved me and I trusted *Him*."

"I'd think by now," Robb answered between his teeth, "you'd know enough not to speak of Catholics."

4

"Quakers have a fine, quiet way of worship." Desperately she tried another tack. "I went to some of their silent meetings with Miss Crandall's black girls."

"So I've been told," he answered, "and was shocked. Quakers haven't a creed, liturgy, even a priesthood. Don't mention Quakers; as you grow in faith you'll forget them."

"I don't believe so," she dared to protest honestly.

"Child, child, I'll make it all clear to you later. But that's enough about piety. Now I want to talk to you about the duties and place of females — "

What he was going to say about females was forever lost to her because they careened around a curve; there was a sickening sideways skid, a massive tilt; far away skirled the high, hysterical *halloo* of the *influenced* driver's voice.

She fell in a thumping crush of bodies, legs, arms, down, down, and then she was alone, arcing through the air. She struck the earth; her whole head turned fiery with pain.

Blackness . . .

She roused to a hand on her cheek, a hand which brushed something from her skin but in the brushing, stung unbearably. Her ears rang, her eyes opened but wouldn't see; she was prisoner to sense of feel and smell. She felt the hand move to her forehead, push back her hair, fumble for her bonnet ribbons. She smelled . . . tobacco? Worsted wool? With the smell came the dim realization of an arm beneath her shoulders, of a big, stooped-over presence.

Sound rushed back. "Bernadette!" the voice kept saying while the hand picked at her cheek. She jerked away protestingly; her eyes flew open, focused.

It was Pastor McIves on one knee beside her. She saw his face wore a look of fervid personal anxiety — nothing demanding, commanding, censorious.

"The coach went over," he mumbled, getting his arm under her legs, picking her up. "You were thrown outside."

5

She peered dizzily around, saw she'd rolled down a slope. Above, the coach sprawled on its side, one of its wheels still turning mindlessly in the air, the nervous animals free and bunched beside it, the handful of passengers standing in a circle watching the Pastor and her. She even saw how the coachman sat, apart, his head in his hands, his whip dangling remorsefully between his knees. With an inward, dotty laugh she knew Pastor must have managed to spill out a scalding kettle of words even in the act of rescuing her.

"She broke any bones?" someone called.

Holding her high against his chest, Pastor looked questioningly at her. Then gently he put her feet on the ground and loosed his hold. She swayed; she stood. Nothing hurt but her head.

"No," he called back, "the Lord be praised."

With his firm hand on her waist, he pushed her up the bank.

"I wish there were someone besides two addled old women to help you," he fretted, looking uneasily at the upset coach surrounded by men deep in argument on how to right it.

"Don't worry about me," she assured him shyly, seeing his look. "I'll sit right here."

She rested her head on her knees, lassitude engulfing her. Faraway she heard his voice raised in command; she looked up once, saw him throw his coat on the ground, saw his shirt sleeves stark white against the pine woods. He began to strain powerfully with the others against the coach body.

Would they get it up? *I'm too dizzy to care,* she mused, her head still marvelously light. What seemed to be in her head? . . . Just memories.

A ten-year-old orphan in Montreal living with old Tante Cécile. Her American mother dead from coughing, her French father lost in a northern silence. Great-uncle Marcus Gray from the Western Reserve of Ohio come to fetch her because Tante had run out of money. She and Uncle Marcus growing to love each other: "*You were slimsy with chestnut-pod hair and moved like a moth in your summer white dress and you wanted to make a proper impress but when you talked English it was shy and funny . . . but pretty, ah, ever so pretty, lovey.*"

The farm Uncle Marcus had brought her to had been laboriously cut out of the dense virgin buttonwood forests of northern Ohio; he and Aunt Leah'd just moved from a log house into a proper New England dream house of sawn siding with insides of shiny black walnut.

There'd been a lot of work on that farm for a girl who'd not known much of toting, weaving, hoeing; Bernadette hadn't even got to attend the settlement school and that'd been hard because in Montreal she'd gone to the sisters since she was four, the nuns who loved to watch her draw, clapping their hands delightedly. (But school was most of all where friends were; in careless high spirits she'd ruled a claque of friends whose faces now floated before her.)

How had she got to school in Ohio? Well, one day she'd come in from the orchard to find the biggest man she'd ever seen sitting in the farm kitchen. He was dark in a different way from her own swarthy papa, fair-skinned with crisp, curling black hair, black gashes for brows, a broad-shouldered, rugged virility warring with harsh spirituality; she — even then — sensed the two must be held together by an iron will. His eyes were a beautiful gray and so level, so probing, she'd fallen instantly captive to them and forgot her curtsy.

He was the fascinating twenty-six-year-old pastor of the settlement church who right now on this Connecticut road was shouting, "Back the team into the traces, easy now!"

Robb McIves had asked her spelling and arithmetic questions. Later she'd overheard him saying to Uncle Marcus she was bright and comely and being foreign and

7

orphan, school would keep her from sinking into a bad end, whatever that was. The very next day, Uncle Marcus had sent Bernadette to the rough little settlement school where, looking up the word "comely" in the dictionary, she'd been amazed to find it hadn't a thing to do with going somewhere.

One time Robb McIves had galloped by that schoolyard, put her up on his horse and ridden through the deep forest to that scandalous school called Oberlin being hacked out of a damp plain a few miles from the farm. Oberlin would be the first college in the world to take girls. "Bernadette, if you went here, you could have a proper young ladies' seminary in a proper New England village, a safe, genteel life for a lone female," he'd said.

In the twilight, with fires burning and pungent smoke rising from felled logs, she'd tried to imagine the buildings and lawns of a college. Studying the disordered clearing, a primal seed took root in her. Bernadette Savard, French orphan, mistress of a proper school? Most of all, mistress of her own self, beholden to no one?

But Robb hadn't let her savor her new daydream long. They'd taken supper with a family in one of the clearing's crude huts, where he came to visit golden-haired Emma Reece of Cincinnati, seventeen summers old and exquisite as a bird. When folks around that table talked soberly of how a few women would walk seven miles every day to Oberlin, Emma had smiled sweetly at Pastor McIves and declared there were more ways a female could serve the Lord than hiking to college. Later, Pastor's hand had rested briefly on Emma Reece's waist as the two had stood together, he looking far down, she with her fair head tilted up. His face had worn a tender intensity; on the beautiful Miss Reece's pale face Bernadette had thought there'd been a puzzling expression — something like the way the hired man looked when he got first crack at the cherry cake.

8

Hugging her romantic discovery, Bernadette had clung to Pastor McIves on the rough horseback journey back to the farm. When the hunting cry of a hungry bobcat had screamed close by, he'd shown no fear. She'd dozed, head on his scratchy back: in her dream she wasn't twelve and gangly and beginning to be more swelled out in front than was handy, but compact and fair and seventeen and never said Z for *th.*

She'd lived just a year in Ohio, though. One night she'd gone out to the barn to fetch Uncle Marcus and, much upset, he'd told her she was to travel to Connecticut to live with his daughter Hester and help care for her when her second child came. Uncle Marcus had said the young pastor was set on the plan, too — Canterbury had a fine female seminary that would ready her for Oberlin.

A year before, when she'd been taken from Montreal, she'd cried "Why?" in anguish, but nothing had saved her. This time a great nothingness — a great no-feeling — had filled her. "It's all right," she'd said quietly, putting her arms around Uncle Marcus's neck while he wept. "Uncle Marcus, it's all right . . ."

Farewell to Pastor McIves had been different. It turned out everyone already knew he was going to marry Miss Reece, so Bernadette hadn't had the grand importance of passing out exciting secrets. He hadn't said anything to her of this, though, when he'd ridden out to wish her Godspeed.

"I'm leaving, too," he'd confided as they'd walked up the lane together, he leading his horse. "I've a church in the fine township of Salisbury in the mountains of western Connecticut."

The young pastor had suddenly looked down at her; their eyes had fastened in that tangled, disquieting way she'd never understood. "Come back to Oberlin, Bernadette. Without proper goals people drift into paths of sin. You've mind and

9

heart enough to be a teacher; now let's see if you've backbone enough."

Her chin had come out at his challenge. "I *will* come back."

"Good!" he'd exclaimed, slapping his boot with his crop. Then he'd slung his body up into the saddle and sat looking down at her. To her amazement, he'd pulled from his coat pocket her little Bible he'd once confiscated because it was French and Catholic.

"Read to me from this Book," he'd commanded.

"What shall I read?" she'd stammered.

"Try the thirteenth chapter of First Corinthians."

Hurriedly, she'd found the place, her hand trembling.

"Quand je parlerais toutes les langues des hommes, et même des anges . . .", she'd read breathlessly.

"Go on," his voice had urged, far above her.

" . . . la charité est patiente, elle est douce, la charité n'est pas envieuse . . . "

She'd stopped, looked up, been struck dumb by an emotional expression she couldn't fathom. "Your words," he'd said tersely, "sound like music."

He'd leaned down, put his hand on her head, took it away quickly as though her hair burned his touch.

Then he'd flicked his reins and galloped down the road.

Watching him go, she'd been sure she would never see him again.

"Wake up!" his voice called. She lifted her head out of her arms, blinked. The stagecoach, upright, stood waiting. High on the seat was a subdued, white-faced driver.

Like two fates, the maiden ladies, remarkably undamaged, sat upright in their places. With their bundles, reticules, mantles, bonnets, flannel petticoats, galoshes, mittens, peppermints (not shared), smelling salts, spectacles, nods, smirks, frowns, stares, they were ready for more pious busyness.

2

THEY JOGGED ALONG like a farm wagon loaded with egg buckets. For an hour Robb had been talking about the duties of women, Bible phrases rolling from him: "The head of every woman is man"; "Ye wives, be in subjection to your husbands . . ."

Still, training her was going to be difficult, he was concluding, because, while she must be as obedient to him as his wife, Emma, was, as a lone schoolmarm he must create her strong enough not to be tempted by an "unsupervised" life.

He fell morosely silent as he thrashed around in this psychic thicket; the old ladies sucked peppermints in a grim delirium of waiting.

It gave Bernadette time to feel her inner loneliness; the pain of the farewell to her Canterbury family combined with anxiety over Robb McIves's enormous expectations of her. All the inside pain, mixed up with her outside scratches and bruises . . .

On the wintry Connecticut River, flat-bottomed, cabinless freight scows passed; a log raft from the north spread brown and viscous on the water's surface.

They came spanking into Hartford, its busy streets full of carts, chaises, horses. Let loose from the shackles of Pastor's admonitions and the absorption of the ladies across the aisle, Bernadette eyed the city. In the twilight it seemed a

fascinating collage of motion, color, sound; her leaden spirits
— always hard to weigh down — took flight.

A pox on despotic gods and meek women! she decided
sturdily, wanting to run up and down the dusky Hartford
streets, peer into windows full of fancies and foofaraws. She
was a French girl; French girls set store by fancies and
foofaraws.

She shared a frigid hostel room with the two maiden
ladies. Since it seemed they knew as much about the making
of Christian females as he did, the door was hardly closed
before they began to lecture her where Pastor McIves had
left off.

It was rude of her to close her eyes before the candle was
snuffed, and right in the middle of sentences issuing simulta-
neously from both old ladies.

But her bones ached, her head throbbed.

She fell asleep.

Sun in a brilliant sky, she chased after Pastor McIves on his
business — to the booksellers, the bookbinders, the bell-
maker (for the church), to a seller of whip lashes and one of
morocco leather, even to the wallpaperer for a scrap of
wallpaper for Emma's entry. She was lingering in front of a
bonnet shop when he took her by the arm.

"Hurry, Bernadette. I must see Lewis Weld before we
catch the stagecoach."

The house he took her to was small and plain, the
sober-faced man who met them at the door the same.

She knew she must absolutely not distract talking gentlemen; so she sat primly on the edge of the slippery black
couch, feet together, skirt spread properly to hide her scuffed
shoes, hands piously folded, her gaze fixed in careful
blindness on a picture on the opposite wall. With a shudder,
she suddenly realized this was an engraving of Abraham

12

about to sacrifice his son Isaac on the mountain at Moriah, and her attention fled this savagery. It was boring simply to look in her lap; she wished she had something to draw with — drawing rescued lots of bored hours. But without paper, without pen, she began to eavesdrop instead on the two men in the adjoining parlor.

"What did Theodore write you about the Lane Seminary debates?" Robb was asking.

"My brother said he frankly planned them to advance antislavery and to undermine the Colonization Society's grip on the Lane students."

"Colonization's plan to send a trickle of blacks back to Africa is nonsense and no solution to slavery. Do you realize Theodore's debate could wake a sleeping nation to the slave issue?"

Bernadette had to lean forward to catch the two men's excited murmuring. She wasn't sure she was making proper sense of it, but if she were, at a divinity school called Lane Seminary in Cincinnati a man named Theodore Weld — brother to the man in the next room — had defied the president of the school, the famous clergyman Lyman Beecher, led eighteen nights of hot debate on slavery and brought the reluctant students — many of them southern — to a rousing stand against it. Triumphantly, Robb was predicting the country would hear of these debates; agitation for free speech and antislavery was already erupting on northern campuses, he claimed.

Antislavery. *Abolition*, it was called. In Canterbury, Bernadette herself had come to believe in abolition. Terrible things had happened last year in Canterbury.

"Who's Theodore Weld?" she asked curiously as they hurried back to the inn.

Robb shot her a surprised look.

"You were listening?"

13

"Yes, sir."

"Well, I suppose it's instructive even for a girl to learn of a saint who makes religion and antislavery identical . . . Brother Weld's dedicating his life to purging slavery from the land."

"Where did you meet him, please sir?"

"At Lane Seminary during the cholera epidemic. For nights Weld went without sleep to hold sick and dying men. Weld and I worked there together, Bernadette."

"Yes, but where is he *now?*" she persisted.

"After the Lane debates Weld and his student followers began to teach free Cincinnati blacks. But Cincinnati folk finally accused them of consorting with black females; so the seminary banned all consideration of slavery. Weld advised the students to ignore the ban. Bernadette . . . you're dawdling."

"Then what happened?" she panted.

"The faculty wouldn't lift the ban; so last summer Weld and fifty-one students walked out."

While their baggage was being stowed she wondered about this Mr. Weld, this man who declared slavery was everyone's religion and boldly associated with blacks. He couldn't look like his Hartford brother — safe, dull, and middle-aged. No, she was sure a man who'd hold dying cholera patients would have a totally different aspect. A vague picture flashed into her hungry girl's mind — a face burning with inner flame, fair, curling hair, a clear, ringing voice, lean, young, leonine grace . . .

Once they were settled on the stage, Bernadette's wonder overcame her fear of starting Pastor McIves to lecturing again.

"Well, where did he go when he left?"

Pastor's face was a study until he remembered. "Theodore, you mean?" he finally grunted. "The students who

14

followed him are living in Cumminsville, working again among free blacks."

"And is *he* with them?"

Robb sighed impatiently. "You're remarkably insistent. No, he's not. I had a letter from Theodore saying one of Oberlin's founders was urging him to come to Oberlin as professor of theology and bring the other Lane antislavery rebels up there."

Oberlin! I'll be there in just a few years! "Will he do that?"

Robb shook his head. "He's going to be an agent for the new National Antislavery Society. Theodore intends — single-handedly, if need be — to convert the whole Ohio country to antislavery. He begs rides, walks in all weather, lives on less than eight dollars a week. The rest of the Lane students may go up to Oberlin, though."

"He must be *very* brave," she breathed thoughtfully.

"Who, Weld? My dear child, Theo's lit by a fire. It won't take long for *him* to abolitionize Ohio — *combustionize*, he calls it . . ."

Eventually they got off at Litchfield, a peaceful town with mountains for a backdrop. Robb pointed out to her the fine law school and the big house which had once belonged to Ethan Allen. They walked carefully around Litchfield girls' academy, where she observed every brick and pillar and stared shamelessly at a procession of marching girls. In bright fantasy, she herself was the proud and independent young teacher at the head of their column.

At Limerock next day they lost the last passenger. Now that they were at last alone in the thickening dusk, Robb seemed to change.

"It must have been fearfully hard to leave Canterbury. You don't know me very well; you don't know Mrs. McIves at all."

15

"That's right," she allowed in a low voice.

"Well, then, perhaps you wouldn't feel so strange if I told you about us."

"Maybe I wouldn't," she agreed hopefully.

"There's not much to know about me. My brothers and I were brought up on a farm near Hartford. Father was a minister in the days when the church ran Connecticut; he and his friends used to pick the governor over their ale and pipes. Father wanted me to go to Yale, but I wanted to convert the frontier so I set out for Ohio and Western Reserve in '26. It takes strong character to stand the rough conditions of a backwoods school; remember that at Oberlin, Bernadette. Well, in three years I was done in Ohio and back to Yale Seminary, but done at Yale I went right back to the Ohio frontier. My first charge was the settlement church, and frankly, I couldn't have lived through those two years without your Uncle Marcus."

He sounded as though he were flipping the pages of a book.

Where in his telling was a small boy, a boy running and hollering with brothers, a venturesome country boy, a dawdling schoolboy; yes, a bad boy, too? she wondered.

"Was your mother alive to be with you?"

He was amused at her anxious orphan's question. "Yes, she's alive; she does my father's bidding."

What must it be like to remember only that a mother does a father's bidding?

"How did you decide to be a pastor?" she asked after a time of looking out the window, thinking.

"Living under my father's roof, I never thought of being else, Bernadette. I started to worry about God when I was a child playing in my father's study. Endlessly I thought about my inner self, judged myself by divine rule."

A rush of feeling overtook her for that hagridden little son.

"Inevitably, doubts later swamped me. My seminary days were agony; I was often sick with despair." At last his voice grew personal, passionate. "But finally I realized no matter how I battled, I could never find the final answer to my search because that truth was the Lord's. So I laid down my inner struggle and it's never overwhelmed me since. I was able to pass my ordination examination at Presbytery."

There was a long silence during which she tried to make meaningful what he'd told her. Tried, failed. Failed because his God was different from hers and had made a different boy and man. A merciful and reliable God watched over her; His face seemed to shine ever more luminous in her. *Despair? Doubt? Battle? Why?* She longed to reach out and touch this man whose young memories seemed to her so thin, harsh, comfortless.

But she was afraid to touch him.

"Well, in any case, it's in action that the man of God can make his mark and keep himself from devouring uncertainties," he finally spoke up decidedly. "Think of the problems the world has! A new wind blows in the land, a wind of reform. Frontier evangelism, Indian mission societies, temperance, and now antislavery . . . for a long time I didn't give much heed to slavery."

"Why do you now?" she wondered.

"From Yale one summer I went to Virginia for the American Bible Society and saw my first slave coffle, a line of men marching through the dust beside the road. They were chained from neck to neck and the master had a whip. I couldn't love those low, dirty, sore-covered slaves, yet my rage cried out for them. Often I'd been disappointed in my search for a God of mercy but up to then I'd always felt Him just, Bernadette. It was unjust to drive human souls down the road like animals. It was unjust, against the laws of God."

17

His voice shook.

"Yes, sir," she murmured in sympathy.

"Still, even that coffle slowly sank from my mind. Then I went to Cincinnati to Lane Seminary and met Theodore Weld. We talked of slavery, and he set me to read and ponder. On my wedding trip I went back to Weld. From that second visit I came out a deep convert to the abolition cause. I'll work for it till I drop, God willing."

"Making friends with Miriam Hosking at Miss Crandall's black school made me believe like you," she confided cheerfully.

How quickly his voice changed!

"I thoroughly disapprove your befriending a black; everyone knows the moral estate of the free black is low. And of course, one can't believe in antislavery just because of personal friendship."

"Why not?" she asked simply. "Miriam Hosking's a good reason all in herself why there shouldn't be slaves."

He moved impatiently, sighed.

"Antislavery's too weighty a subject for a girl. With God's guidance, I want to show you a proper woman's sphere, Bernadette. Trust and follow me; I have your interest at heart."

He put his arm around her shoulder; for some reason he as quickly took it away.

She remembered he'd never got around to his wife.

"What about Mrs. McIves?" she asked.

"Oh, yes," he answered absently. "Her father was a Cincinnati pork-packer. She was brought up a pious child."

"I'll never forget that time I saw her," Bernadette confided. "I still had my French accent and it bothered everyone, and I thought how wonderful it'd be to talk like her. She was so little; she had yellow hair and wore a pewter comb."

18

"She did?" he asked, still in the same offhand way.

"At Oberlin it was. Remember when you took me on your horse to Oberlin?"

"Yes."

And then he didn't seem to want to talk about himself or his wife anymore. But their silence was friendly.

They coached past Salisbury and on to Furnace Village. It grew late, dark. To her amazement, an intermittent ruddy shaft quivered like heat lightning in the evening sky; blast furnaces for iron, he explained. They walked to the livery stable to hire a wagon and an old horse to transport her trunk and themselves to his house on the edge of the village.

He pointed out his new church to her; its slender spire briefly cleaved the red shadows. She looked up at him; his profile was suddenly bronzed. The glow dimmed; his face melded into the mysterious evening shade. With its smoky air and red horizon, Furnace Village seemed to her like a Halloween place.

"You'll find Mrs. McIves unwell," he told her stiffly at his threshold.

He threw the door open. Looking into the drawn, gray face of his little wife, his wife who was more ghost than woman, Bernadette was shocked speechless at the change in Emma McIves. Where was the lively, beautiful, gold-haired, pewter-combed girl of Ohio?

She turned in consternation to Paster McIves.

His glance was cool, impassive, unanswering.

At the very act of crossing his own sill, her new-found Limerock friend vanished.

3

SHE STARED out the window, rubbed her eyes, looked again: sooty mist churned everywhere. Nighttime flicker above the trees had dyed Pastor's face. Iron furnaces! But would all their days be lived in a thick haze?

Dismayed, she threw on her clothes, listening for the noise which had waked her — a pulsating grunt, deep and unearthly. Now came a second sound and this one she recognized — somewhere close by, a screeching water wheel turned.

She ran down the steep stairwell, crossed the tiny hall, unbolted the door and rushed outside.

So this was her new world! she thought, stunned, clinging to the fence.

Across the road were dim outlines of houses and sheds; she had a sense that to the left lay village, to the right open country. Somewhere a road wound through the valley, somewhere were mountain summits, those blue black Berkshires whose shadows the coach had rumbled under. After the sunlit Firelands fields and the Canterbury farm's rolling green meadows, she'd smother here.

Canterbury. She clung to the fence post, shut her eyes, shut herself away from this seething place, remembering a more familiar place.

Canterbury, Connecticut, where she, the orphan traveler, Bernadette Savard, had come a year ago June to live on the farm of her cousins, the Frys.

20

Rachel, the baby she loved, born right after she'd got there . . .

Hard work. Wondering if school would *ever* begin and lift the yoke . . .

And then the door of Miss Prudence Crandall's fine Canterbury seminary shockingly slammed against her — because the Abolitionist schoolmarm, angered by Canterbury's starchy objection to her one black student, had dismissed all her white girls and turned the seminary into a black one.

At first, Bernadette had felt just as mad and balked as everybody else. Then, listening to all the abusive talk, frustration began to war with secret sympathy for the put-upon schoolmistress.

About then, the black seminary student, Miriam Hosking, was stoned on the Scotland Road and Bernadette had helped her. Afterwards had begun the slow growth of a trusting friendship . . .

And finally Bernadette was at the seminary the night vandals had smashed the windows and downstairs rooms. After the terrifying attack, letting go Miriam's hand, jumping into a dark sea of grass, running home, she sensed the hurried goodbye would be their last . . .

The school brought down, the girls and the mistress fled, the great house empty.

Oh, Bernadette had visited the schoolyard, scuffed through the leaves, sat by the mossy dead fountain, thought of how Miriam at one of Miss Crandall's court trials had testified Canterbury was a beautiful place except for the want of civilized people. Rubbing the moss, thinking how the empty house must echo inside, it'd come to Bernadette that civilized people were the best thing there could be in a place.

Soon after, Robb McIves had dropped in to visit Marcus Gray's grandniece. "But she *must* go to a good school to get into Oberlin," he'd first said urgently; then later thought-

21

fully, "My wife's been ill and we've no reliable help. We've a *very* good female school."

Knowing in her bones there'd soon be another move . . .

Canterbury, she sighed, her mind coming back to the murk around her. Canterbury hadn't smelled like this sooty bog; in Canterbury you could see to get around, didn't have to creep like a blind bat everywhere.

Footsteps sounded on the path behind her. "Without a shawl you'll take a chill," Robb McIves remarked matter-of-factly.

"Is the air always like this?"

"No. Wind's wrong this morning. Usually we see across the road, past the meadows to the forest and a mountain ridge. The furnace is behind us, at the mouth of the lake. The noise of the bellows bothers Mrs. McIves but I'm used to it."

So the air wasn't always like this! She breathed a gusty sigh of relief, turned, inspected his still-impassive face. "I'll go in and light the fire," she offered hastily.

But when she entered the kitchen, a fire already warmed the room; Emma McIves knelt in front of the narrow hearth. By now Bernadette was adept at what she must do in strange kitchens: she took down three plates and cups from the dish rail.

"Good morning, Bernadette," Emma said, straightening up.

By daylight, bone-thin Emma McIves looked poorer than by candlelight. Her hair under her cap was still a glorious color, but as Bernadette helped with the stirring and lifting, she peeked and saw how lusterless it was. The ashy face was all hollow eyes. Bernadette was amazed to observe that the ruffle of exquisite Emma's housecap hung torn and raveled.

Despite her changed aspect, Emma talked brightly with Bernadette, told her how many people were in the church,

22

named the richest members; asked a few questions — desultory ones about the coach's upsetting, about Uncle Marcus; scarcely waited for answers before rushing on in nervous haste as though a spool were wound, then unraveled in jerks. When silences came they were blank, odd — they made Emma McIves seem deep in herself.

The chops were browned, the chicory boiled, the bread sliced when Emma went to fetch Pastor McIves. Bernadette heard her rap at his study door off the parlor, call softly, "Mr. McIves, Mr. McIves." Incredulously Bernadette recalled Uncle Marcus's plain way of calling Aunt Leah "wife," thought of the Frys with their simple "Hester" and "David."

Pastor McIves filled the small kitchen; Emma followed, making skittery gestures of adulation. After the blessing, like a bird beating against a cage, she rushed to get salt, poured cream for her husband's chicory, ran mindlessly from hearth to table.

Under her lashes, sideways, Bernadette secretly watched Robb McIves. He ate stolidly, his vitality paralyzed.

Her young but acutely sensitive instinct told her Emma's chatter must be mainly an effort to enlist her husband's attention. But was Emma also — for some strange reason — trying to prove to Bernadette that everything was admirable in their life? Yes, the house *was* small, but cunningly arranged, the chatter went; yes, I have managed my work with *only* the help of a farmgirl; yes, the life of a village pastor *is* busy . . .

"The new wallpaper delights me. Don't you agree Mr. McIves has excellent taste? When do you think the carpenter can put it on?"

"I'll speak with him this morning," Robb answered, crashing his cup; irritation *did* lie just under constraint.

"But you're going to stay here and work on your sermon, aren't you?" Emma inquired, alarm tinging her chirrupy

23

voice, something more in her than the age-old female lament of being shut out of the tribal mystery, *where does he go in the morning?*

"Emma, you know I must take Bernadette to Dame Miller's. I promised I'd bring her to school at ten."

"But there won't be any school today."

Patience lay heavy in the husband's voice, patience leashed and bridled; fervidly Bernadette hoped Pastor McIves would *never* have to use that patient impatience with her.

"I'll bring her back soon. She starts school Monday and can't do without a visit to the schoolmarm first. We need to pick up her books, too."

"By noon?"

"Certainly." He rose; the bright-eyed girl felt he wanted to escape this little room. Escape his young wife? *But why?*

They walked the narrow, rutted road in silence. Finally Pastor McIves said gruffly, "After the loss of our first child, Mrs. McIves wasn't herself; she's having the same difficulty after the loss of this second. I never speak to her of her condition and it goes without saying I never mention it to others. She'll mend — she did before." But why were uncertainty, bitterness, unaccustomed humility mingled in Pastor's seemingly confident words?

Whatever Emma's mysterious condition, all wonder about it vanished from Bernadette's mind as they came into Furnace Village whose houses lined the road which split the valley; Pastor turned north on a cross street, strode up the hill till he came to a square frame house, clanged open the iron gate, marched her up to the door.

Miss Miller — rumpled, plump, little steel-rimmed spectacles bridging bobbing gray side curls — looked jolly until Bernadette took in the appraising gaze. There were two rooms, bare-floored and sunny, with small tables for desks, a globe, shelves for rocks and seashells, a shiny, not-battered piano. But Bernadette had hardly glanced about before Dame Miller began to fire questions at her.

"What is an elliptic?"

Panic chased around her head for a moment; went its way. "The elliptic is what appears to be the path of the sun in the heavens but is really the path of the earth around the sun," she replied from facile memory.

The young minister's face grew still; carefully, he sat down backwards in a wood chair, leaned his arms on the back, his chin on his fists.

"What's the zodiac?"

"The zodiac is a space in the heavens of eight degrees on each side of the elliptic, in which the planets perform their annual revolutions around the sun."

Zut! She had to let out her breath after the scurry of that one!

"Name me some prepositions."

No trouble on those. "About, above . . ." she raced on.

The barking teacher made no sign; Robb never took that clear, considering gaze off her.

"Give the rule for dividing. . . . Ah, yes, but can you do it?" Dame Miller challenged. She set Bernadette to work with figures, first in her head, then on a slate.

After that she spelled, carefully suppressing French things.

Finally there was the triumph of Miss Miller's curt nod, Pastor's relieved stir.

"What do you like best about school?"

"The people," Bernadette artlessly answered. "The girls. *And* the boys. In Ohio I ran with the boys in their foot races."

Robb cleared his throat.

"What *studies* do you like best, I mean?" Miss Miller scribbled names of textbooks on a paper while she talked.

"Drawing," Bernadette began; then guilt stopped her.

25

How would Miss Miller feel about drawing? In Montreal the nuns had adored her drawing, but in Ohio old Jimmy Henderson, the settlement teacher, had made her stand with her nose to an auger hole in the log wall as punishment for what he called her incessant "scribbling." She'd had to bend her knees to make her nose fit the hole and it'd been a terrible hour.

"Geography, I guess," she amended, "and declamation." Then impatiently, "Well, I really like it *all* . . ."

Robb relaxed against the chair back; Dame Miller allowed a faint running off of her clayey features, indicating Bernadette had *finally* arrived at an acceptable response.

When they came away from Miss Miller's Female School, Bernadette yearned to throw her skirts up in the ecstasy of a cartwheel. Back to school after a year of mark time in Canterbury! Relief washed over her in waves; she literally hugged the books she was carrying.

Hurrying, Robb caught her excitement, threw back his head and laughed, declaring he'd never known a person so glad to go to school. "Well, I suppose it's natural. Being female, you couldn't expect such advantage." Then, with a hesitancy most unlike him, he said his own Latin needed brushing up; he'd review hers with her every night. "Oh, yes, and I've always been partial to mathematics. I'll go over those lessons with you, too."

At noon Emma's only comment was a censorious "I pray she'll not be made into a clever woman, Mr. McIves." Then abruptly the young wife changed the subject, deploring that no one had put the girl into grown-up, front-buttoned dresses. It was disgraceful, Emma scolded.

Pastor looked frankly at the subject of his wife's remarks while Bernadette blushed furiously for the two bothersome things which stretched her bodice calico and drew his pointed glance.

26

"She's coltish," Emma complained.

"She's tall for twelve," he answered matter-of-factly.

"I wasn't like that at twelve," Emma replied firmly.

But Bernadette didn't have long to stay self-conscious; new things kept happening to her.

After they'd eaten, Pastor brought the horse around. "I'm taking her up the mountain," he explained to Emma, who watched bleakly from the window as Pastor helped Bernadette up on his horse.

This time they rode straight through Furnace Village, through a brief countryside, then into the village of Salisbury, the township center.

At first Salisbury seemed not such a grand place as Canterbury because it wasn't laid out in an open green space. Like Furnace Village, its buildings lined the coach road, clinging close to it, a mountain ridge crowding in from the north. Still, there was a very grand white church with a fancy octagonal tower for a steeple. Directly across from it stood a great, pillared town hall. That part was better than Canterbury, she had to admit.

They turned off Main Street near the church and jogged up a road which Pastor called Washinee. Soon houses fell away as Washinee narrowed into a trace; they entered a woods.

They climbed; he slipped back and she had to fight to keep from sliding off the pillion. She bunched his coat, held on. Impatiently, he reached around, loosed her fist, pulled her arms around his leaning, muscular body. Memory of a night in Ohio: silver combs, bobcats . . .

Beside the trace a stream sounded; the leaves were down, so she could see to the coursing water. It was a wild, dark place, this deep ravine. But not lonely, she soon realized, amazed.

There was traffic on this mountain road, oxen laboring

27

with loads of rock, men on horseback; even foot travelers were common, even women. Whatever was at the top of the trace, it must be very busy, she surmised. But wondering what might be ahead didn't blind her to sudden tunnels where the trees had been strangely felled, allowing a view of the mighty Berkshires cascading under roily skies.

"What are those smoking places?" She pointed to a half-dozen white plumes spiraling on the horizon.

"Charcoal pits," he answered. "Except they're mounds, really. You'll see them smoking on the hills everywhere in Litchfield County. Men called burners fell the trees, burn the wood for charcoal, bring it up for the forges at the top of the mountain." He reined in, nodded across the valley. "Those mounds are forty feet high. I sometimes wonder if there'll be any trees left after the burners are done."

Counting the fires, she silently agreed with him. He clucked at the horse, moved on, sighing, "But iron takes charcoal. Takes good ore, too. They dig that down below, out of Ore Hill. That ox wagon up ahead is carrying ore. Then iron needs limestone for flux; limestone comes from the valley floor, too; that horse with saddle pouches we just passed was hauling it. On the mountaintop is the last essential — water power. Litchfield County makes the best iron in the world, Bernadette."

She listened politely, absently, caught up in the life around them. A horse pushed past, detoured two trudging ladies, skirts held up. The mountain traffic thickened into a crowd.

The first forge she ever saw close up was a terrifying compound of smoke; fiery vents at the foot of a rock tower; grunts, squeals of strange but not visible machinery; oxen, horses, workmen rushing. Robb said indifferently over his shoulder, "That's one of the smaller forges. No point in wasting time on it."

They passed a second forge; its noise, smoke, blaze, smell blended with the noise, smoke, blaze, smell of its brother. For half a mile along the stream there were a fantastical number of forges for her to study. Then the trail widened suddenly; as suddenly, she was peering around Robb McIves into open space. She felt cold air, had an impression of a vast, wind-swept summit.

Mount Riga's great furnace reared straight ahead, lying by a pond below the dam-up of a long black lake. Awe-struck by its high, conical tower, by the dramatic gas cloud suspended over it, for a moment Bernadette didn't take in the village on the rolling slopes above it. When she tore her fascinated eyes away from the furnace, it was then the village struck her.

A cunning town on the high, remote top of a bald mountain! Rutted roads, little wood houses, large buildings which looked like barracks — even a big general store, a schoolhouse, cows staked in settled yards. At the far end of the long black lake, a great white house was mirrored. She scarcely had time to absorb it all before Robb reined in beside the vast tower.

The furnace rose three stories high. On the slope to its north, a ramp led from sheds filled with ore and limestone to the top of the furnace. Over this ramp two horse carts lumbered, a man ran with a loaded wheelbarrow.

"They dump the ore, the limestone, the charcoal into the maw at the top. The combination heats, mixes in the broad middle part, then falls to the hearth. Molten iron flows out the hearth doors into those molds. Tapping the hearth, they call it. It's not a spot for a female."

She ignored his judgment of female places. So far as she was concerned, a furnace top looked too ominous and hellish for *anyone.*

"It's dangerous up there," he confirmed her suspicion.

"Gases generated from the smelting keep on burning high up in the air above the furnace. At night that cloud you see is a torch — gorgeous sight."

She peered, eyes shaded.

"Have to have a good top man," Robb summarized. "He's in charge of the mix; wrong mix, there could be an explosion. And if he doesn't keep the cylinder clear inside, there can be a jam-up. A jam-up can kill a furnace; so can a plug farther down if ore cools in the hearth."

She tried to visualize the mysterious hot innards while he explained that the big furnace made the pig iron bars, which the smaller forges turned into anchors, plows, chains, hinges, latches, kitchen utensils.

The horse ambled on; stopped in the shadow of an enormous water wheel. Fascinated, they watched as the water fell in orderly silver threads from great wood box to box. But the wheel's screech was nothing compared to the rhythmic pulsation of a huge pair of bellows on a beam frame nearby.

"Supplies the air blast for the furnace flame," Robb said. "Promotes burning, speeds the process."

Urrr . . . hawhaw . . . urrr . . . hawhaw . . . That was the pulsating grunt, deep and unearthly, she'd heard in the morning!

They sat, both watching, breathing, listening, living that sound in their viscera: *Urrr . . . hawhaw . . . urrr . . . hawhaw . . .*

"We must get along," he announced, distaste in his voice.

Distaste. Why didn't Pastor like this novel village hanging to the slope of the mountain? She was amused, enchanted. How venturesome to come up here to live in the clouds!

As they rode, Robb seemed to be counting. "One . . . two . . . three . . ." What in the world was he counting?

30

Wondering, she watched two blackened, knob-eyed colliers slouch by, then a buxom mother, handsomely dressed in heavy skirts, followed by a covey of ruddy-cheeked children in strange embroidered hats.

"*Mes chéries, vite, vite,*" the woman called. At the French Bernadette nearly tumbled off the horse to tear after the mother who spoke in her own familiar tongue.

"Where do they come from?" she gasped.

Robb stopped counting, looked around at her curiously.

"This is a company-built town, Bernadette. It's full of Liths and Swiss. The smaller forges and the big furnace are owned by Holley and Coffing, the iron manufacturers. Years ago, when the company couldn't work our New England valley folk to suit itself, it brought over colliers from Lithuania and Switzerland. Many still speak their own language. Lots are single men, carousers who live in these big barracks or board with families. They and the native Raggies drink like fish," he added disapprovingly.

Who cared how they drank! The question was, were they on the list of people her new guardian disapproved of?

"Which of them speak French?"

"French? Switzers, I suppose, or at least a few of them." Then his mouth thinned. "Bernadette, these aren't people with whom you'll want to have commerce. Once you're acquainted with the girls at Miss Miller's — young women from Furnace Village's and Salisbury's best families — you won't even think of Mount Riga."

Her excited spirits went down like a punctured bellows; wistfully, she watched the retreating figures of the mother and children. To Pastor McIves, Catholics were anathema; free black Miriam was of low estate; Quakers had no theology; Mount Riga's French were not of good family. What *was* the matter with her, Bernadette? Ever since she'd been in her mother's country she'd found the wrong people the most appealing.

"Anyway, we're not here to meet the village population," Robb assured. "I've come to count the rum shops and plan how the church children should march to Mount Riga next week."

"March?"

"I'm forming a Children's Cold Water Army."

"Cold Water Army?" she asked in confusion.

"Drunkenness is so common, the American Society for the Promotion of Temperance is campaigning to get people to sign a promise to drink just water; if people shouldn't drink cider, whisky, or rum, the common-sense thing for them to drink is water. That's why signers are called members of the Cold Water Army."

"But what can marching children do?"

"They carry banners, parade, sing songs I've taught them about the evils of drink. Already we've closed a rum shop in Salisbury."

"Just by marching and singing?" she asked incredulously.

"Indeed, yes. When we come to Riga next week I'm expecting you to march behind me and help with the youngest ones, Bernadette."

She tried to think of herself carrying a banner and singing about cold water while people stared. If she couldn't imagine *herself* doing such a thing, it was equally impossible for her to imagine *his* leading such a strange band.

"Will you feel funny marching for cold water?" she finally asked timidly.

She never forgot his terse reply. "I've no desire to make myself a fool, but for my beliefs I'll make myself appear any way necessary to further them."

Deep in conversation, they'd skirted the long narrow lake and were approaching the white mansion she'd seen reflected in the water.

It was a beautiful house, proud, high, designed in classic baronial proportions like Miss Crandall's. How had it ever come to be on this barren blue rockery?

As if he'd read her mind, Robb said softly, "It was built for Ironmaster Joseph Pettee. I understand it has a ballroom."

She looked back over her shoulder to get the view the house commanded. To one side, the village on its slope, then the fiery furnace rising like a giant battlement beside the jet lake glittering in the November twilight . . . the Ironmaster's house kept watch of it all.

"I wish I could enlist the Ironmaster in my reforms," Robb reflected in a hushed voice. "Among other things, I'd have money to send to Weld then. Theodore was just caught under swimming horses while fording a creek in Ohio. By a miracle he escaped with his life, but he lost everything."

Mr. Weld. She sat there, the picture in her head of what Weld must be like struggling to grow clear.

Pastor jerked the horse around. "No use to think of the Ironmaster," he concluded. "Someday perhaps I'll have the ear of the mighty, but I haven't now — at least, not the very mighty." He laughed; she sensed hunger in that sound.

It was a lonely trip down; the traffic seemed to have vanished as shadows lengthened across the Mount Riga trace.

Full dark had settled by the time they turned in at their yard. Before Robb took the horse to its shed, he swung her down to the ground; his big hands held her for a moment.

He nodded curtly, dismissed her.

❋ 4

"**A**NNIS, catch Noah!"

Her zestful new friend, Annis Atchison, swooped down on the straying seven-year-old, nudged him into line.

Twenty-three children slogging through the rainy mire, marching up the mountain for cold water . . .

Bernadette dived for a dipping banner, saved it from muddy extinction, hardly dared to take her eye off that tall hustling figure ahead, remembering for courage his sober words of last night: "I know it's a hard thing I ask of you, Bernadette, but it's necessary we put an end to bibbing. In Furnace Village, overseers of the poor, the jailer, the doctor know how much misery, crime, death drink causes. Twenty years ago folks spent more than the government's national budget on spirits. Perhaps telling you this will make tomorrow easier." His eyes held a pleading.

She'd melted into his softness; as soon as she had, he'd hardened. "See the children march properly, sing out. Annis is a flibbertigibbet; Otis spoils her."

At the forges, total disunity threatened while the children ogled; Robb waved impatiently.

On the windy summit of Riga, she breathed a sigh of relief.

But not for long. The town slopes turned out to be more unnerving than she'd imagined. Face into the squall, they marched with their drooping muslin banners which said SIGN THE TOTAL ABSTINENCE PLEDGE, JOIN THE COLD WATER ARMY

34

from rum shops to boarding houses, while Rigans smirked. At the first barracks several Raggy men drifted out on the porch, listened to their singing

Clear the house, the tarnal stuff shan't be here so handy;
Wife has given the winds her snuff so now here goes my
brandy . . .

then simply burst out laughing. One shouted to another, "Reminds me, Dan, I've a thirst. How about a whisky?" and in plain view took off for the nearest rum shop.

Pastor's profile turned white with fury, but sarcasm didn't stop him. The army trudged to the second barracks, entrenched itself in in front of it.

In wavering treble the children sang,

Bright water for me, bright water for me,
And wine for the tremulous debauchee . . .

"I never *could* sing," Bernadette grumbled, pushing away the rain-soaked hair that plastered her forehead.

"I've noticed that," Annis whispered back amiably. Then, "Look at him. He's staring at us . . . nò, he's staring at *you.*"

"Who? That old man?"

"No," Annis hissed dramatically. "The one over there."

Bernadette followed Annis's pointed stare, saw a young boy leaning alone against the clapboard porch front. One foot was propped deliberately under him, his arms were akimbo, he bent a little forward from the waist. He wore a seaman's visored blue wool cap; its tassel hung rakishly beside his cheek, drawing a line between his long, shining black hair and the ruddiness of his skin. He was short and square and, she was sure, much younger than she.

It didn't take more than one upward glance to make sure he was *indeed* staring at her.

"Who is he?" she hissed back.

"Pettee Trevelyan," Annis said at her ear; then, silenced by Robb's staring around to see where his main supports had gone, both girls began to sing lustily,

We pledge perpetual hate to all that can intoxicate . . .

Petit flashed through her wondering mind; *Little* who? How could a boy let himself be cursed by such a demeaning name? He didn't look the sort to play the fool.

Under his insistent bold stare she began to feel the red rise up her throat, crawl all the way under her wet scarf.

Then the boy, whistling to himself, lounged around the barracks and was gone.

She let out her breath; tried to find her way back to the tune.

Finally, banner slogans soggy, young voices hoarse, the troupe had had enough; Robb headed them away from the embarrassed colliers, laughing Raggies, women who tittered and nudged. "Bernadette, you and Annis run to Mrs. MacDonald's to pick up the money she's giving our ranks," Robb instructed. "Catch us on the trail."

"Who was that little boy, that *Petit?*" Bernadette asked as she and Annis scurried off.

"He's the Ironmaster's relative."

"Well, why do they call him *Little?* Is the Ironmaster French?"

"Little?" Annis breathed her mystification. "His name's P-E-T-T-E-E. That's American. No, the Ironmaster's not French. What gave you that idea?"

Bernadette rearranged her thoughts hurriedly; how hard it was to learn the ins and outs of another country!

"The Ironmaster lives in that big house, doesn't he?"

"Yes. And that's where Pettee Trevelyan lives. He's some kind of family member, I think. He's younger, he's ten. My sisters say when he grows up he's going to be the handsomest rich gentleman in Litchfield County. The wildest, too. He's a terror, always racing his pony or upsetting his raft, always shooting folks' geese when he's supposed to shoot pigeons. He cusses in a foreign language so he can say anything he wants. I like him; I wish he'd stared at me."

"Why? It made me mad."

"Well," Annis fumbled for words, "he's kind of *wicked*."

"You'd like to be stared at by somebody wicked?" Bernadette asked, slowing down, not even noticing the water dribbling off her kerchief into her neck.

"He's only interested in wicked things," Annis floundered helplessly.

Wicked things. He'd stared at *her*, Bernadette. But then she shrugged it off. She was going to be a schoolteacher. Nothing wicked about *that*.

"A schoolteacher like Miss Miller?" Annis asked.

Briefly Bernadette quailed before a vision of bouncing side curls, heavy breath, weak eyes peering behind spectacles, a sweet lady-voice that was a coating for cold severity. Then optimism swept her. "No, not like Miss Miller," she finished decidedly. "A schoolmarm, but like myself."

"Folks'll hate you if you're clever. If you learn algebra, boys won't care for you, nor will men. Already you're my best friend, so I can warn you," Annis confided, brow puckered. Annis was freckled, red-haired, teeny; Bernadette felt like a moose beside her. *Moose, foreign, coltish, brainy* . . .

Bernadette ran from Annis, jumped for a tree branch. If only Annis and Emma McIves wouldn't harp on the dangers of cleverness! What was she to do? How was she to reconcile their warnings with her own driving curiosity, her need for independence? And how was she to figure out Pastor, with his same abhorrence of clever women but his strange relish for teaching *her*?

37

Her brief spurt of running had set her chilled blood pulsing; her temples pounded. *I don't care. I want to. Will I be like a man if I do? A little. But I want to be a woman. Only one who takes control of her own life, says who she is and likes what she says . . .*

Not pretending. I'd like a life of not pretending . . .

She heard Annis shouting. "Wait! I didn't mean to hurt your feelings, Bernadette. I know orphans are different."

She slowed, turned, waited impassive-faced for Annis to catch up. "Orphans aren't different," she spoke matter-of-factly.

Housewife MacDonald wasn't at home when they rapped at her door. A passing woman called, "She's gone to the bonnet-maker's, Emilie Glaudin's. Try there."

So they knocked on the bonnet-maker's door.

A wheat-haired matron smiled at them. Peering around the woman's skirts were a covey of children. *Vite, vite, mes enfants!* the mother had called to them while Bernadette had nearly tumbled off Pastor's horse wanting to rush after them.

Looking into the woman's smiling face, Bernadette knew the truth instantly. *No matter what Pastor said, I intended to find her one day.*

"Ah, yes, Mrs. MacDonald is here." The woman called Emilie Glaudin stepped back, beckoning them in. "She is just now going."

Housewife MacDonald said in her thickest burr that she was gieing temperance tracts to her mon to take to the worrrkers at the forrr-ge. "We were havin' a spot of tay . . ."

"Would the young ladies care for a cup?" the bonnet-maker inquired when the other had taken her leave. "You are wet and it is cold. You have come from the valley, have you not?"

How warm and cozy it was, with tumbling babies and blazing hearth, bonnet frames and braid scattered about — and yes, on the table a soup tureen exactly like Tante Cécile's!

"Yes, ma'am, if you please," Bernadette accepted softly, eyes only on Emilie Glaudin, French mother, when Annis poked her sharply in the ribs. Bernadette jumped, turned a startled look on her friend. In doing so, her glance took in a stool by the far side of the hearth.

A boy, eating. Licking his fingers deliberately, wiping his mouth with the back of his hand. Then rising without haste, with an air of absolute aplomb.

A short, red-cheeked boy with curling black hair under his tasseled sailor hat, eyes bright and bold as polished jet, white teeth flashing in his brown-skinned face.

"It's Pettee Trevelyan, Bernadette," Annis whispered, "the one we were talking about."

"Madame Emilie Glaudin's her name," he explained, nodding toward the Frenchwoman. "She's wife to Mount Riga's best blacksmith. She makes bonnets. They speak French here. I can help you understand."

"*Mercie, jeune garçon,*" Bernadette teased him. "*Mais je parle français aussi. Et vous?*"

For the first time his calm expression changed visibly. "Are you Swisser?" he asked, astonished.

"No. My father was French; he came from Montreal. I lived there until two years ago."

"Well," the boy summarized bluntly, "I guessed you were different. French and Iroquois, maybe . . ."

Annis let out a smothered shriek, covered her mouth. "Injun?" she asked in horror, looking straight at Bernadette. "She don't look one *bit* injun to me."

"She don't exactly to me," Pettee Trevelyan allowed. "But how come her eyes are slanty?"

"Bernadette, *are* you part-injun?"

"No, Annis, of course I'm not, or my mother would have told me," Bernadette answered crossly. "But what if I was — what difference is that?"

"That's what I thought, watching you," Pettee Trevelyan agreed. "Having some injun would be ripping. I know I'd like it better than being just somebody from Philadelphia who lives with Mr. Pettee. We're kin but he's not really my uncle, though I call him that — he takes care of me."

"I'm ward to Pastor McIves down at Furnace Village."

"Well," the boy answered, not without humor, "I guess that makes us alike. Madame Glaudin baked today; ask her for bread. She bakes better than our cook does." He pulled on expensive lambskin mittens, said a few words to the bonnet-maker, didn't even say goodbye to the girls. He opened the door; it let in a rush of raw air.

Madame Glaudin was taking long, gold loaves of bread from the round brick oven. Watching the bending body in its swaddling apron, Bernadette's heart exploded in her. She grabbed up a paddle, joined the woman, deftly drew out a loaf.

"*Voilà!*" she smiled into the eyes of this compatriot. "I speak as you do. But from Canada."

"Ahhhh," Emilie Glaudin breathed, her eyes and teeth glinting, her smooth cheeks bursting with a smile. "And so you live with the handsome, tall pastor down at the foot of the mountain! The pastor who works against spirit-drinking, the one who marched up here?"

"Yes, I live with him."

"Well, then, is he your brother?"

"No."

"Your uncle, perhaps?"

"No. He's a good friend of my great-uncle out in Ohio. I'm living with him till I get through school, then I'm going back to Ohio. I help take care of his wife and do his housework . . ."

"His wife's been sick," Annis spoke up.

"Sick, ahhhh. So hard for a young man. Tall, he is, *oui*, and 'bonny' as Mrs. MacDonald says. But he frightens me. *Trés sérieux* . . ."

Emilie put plates on the table, tore the hot bread in chunks, brought a circle of cheese. While the girls ate, the five little children hung about insistently, the smaller ones leaning on the benches, watching, bright-eyed.

Bernadette had learned from Rachel in Canterbury never to swoop down on a baby; children took sidling up to before you could lift them. Very casually she held out a piece of cheese for the baby, a girl about Rachel's age in a long challis gown and close-fitting cap. The baby chewed solemnly, just as solemnly spat the cheese out on the floor.

"Ah, bad child!" Emilie scolded. "Give her the bread." After that, the baby climbed into Bernadette's lap, settled down to suck comfortably on a crust.

A sharp whistle of wind in the chimney reminded Bernadette of the need to hurry.

"Dear young girl, please come back," Madame Glaudin said with special meaning to Bernadette.

"Pettee Trevelyan hardly paid any mind to us," Annis grumbled when they were outside.

"Oh, him," Bernadette answered. "Well, he was in a hurry. Did you know Madame Glaudin's not Swiss but French; she comes from Tours."

"Oh, her," Annis said.

Luckily, Pastor was late getting home to supper from delivering the children; when he came in, Bernadette and Emma were browning salt pork.

"You were very helpful on the march. Come with me."

"But she's minding the meat," Emma protested.

41

"It'll just take a minute, Emma, dearest. It's something I keep forgetting."

She followed Pastor into his study. He handed her something, mumbling he'd picked it out for her in Hartford. It was a beautiful gift, a morocco leather book with blank pages. Holding and feeling it, she knew he could ill afford it.

"It's the journal I spoke to you about in the coach, Bernadette, the one in which you're to record your spiritual progress. After you read your Bible, let God guide your pen; as His servant, I'll then review what you write. Tonight's a good night to start — you've done the Lord's work in marching with the children up the mountain."

"Bernadette!" Emma called querulously.

"Thank you for the beautiful journal," she said simply.

His face was luminous when not set hard by lines of guardianship duty. He smiled; then his expression turned frosty as though he reminded himself that overseeing an orphan was a weighty responsibility.

"Of course, most of the time," he warned, "you won't be noting your worthy deeds. A sense of your own sinfulness is a first step to Christ."

"Yes, sir."

"I'll ask you to bring the journal to me from time to time."

By the candle in her cold room she wrote: "After the Cold Water March, Annis and I went to get money from Mrs. MacDonald. She was visiting the bonnet-maker, Madame Glaudin. I helped Madame Glaudin take out the bread. I held the baby, a girl like Rachel, just learning to walk."

She ran the soft feather quill over her cheek thoughtfully. "I wonder," she scribbled, "what Theodore Weld is like?" Why had she written that? She didn't know.

Then hurriedly she flipped over the page and began to copy the first Bible passage which caught her eye: "Save me, O God; for the waters are come into my soul. I sink in deep mire, where there is no standing; I am come into deep waters where the floods overflow me . . ."

Was that what it'd been like for Mr. Weld when he'd nearly drowned under the horses at Alum Creek? She shuddered, thinking of it.

After that, she forgot about Emilie Glaudin's warm French kitchen, redolent with maternity, forgot it had somehow led her musing thoughts straight to Mr. Weld. Forgot completely about that boy, Little Trevelyan.

 5

THE FIRST heavy snows were melting in an unexpected thaw.

After the supper dishes were washed and dried, Pastor McIves went to his study. Emma took to the rocking chair by the kitchen fire, inviting Bernadette to bring her books to the hearth rather than go up to her cold bedchamber. Soon Bernadette was lost in study; after a time, she noticed Emma got up and walked around the kitchen, walking, walking . . . then pacing.

The clock ticked, a log fell with a burst of sparks, Emma muttered to herself. Algebra proved a hard subject, but fascinating . . .

A long time later, from thousands of miles away, Bernadette came back to the world of the little room. Emma was gone. The clock hand pointed to ten — a shocking hour to be still up. With a rush, Bernadette gathered up her books and climbed the stairs.

The door to the McIveses' bedchamber was closed; as she

passed it, a muffled thud caught her ear. Bernadette paused on the threshold of her own room to listen. After the first thud came another, then came a woman's voice raised in rapid speech. It sounded eerie, that voice.

Where was Pastor McIves? Bernadette realized he hadn't yet come out of his study downstairs. She paused uncertainly, wondering what she should do. There came a smothered exclamation, the crash of something small and light, a glass dish dropped, or . . . thrown?

Bernadette turned, hurried downstairs, rapped at the study door. Pastor opened it, a book in hand; Bernadette could see that he, too, had been miles away.

"It's Mrs. McIves," she stammered. "I think she's talking to herself."

All at once, penetrating the walls around them, came a scream. Robb leaped past her. She tried to keep up but he took the steps three at a time.

When she got to the upper hall, he was pounding on the bolted door.

"Emma! Open up!"

Inside there was more talking, more laughing, sobbing.

Robb McIves lunged at the door. With a splintering sound it leaned inward, then the bolt gave. Close behind him Bernadette saw into the bedroom.

Emma rocked on the bed, hugging her knees, her gown tangled, her head uncapped, her hair tumbling down her back. She turned to them and froze, her face all enormous eyes.

"Merciful God, Emma," Pastor breathed.

"Don't you come near," his wife shrilled, flouncing off the bed and running to a corner of the room, her iceberg immobility dissolving as though sun-scorched. "Don't come near me or I'll hate you. I don't want to hate you . . ."

Bernadette's heart beat with terror at the sound of that strange, shrill voice.

All the while, the husband's big bulk was moving closer, closer to his wife . . .

When Robb cornered Emma, she screamed one brief, unearthly scream; the smart sound of his slapping her face was nearly lost in that scream.

She collapsed against him, weeping wildly.

"Don't leave me. Help me; hold me," she wailed.

Robb lifted Emma, put her into the bed; his body leaned over her for a concealing minute.

When he straightened up, Bernadette saw Emma was just a small heap under the covers, knotted and huddled. Robb looked over his shoulder to Bernadette, his face stricken.

"I had to strike her, she was hysteric. I think she'll be quiet for a while. Stay right beside her while I go for Dr. Turner."

Knees shaking, Bernadette pulled up a chair and sat close to the great high bed, listening as the crying turned into a pitiful mew. Below she heard Robb's horse beat down the road.

Emma McIves hate her husband? But why? And hating him, how could she want him never to leave her?

Finally all was quiet; Bernadette didn't dare get up and look to see if Emma slept.

"Bernadette?"

"Yes, ma'am?" she jumped, startled.

"A woman must follow her husband in *all* things," the small voice from the bed quavered. "Nothing's more precious to a woman than a good husband . . . I couldn't live without Pastor McIves."

Silence.

"A wife gives up everything for a husband and isn't afraid

45

to do it. *He* isn't afraid. *He* fears nothing and no one, except yes, sometimes himself . . ."

Bernadette scarcely heard the words for fear that Emma might grow strange again. She stole anxiously to the window, looked out on the front road, saw it was lathered in moonlight. When she turned back, Emma rested with her face up on her pillow like a carved thing.

Despite his dishevelment, the old doctor was heavy with authority. Bernadette drew back when he and Robb came into the room, slipped to her room but kept the door ajar so that Pastor could call if he needed her.

Thus it was she heard — though to understand it was another matter — when the doctor and Pastor McIves came out and stood in the hall.

It was Robb's tormented voice which caught her ear, a voice to match his face.

"We haven't been wed two years and already in threat of death she's borne and lost two infants. The first came to us without intent; the second you urged on us for my wife's well-being. There mustn't be more for a time."

There was a long, professional silence. "Nonetheless, my dear young man, this excess of delicacy — both mental and physical — won't be overcome till your wife holds a sturdy child in her arms. How well I know these young women! Frail in health till motherhood rends them hearty; fearful in mind till their every thought bends to the nurture of young."

"You're right, I'm sure you're right. God willing, in time we'll have a living child, but not now, not for a time."

There was a disapproving sigh. "Very well. But remember she wasn't hysteric when she had a confinement to look forward to — only afterwards, with no infant to hold. And I need not remind you, sir, that the Lord commanded us to be fruitful and multiply; fill the earth, subdue it . . ."

"Yes, yes," Robb replied in a miserable way. "But first my wife must have time . . ."

They went down the stairs together.

Listening to their heavy, fading footsteps, Bernadette knew she must put the picture of Emma crouched on the bed into that closed-off part of her memory with the other things she couldn't understand: her mother's coughing death, her father's vanishment, Uncle Marcus sending her away, Hester Fry giving her up . . .

That part of her mind was growing to be a desperately crowded place.

She heard Robb shut the front door, heard him walk through the parlor. But tossing, turning, she didn't hear him come back upstairs.

Miss Miller put away the arithmetic drill cards and Bernadette could almost hear the younger girls heave sighs of relief. Nothing brought out Miss Miller's well-bred sarcasm so much as hesitation over 9 X 12 or 7 X 7.

Galileo said planets were perfectly round globes looking like little moons, while fixed stars blazed. She was supposed to be memorizing that, but instead Bernadette doodled on the margin of her workbook — little round globes, circles with blazing zigzags.

She stole a secret look at Annis, who stole one back.

She wished she could hunch and relieve her spine from the exhausting straightness Miss Miller required of sitting young women.

Then, unbelieving, she heard Miss Miller's early dismissal, because, as the teacher said, snow was expected and most were without gum boots.

She and Annis marched sedately out the door, waited until they were safely in the yard to grab each other and spin around in exuberant whirls. Global communiqués — suppressed since noon — poured from them in torrents.

"They played blindman's bluff and do you know who caught my sister? Lardy Dunkel. She said it was like being hugged by a jelly bowl!" Shrieks of laughter . . .

She and Annis parted at the crossroads.

High off the mountains, a winter wind blew out of the swollen sky.

She rushed.

Just this morning Emma had admonished her feebly from bed, "You mustn't walk so fast. The Lord meant ladies to be languid."

How, Bernadette wondered, did one combine languor with Miss Miller's ramrod blandishments? *Zut!* If she had to figure out how to walk drooping-slow but back stiff she'd never get home to her housework!

"Why are you walking so funny?" a voice suddenly asked behind her, stopping her in her tracks. She whirled. Master Pettee Trevelyan looked up at her with his impudent black eyes, Master Pettee Trevelyan materialized out of the wintry air. . . .

"You gave me a start! Why are *you* in Salisbury?"

He walked with his hands stuffed rudely in his pantaloon pockets, his school cap pushed carelessly back on his head. "I came to see what you were doing this afternoon, spend it with you," he answered casually. It didn't sound like an invitation; it sounded like a command.

She minded his aspect and tone. "I've got work to do," she told him haughtily, forgetting to slouch and sidle, skimming instead.

"Wait up. What work?"

"Dusting, starching."

"I'll hang around till you're done."

"Mrs. McIves wouldn't like it."

"You mean the one who's shatterbrained?"

Her defenses flew up, defenses part-caused by the hushed voice of fear within her. "How dare you say a thing like that!" she stamped her foot in fury. "It's easy to see you're a perfectly dreadful boy."

"Maybe," he answered imperturbably, "but if it's true, most folks don't have nerve to tell me. I'll wait in your backyard and you come out when you're through. I've got something to show you . . . I keep it not far from your place, keep it with a friend of mine."

"What?" she asked, slowing.

He glanced at her slyly. "Have to come out and see," was all he'd tell her.

Thinking of his waiting, she made the starch too thick. The feather duster flew nervously from table to mantel to cupboard. What *was* there about Pettee Trevelyan that nettled but drew her?

She finished ahead of time. Emma would probably drowse through the rest of the afternoon from the new medicine Dr. Turner gave her.

Dinner was warmed-overs . . .

Oh, all right, she told herself, throwing her shawl in an impatient swirl over her shoulders. Just this once. Just to get rid of him . . .

"Still here?" was her grumpy greeting. But *he* didn't seem grumpy; he whistled cheerfully as they went out the yard. (She couldn't help but notice he led her out in such a fashion that they couldn't be seen from Emma's upstairs windows. Hanging around, had he coolly figured that out?)

"Ever been to a furnace?" he asked.

"I haven't had time."

"Haven't had time!" he exclaimed, unbelieving. "Well, what've you been doing?"

"Studying and working."

"And going to church, I'll bet."

"Yes, that, too."

"Well, all I know is, if I lived in Furnace Village I'd have been all over every forge by now. Top to bottom."

"I'm not supposed to," she squelched him. "Pastor McIves says it's no place for a girl."

"Girl?" There was something in his startled tone that made her think he'd hardly noticed her girl-ness, wanted to be with her for some quite different reason. She looked over at him thoughtfully while he went on, "I never heard anything so silly. Would you like to go up top? I know a good top man . . . Antanas."

"Maybe," she allowed casually. But shuddered; a forge top looked fit only for demons.

"Then I'll take you," he promised. "But not today; I've got to be somewhere else."

They skirted the forge which lay at the outlet of Wononscopomuc Lake; Pettee Trevelyan told her it was an old forge built long ago by a man named Ethan Allen. It was owned now by Holley and Coffing. Pastor said the Holleys virtually owned Furnace Village, Salisbury, Mount Riga; they didn't belong to Pastor's struggling new church.

Pettee Trevelyan turned into a farmyard, headed behind it to the barn. At the barn door he turned to her, put his finger to his lips. "You won't tell?" he asked, his black eyes inscrutable, sparkling.

"Tell what?" she asked impatiently.

"I keep my shawlneck here. I'm going to fight him this afternoon, take on a fellow's mugwump. Ever seen a cockfight?"

"No." Something inside her gave a brief quiver. She shouldn't; even among men, the civilized ones, chickenfighting was deplored.

50

And then somehow she was inside the barn with its cold, still air, its circle of kneeling boys — yes, and a tousled girl who didn't go to Miss Miller's seminary.

They murmured his name — *Trev . . . Trev*; it went admiringly around the circle. So Pettee Trevelyan was *Trev*, she noted; begrudgingly, she admitted the short, smoothly imperial name fitted him.

She leaned on a post watching intently as Trev opened a cage, lifted out a white-legged, black-breasted cock with a coppery back, and hackles that fell all the way to its shoulders. Another boy was holding a dark red cock which he now let go to strut in the boy-made ring. The cock stretched its neck, minced round and round.

Trev came back in the circle, his bird resting in the curve of his arm. There was a terse conversation. "Take up the mugwump," Trev said to the other boy.

Trev and the boy faced each other, both birds held in arm. Then someone shouted, "Bill your cocks!" and Trev and the boy stepped out, faced each other again, let the birds see each other.

There was an excited murmur.

"Mugwump's a dunghill, he won't fight."

"Look what he did last week to Billy's spangle. He'll fight the shawlneck, all right."

"Anyway, the shawlneck's a wheeler . . ."

Bernadette had scarcely crowded closer when something happened inside the ring. The birds stiffened, their eyes bulged murderously; Trev's stretched its neck, struck at the mugwump.

"Pit 'em!" someone shouted hoarsely.

Trev and the other boy threw their birds to the straw; what happened next her eyes scarcely followed. The cocks leaped in midair; their neck feathers ruffled monstrously. There was

51

a confusion of bird-colors, boys' calling, everyone leaning forward. The mugwump suddenly sprawled on his side in the straw.

Trev scooped up his bird, stroked it, blew into its face. His face was tense, excited; somehow it held gentleness, maleness. Bernadette knelt on the straw, mesmerized.

The tousled girl finished counting to ten, the boys set their cocks on the straw; again there was that incredible motion which she could perceive only as streaks of color, except for the feathers gently floating afterwards . . .

Again the mugwump fell on its side.

"Handle!" the tousled girl cried.

"Blinked him. Took his eye out . . ."

The owner of the mugwump lifted up his bird; she couldn't believe what he did — he put its whole head in his mouth. Trev waited, again stroking the shawlneck. He looked over at her, nodded in that quick salute he had.

"Breast 'em!" someone called.

Again Trev and the boy scrambled to face each other; the cocks were beak to beak.

Then somebody cried, "Hey, Trev, let up! You've won. He don't have any other cock; he couldn't get another one like you."

"Fair enough," Trev said, backing off, pushing his cap up, full of boy dignity. "Mugwump's blinked anyhow."

Bernadette couldn't look at the bleeding bird. Trev took his cock to its cage, boys were gathering up gear, schoolbooks, mittens. Bernadette tried to talk to the tousled girl but somehow nothing came out; all she could think of was leaving.

Out in the wintry air she asked, "Do the cocks ever kill each other?"

"Oh, sure," he assured easily. "But not much when we're fighting. I can get more birds but the boys can't lay hands on good fighters. Lots of dunghills around. Did you like it?"

"No," she replied grimly.

"I didn't think so," he observed dispassionately. "I watched your face; you looked sick. You're right — you're no injun."

"I said I wasn't."

"Yes, I know."

They stopped and watched two men fishing through the ice on the lake. The shadows were growing. He had to get back to Mount Riga way up there. And even warmed-over, the dinner couldn't be got at the snap of a finger.

In the backyard he said matter-of-factly, "I won't take you to any more cockfighting. Ever seen a charcoal hearth close up? Out in the forest, colliers pile the wood big as a house, cover it with leaves and dirt so the wood'll burn slow, char. There's lots more things to show you."

She was about to tell him she'd be too busy but something stopped her. All she said was, "Trev . . . good night."

He made a brisk gesture at his cap brim; there was something unfathomable in his smile. "Madame Glaudin asked me to bring you to her."

That night she couldn't think of anything to write in her journal; she was getting sick to death of copying chunks out of the Bible.

Well, she *could* write about going to a cockfight.

Unthinkable! In this journal went only things which God and Robb McIves approved.

Theodore Weld. A man; no crude, cockfighting boy. And even as a boy, not one for barbarous animal fights. A boy with a tenderness, a stripling godliness. A fair, winsome boy, intensely serious. A David turning into someone beautiful — a romantic zealot hurrying down the streets of Cincinnati, cloak unfurling behind him.

53

She thought of his blond hair rolled at the back of his neck just above his high white collar.

Couldn't know that idealizing lead only in one direction: to disappointment.

She shut the journal helplessly.

In imagination she could feel his hair, silken and springy; her fingers tingled as she lay in bed.

Weld, she whispered, experimenting with the soft, out-loud murmur of it.

Weld had a loving sound, a joining sound, she thought sleepily; she slipped off, her mouth still in a *moue* from saying his name.

 6

THE MEAT CAKES were smoking when Bernadette came into the kitchen; for a time Bernadette had hoped Emma would learn to cook from watching. Emma habitually now took up her fancywork as soon as Bernadette appeared.

"Mr. McIves is talking tonight to the Home Mission Society so I put the meat on early," Emma explained blandly.

"It's his fourth meeting this week."

"That's the truth," Emma sighed from the rocking chair, searching for her thimble. "I'm afraid he'll break his health. The Temperance crusades, the Tract and Bible Society, General Union for the Christian Sabbath, Society for Promoting Manual Labor in Colleges . . . Do you know he's just accepted a national office on the board of the American

Society for the Observance of the Seventh Commandment?"

Bernadette, distracted by trimming the burnt cakes, tried to remember which was the Seventh Commandment.

"To redeem strayed maidens," Emma added hastily, seeing her blank expression.

"Oh."

"No, I never dreamed what a success we'd have so quickly in Connecticut. It's a real responsibility being married to such a promising man."

Listening absently to Emma's boasting, Bernadette marveled at the change in her. Gloss had returned to her hair, her cheeks had filled out under an exquisite high flush, her arms and bosom swelled. As Bernadette had once bravely promised curious Annis, Emma now sat in her church pew, eyes fixed adoringly on the pulpit.

All that was left as a reminder of that mystifying November night was Pastor McIves's still sleeping on the couch in the downstairs study. It seemed very curious to Bernadette after the habits of the Grays and Frys, but she allowed herself only the worry of how Pastor ever made his long length comfortable on the short horsehair slab.

"It's not just proper attention to a husband's comforts, it's tender regard for his spirits," Emma was declaiming when Robb McIves came into the kitchen.

"I'm glad to hear you say so, my dear," he commented pleasantly. "Confidentially, the elders just voted with me to read Jonah Bell out of church for drunkenness. I'll take him by surprise next Sabbath service."

"Good!" Emma exclaimed. "He's a disgrace to all of us."

Bernadette served the dinner in a brown study. *Read out of church by surprise! How awful!* A sympathetic vision of Jonah Bell's face rose in her. He was one of Otis Atchison's tanners; he was a shy man everyone insisted on teaching. But with Annis and her — on their nose-holding tannery

55

expeditions — Jonah was full of salty little wisdoms like the time he'd caught them plotting and smiled, "Ain't it tingly to do something nice for someone in secret what gets found out!"

"If his friends desert him, won't that make him drink worse?" she asked.

"You know what Ecclesiastes says about drunkards, Bernadette," Robb spoke testily, sitting down at the table. "Ah, burnt again?" he looked at his plate.

The young wife answered nervously that the hearth was too small. Night after night she talked of parishioners who had cookstoves — those new, cast-iron inventions. Then stopped. Why didn't she ask him for a stove straight out? Bernadette wondered unceasingly.

Pastor ate heartily, burnt cakes or not, and appeared to be thinking of other than charred things. "Otis Atchison and I were agreeing this afternoon that southern members of Congress may gag our northern antislavery petitions."

"Gag, Mr. McIves? Pray, what do you mean?" Emma asked absently, stirring his tea.

"Dear little wife, you've heard me explain what petitions are."

"Whatever they are, I don't think they're any affair of ours," Emma murmured.

"What about the petitions?" Bernadette insisted softly.

"Southern legislators may ram a vote through forbidding northern people from sending petitions against slavery to Congress, Bernadette."

"Did you see it when you were at the Atchison's?" Emma interrupted.

"It's infuriating the way those arrogant planters hold a gun to Congress. Did I see *what*, Emma?"

"The stove. Did you see Mrs. Atchison's stove?"

"I wasn't poking around their kitchen, I stepped in the

56

parlor," Pastor answered impatiently. "I mean to lead a campaign here in Furnace Village, get people to gather antislavery petition signatures."

"Gather signatures? But Mr. McIves, that's radical! Our churchfolk won't like it." Emma was no risk-taker.

Robb McIves started to touch Emma's hand in a soothing gesture, stopped (since November, they didn't touch each other). "Now, Emma, I'm doing nothing compared to Weld in Ohio. Single-handed, he's founded the Ohio Antislavery Society, even called a convention in Zanesville."

"Zanesville's a rowdy place," Emma answered distastefully.

"So Weld's just found out. His first lecture there, a mob met him with stones and clubs, battered the door down."

"Was he hurt?" Bernadette asked carefully.

"No, by a miracle he wasn't. Theodore wrote an interesting thing, Bernadette . . . said the best way to face a mob is to come out of the meeting place, fold your arms and simply stare at your tormentors. He jokes that for some reason mobs won't attack a man with folded arms."

"Well, I don't believe that," Emma declared. "Besides, it's irresponsible to anger folks. Bernadette, Mr. McIves's cup needs filling."

"I'll get it," Pastor said, rising, stretching, bending over the kettle on the crane. "By heaven, the fire's hot, Emma. No wonder you scorch things."

Bernadette pushed back her chair, went to the hearth, roughly poured tea for his cup. Suddenly sick of all the unfathomable, obtuse female maneuvering, she blurted out, "Mrs. McIves wants a stove."

"Stove?" Pastor exclaimed, unbelieving. "But Emma, it'd cost a fortune!"

"Twenty dollars," Emma quavered.

"Where would *we* get twenty dollars?"

"Well, I thought . . . I thought we might use the money Mr. Gray sent for Bernadette's winter expenses. Borrow it, I mean. By spring we could pay it back."

He looked down from his great dark height on his wife. "There'll be no tampering with Marcus Gray's money," he ordered quietly. "And no risking Bernadette's education. Why didn't you tell me you wanted a stove? I'll borrow the money from Otis Atchison; he might as well add it on to what he's lending me to go down to Pittsburgh in May. Theo Weld's going to be there, Bernadette. He's written that together we'll mount a church campaign for abolition at the Presbyterian assembly."

"In May?" Bernadette murmured; she stood at the dry sink hiding her face, thinking of Weld at Pittsburgh in May — when the maple trees budded, burst open with long, hanging, coiled leaves, tender-green, tight-furled.

Behind her, Emma McIves said, "Well, of course when you're gone, Bernadette'll be here so I'll be all right. As for the stove, the ladies I've talked to recommend Campbell's made down near Hartford. Clara Currie showed me hers yesterday, explained all about drafts and things I've forgot. The main thing is, there's less burning your arms, less wood-lugging."

"What do you think of a stove, Bernadette? Do they cook well?"

"Stove?" Her racing mind was a thousand miles away in Zanesville. "Cook well? Yes, they do. Aunt Leah had one."

"Would you like one, then?"

"Yes, sir, if Mrs. McIves does."

"Very well," he answered, "I'll arrange for a stove. Now come in the study with me. I don't have much time before my meeting."

Every night when they sat down, he inspected her journal

58

carefully; this wintry evening Pastor McIves flipped the pages hunting for something he always seemed to find missing.

He spun the book across the desk top, leaned back in his chair, his long legs stretched out beside her, put his hands behind his head and looked at her searchingly.

She squirmed.

"Bernadette, I see small evidence of spiritual growth in what you write. Shame for transgressions, yes, but no hunger for the Lord, no fervid reaching out to find Him."

How could she make him understand the Lord did not require Himself to be rediscovered by her in a flaming burst of painful emotion? Couldn't Pastor be satisfied with her asking forgiveness for her countless mistakes? There were ever so many of them — never had she felt herself reproved, improved so assiduously! By Emma, by him, just today by Miss Miller who'd caught her sketching Flora Schultz and once more delivered a lecture on how females must shun like the plague a public talent like art . . .

Couldn't they soon get to Latin? Her Latin, at least, seemed to please him . . .

But he took the journal back, held it up before him, squinted at it critically. "And why do you always put down everything I tell you about Brother Weld? I already know all those things."

"Mr. Weld seems like a hero," she stammered. *But elusive,* she didn't add; didn't add that's why she had to pin Mr. Weld down on paper, get him into the finality of words.

"What he does *is* heroic," Robb McIves agreed, "and it's very important for young men to have heroes. But girls? Well, they don't need them; they've usually got good family women for examples. Anyway, I'd certainly never recommend Weld as model for a young girl."

No, he wasn't her model, she denied secretly, fervently. He was her comfort.

Oh, please, would they never get to Latin?

For a long moment Pastor studied her. Then abruptly, he sat forward in his chair and reached for her school copybook. "Write what you like about Weld," he ordered. But his face said clearly she was beginning to puzzle him.

And so, against all bidding, Theodore Weld came to live in her — first as a passing wonder, a fleeting idyll, but as winter progressed and she heard constantly about him, he grew to be a compelling absorption, shielding her from the harsh, shackling realities which bound her. Her feeling for Weld made her sense infinite possibilities in herself, possibilities brought out by that intense and trusting state special to first love — imagined or real. Often she felt herself a magnificently different person, daring, confident, graceful, secure; anything was possible to her because of *him*.

She daydreamed. At night she lay awake and imagined herself with Weld, seductive imaginings of timid, untutored hand-holdings foreign to her unexplored but explosive temperament.

Annis finally decided she was lovesick for "Sheep's-Eyes" Will Ainsworth, the constable's son, and badgered her. Shy, Bernadette was ashamed to confess she was in love with someone she'd never even seen. So she fended Annis off crossly one moment but ached the next to confide her consuming secret to her dearest friend.

7

Bernadette took a quill from the bundle on the table, dipped it in the ink, began to scrawl hurriedly . . . the church's October festival had been successful — her new friend Pettee Trevelyan had brought her a set of cast-iron jackstones — she was done with candle-dipping — the new stove had been delivered but now Pastor must go to the expense of replacing the three-legged hearth pots with flat — she and Annis were making hairnets of silk thread, over a pencil — dancing school would soon start but she wasn't allowed to attend, mostly Episcopals could — a committee of churchwomen had complained to Emma she wore too many ruffles — Pastor said to pay it no mind, but, furious, Emma'd been ripping for days — Pastor wanted to teach Bernadette Greek and when Emma declared Bernadette's female brain would crack, Pastor had stamped out of the kitchen announcing he'd risk it . . .

"Cousin Hester," she scratched on, ignoring blots, "it's funny you're carrying an antislavery petition around Canterbury, too. Just this morning I picked one up from Pastor's desk and mean to get it signed for Pastor's petition campaign in Furnace Village —"

A thud on the side of the house made her jump. She leaped and rushed to the window, looked out. Leaning against a tree trunk was Pettee Trevelyan; he was juggling two more snowballs, grinning up at her. She threw open the sash.

"I saw Mrs. McIves ride off in the Curries' sleigh. You working?"

"No."

"Come up the mountain with me. Emilie Glaudin's been after me like a dog digging a bone. She says she won't give me anything more to eat until I bring you."

"I'll be down," Bernadette shouted, crashed the window down, ran in a fever of haste to find gum boots and tossed mittens.

Closed up the ink bottle, saw the petition sitting beside her letter. Thought of Hester, thought of Weld, of black Miriam Hosking whom she missed; a welter of impulses made her stuff the petition inside her cloak pocket. She'd like to tell Emilie of antislavery and Weld. Well, something of Weld anyway . . .

"You got snowshoes?"

"No, do you?"

"Well, of course I do," Trev answered. "Next time I come down I'll bring you a pair. Makes the going faster. I guess we can walk in the ruts."

When they left Washinee and started up the mountain, the sharp light cast blue shadows on the patchy snow; beside them the creek was gray. They followed a partridge track, dug out a nest in the thickets heaped with snow, trudged upward. He was a boy, so of course he began to snowball her and she had to turn on him, try to rub his face. Though he was shorter, younger, she was surprised how strong he was — no snow of hers made *his* cheeks ruddy. While she was trying to grab him, she tripped; he said, "Ho, you've dropped something!"

She saw her slave petition had fallen out of her pocket. He scooped it up, unfolded it, handed it to her. "What is it?"

"It's a petition to send to the federal Congress," she answered.

62

"What about?" he asked curiously.

"About slaves."

"Oh, blacks," he replied vaguely. "We haven't got blacks hereabouts. They've got 'em in Philadelphia, though."

"Those are free blacks. This petition's for slave blacks."

"Well, what *does* it say?"

She climbed up on a fallen log, balanced herself against a low tree branch, squinting severely to see if he listened. He listened, not looking, crouched down in the snow, rolling a snowball bigger and bigger while she read that "The undersigned most earnestly petition Congress immediately to abolish slavery in the District of Columbia, and to declare every human being free who set foot on its soil . . ."

"Do they just want slavery out of the District of Columbia?" he asked, looking up at last, his dark eyes sharp on her face.

"No, but they're beginning there because Congress can change that quicker."

"The paper's a blank after the words."

"That's for the names, Trev," she explained patiently. "The people who'll sign because they agree with what I've read."

"Are you going to get names for it?"

"I'd like to; I'd like to help Pastor McIves. He says Salisbury folks get upset because they think the petition'll tear the government apart. Or they just think the slave should have a master, it's ordained. Or that northern business will suffer. But mostly, Pastor says it's slow going because people are cowards and won't mix in with anything hot."

Trev threw the snowball into the bushes, jumped up. "I've got a lot of friends at Mount Riga. They'd sign what I say, hot or not. I could help you get names, if that's what you want."

63

She jumped off the log, rushed up to him. "Trev, *could* you?" Then, eye to eye with him, ardor dimmed in her. It wasn't right somehow. *He* wasn't right.

"You don't even believe it, do you?" she asked wistfully.

"Believe what?"

"The slave should be free."

"If enough people have a mind to free him, I expect it's all right. I don't think about it much one way or the other," he drawled bluntly.

"I lived in Canterbury last year where people wrecked a black girls' school. I had a black friend who went there . . . that's why I know slavery isn't right," she ended lamely; how could she ever explain to this wild, careless boy about Prudence Crandall's school or Miriam Hosking?

He was silent, poised, not hearing.

"What I mean is, if I came to Mount Riga with a petition, and you helped me, I'd want you to *believe* what you're doing."

"I don't believe in the Cold Water Army," he admitted at last. "Everybody hoots at it. Still, I'll believe what you say about the nigger," he assured her, never batting an eye. "Come on, it'll be fun racing around, getting names."

But her friend Trev was easily distracted. And on a blue, bright day like this — wind blowing white streamers off the snow patches, Mount Riga's lake riffled with snow — she found she was distractible, too. Before they got names on the petition, before they called at the Glaudins', Trev asked why they couldn't detour around by the icehouse, watch the men carving out the lake. Casually, he borrowed a sled from a little boy, said they'd wait for the nearest sleigh, hitch a ride behind it.

One came, jingling delightfully. "Get on!" Trev shouted.

"But I can't — I've never lain down on a sled before! I've always had to sit up."

"Oh, don't be so prissy!" he shouted back, and suddenly

like a regular boy she slammed herself down on the sled; the air went out of her as he fell on top of her, reaching, grabbing the runner brace.

Off they went on a splendid ride, wind roaring, bells singing, Trev hollering jubilantly in her ear.

At the icehouse, men were stacking the silvery blue chunks in straw; the pair of them peered around the door, feeling the still cold, breathing to see their breath. Then they went down by the lake's edge where the wagon was, the horses steaming and stamping, men lifting the ice blocks up, heaving them into the wagon bed.

"You mean that's the first time you've ever hung on a sleigh with a sled?"

"I never lay on a sled. Girls steer with their feet."

"Good grief!" he exclaimed in disgust. "You can't have *any* fun that way! I'm glad for once you got to do it right." They delivered the sled to its worshipful young owner, struck out for the Glaudins' house.

"We'll get warmed up first," he said. "Have some bread or cake. My fingers are icicles, how about yours?"

"They're cold," she laughed.

"Still," he observed, "you don't fret about it. Girls can be awful frets."

"I know," she agreed uneasily. *I know. I'm girl, but I must be boy, too, at least when it comes to sleighs and sleds, cold fingers, Greek . . .*

But Weld? That was different.

Madame Glaudin hugged Bernadette, bustled for plates, forks. Bernadette hung her cloak on the peg, picked up the baby. Trev threw off his sheepskin, shoved back his tassel-cap, blew on his fingers.

She and Emilie lapsed into French, Trev too busy munching to care. After a while they got around to petition-signing and Trev fetched the petition from her cloak pocket. Painstakingly, he explained to Madame Glaudin exactly what the paper was about.

"The wind blows too cold for Bernadette to knock on the doors, Trev. You take the paper, get names for her. But first let me sign." Emilie Glaudin fetched quill and ink; awestruck, Bernadette stared at the name which flowed across the white blankness of the paper. Her heart thumped suddenly inside her. A blow struck for Miriam, for Weld, for Pastor . . . for freedom!

Emilie commanded Trev to run to this place and that. "Tell them to sign for Emilie Glaudin. Most can't read but they'll sign if I ask. Now go, Pettee, but hurry back; Bernadette mustn't be on the trail at dark."

He came back, his eyes sparkling; it was clear he enjoyed what he was doing. A dozen strange names followed Emilie Glaudin's.

"When you come up again," Trev said, "we can finish it. It's jolly."

"But it's late, go now, go on . . ."

The door closed behind the embrace of the Frenchwoman.

Trev turned back to the village at Forge Pond. When she looked around, he was jumping from rock to rock on the rim of the ice, then he zigzagged and ran among the little silver weeds which stuck out of the bald pate of the white field and filled it with shadows of lace.

It was going to be dark when she got home, Bernadette realized in dismay, but then she reminded herself that Pastor would be so pleased to have the petition names.

He loomed suddenly out of the evening shadows on the road above the house. He said she should get home instantly, he had to tend to his horse.

She held her stiff hands to the smoldering hearth, blowing

to bring up the flame. Emma McIves wasn't anywhere downstairs; that meant she herself must hurry to get the late supper.

He came into the kitchen, big snowflakes on his broad shoulders, some clinging to his black hair. How fortunate the snow had held off till now, she thought, thickening the meat juice.

Without warning, her stirring arm was seized and she was jerked around; juice dribbled off her spoon onto the floor at her feet.

"Where have you been, Bernadette?"

"To Mount Riga. I'm sorry I'm late." Then she quailed. Why, anger literally exploded from him!

"You should have asked Emma, told her where you were going. It's almost six o'clock."

"Yes, sir. Mrs. McIves was off with Mrs. Currie. I got some names for an antislavery petition."

"You *what?*"

She wanted most dreadfully to fetch the paper from her cloak, but he held her arm in such a viselike grip she could only stand there, looking up at him, praying he'd loosen his grasp. He'd struck his wife, Emma. Perhaps he'd strike her, too. She couldn't move.

"We got twelve names for Congress," she whispered, unable to take her eyes from his thunderous face.

He didn't slap her. Instead, he let loose her arm, sat down at the table, put his head in his hands. He rested for a moment, still as stone. When he looked up, his face wore a strange marriage of stern gentleness.

"Bernadette, I hardly know what to say. Emma and I have been worried — Emma's worried herself straight into bed. I was just saddling the horse to find you. You shouldn't have got a petition signed."

"Beg pardon, sir, but you said men and women were taking them around in many places. Mr. Weld's eager to have them signed, you said."

"I never thought to explain. Yes, other men and — the Lord forgive us — a few women. But not children, most especially not female children."

"Children marched in the Cold Water Army," she replied stubbornly.

"Ah, yes; I see what you thought. But Bernadette, you're too young to converse about grave matters with strangers. I shudder when I envision you on that mountain with those vulgar men. Furthermore, I most especially do *not* approve women doing this work. I should never permit Emma, never, nor ask any of my churchwomen."

In confusion, she tried to sort out his words. She was too young. She was female. Neither the young nor the female could get signatures for the slave. On the other hand, children (of apparently neutral sex) could march against drunkenness.

It made no sense. Fearful as she was of him, defiance leaped in her. *I don't believe what he says.*

She looked at him silently out of dark, brimming eyes.

Apparently he mistook her look, thought he'd unduly frightened her. Remorse seemed to overcome him as he reached out for her, dripping spoon and burning kettle forgot. Gently he brought her between his knees as he would a child, started to speak. Then unaccountably he flushed and, looking annoyed, confused, pushed her away. All he said was "I want you to write in your journal about this folly. Pray about it on your knees. Now salvage what you can of supper. I've a meeting."

By the candle in the cold room that night she wrote in a lagging hand: "Today I was wicked, having taken an antislavery petition without permission up to Mount Riga; I was willful in that I didn't ask leave to get it signed and in getting it signed I was late coming home. I pray the Lord to forgive my reckless, unruly nature." She threw the pen down in an agony of self-disgust, picked it up again. "Dear Lord, I'll do it again. And I don't even see why I shouldn't. Theodore, help me."

Then she tore that defiant page out, put it to the candle flame, watched it brown, curl and disappear.

She didn't rebel right away; she even forgot her intention, because winter set in, long, deep. Delicate white vapors blew off low ridges; plum-colored clouds settled on the skyline; snow reared against barn doors; titmice and grosbeaks hid out in tree crooks. In the morning sunlight, sharp frosted pines pierced hoary hills; by midafternoon snow thudded off roofs; in the evening they watched for flu fires from the red-hot stove.

Winter also brought a beautiful fear-reducing discovery. Thrown aside in haste on his study sofa was Miss Miller's first school report to Pastor.

> . . . I send to you marks for Miss Bernadette's first six weeks. I do not need to tell you what manner of student she is — with the application of unwavering discipline she can become a prodigious one.
>
> As to deportment she is headstrong, quick-tempered, not conscientious, and she sometimes embroiders the truth. In a word, she is not yet steady but can, I am confident, grow so. (She is also overintense and could fall prone to nervousness.)
>
> Her worst habit is the persistent scribbling of everything she sees — the girls, the countryside, even my humble self. It is very wasteful of paper and lead. I punish her, for women should not cultivate public talents like art or music. I myself will not even sing with the men in church.

To keep her busy I require her to help with the younger students and they gather about her like flowers to the sun. She is discovering that learning means something to her not because its mastery comes easily but because it is something precious to share — thus will your dream be realized and a true teacher be born.

I implore you to be — as I am — severe. There should be no surcease of character improvement. She could be easily spoilt.

Now I must end by telling you that I find her warmhearted, high-spirited, sensitive, and lovable. She is one of the most appealing students I have ever taught.

Perhaps it is extravagant of me to say so, but has she not the most beautiful eyes ever seen in the human head?

I am, sir, your obedient servant,
Elizabeth Miller

Filled with disbelief, hardly absorbing Miss Miller's particulars, all Bernadette could whisper to herself as she put the paper down, was "Why, she likes me. Miss Miller *likes* me . . ."

March 1835. A blustery time, bare tree limbs cracking. The peepers began in the swamp back of the shed; as she watched, ice gradually retreated from it. Geese honked. Finally, here and there a patch of brown field grass showed. On the way home from school, she and Annis came across a mouse run exposed by the melt. Annis, shrieking and dancing, cried, "What if the mice come out?"

"Annis, are you really afraid of a mouse?"

"I'm afraid one'll get under my skirts. . ."

Yes, Bernadette admitted, she wouldn't like a mouse to do that; then she was suddenly ashamed of her timidity, wildly impatient to see Trev.

Forgot Trev. But never forgot Weld, who was always a presence in her, someone to talk to.

Bernadette and the McIveses ran to church incessantly, rushing between their little parsonage and the clapboard meetinghouse, whose walls still smelled of wet plaster, its pews of fresh varnish. It wasn't a large, stylish church on the turnpike where rich forge-owners, lawyers, and store-owners went, but Pastor was confident his would soon be a ranking congregation because he preached the new-style, reforming evangelism let loose in the land by the great twenties revivals.

She listened to his fiery urgency, spellbound as ever. It wasn't just his arresting physical aspect, nor his expressive man's voice, public yet intimate; it was qualities in him of aliveness, of being caught up in what he said. He made of the world an excitement, he showed a Hebrew appetite for experience, only part-repressed. His was a world of friend or foe: no one was neutral to him. "Such a devoted man," his churchfolk murmured. In the days when preachers — along with politicians — could become national heroes, Otis Atchison summarized bluntly, "He's a comer."

Still, listening attentively, finally hurtfully, she stayed repelled by a harsh, bleak creedal insistence, sensed the Book was not everything; this church was not all. She believed the world was wide and large and many kinds of people belonged in it. She kept thinking of the Canterbury Quakers, kept thinking of Montreal Mass. What larger, more human, more accepting experience was in both which wasn't in him or here?

Fighting him and the churchfolk off, she continued to sense his faith would force on her a tortured existence where sinning seemed keener than loving, obligation outweighed willing respect, shame preempted joy. To feel depraved was alien to her nature; she simply couldn't experience an accusing God.

71

"Should you raise up a worldly issue like that?" Emma pouted after Pastor's first abolition sermon. "Mrs. Currie says *no,* Mr. McIves."

"Of course I should," Pastor concluded cheerfully. "Don't fret, Emma. No minister worth his salt ever preached to everyone's content."

Bernadette looked out the window; a redbird rose from the swamp, shot upward.

It reminded Bernadette of the forbidden petition hid under the petticoats in her drawer.

Trev tore ahead of her propelled by a fever of executive excitement — for all his high jinks, Trev was a driver. As she watched him flicker through sun and shade, Bernadette's guilt subsided. At Mount Riga illegally, she suddenly didn't care; she gauged the spring mud with a practiced eye, jumped energetically to the plank walkway.

"Let's go to the blacksmith shop," he suggested. "There are lots of men there. Charles Glaudin'll *make* them all sign."

She paused, considering. Something was changing in her, some subtle imbalance which went with front-buttoned dresses, Sir Walter Scott's contraband novels, and everyone at school not hating boys anymore.

Grown women never went to smithies.

Trev's eyes dared her. "Come on," he pressed.

What decided her was simple: she *wanted* to go.

She followed Trev boldly into the smithy shed, stood there, eyes downcast. The smithy floor was black with grime, scattered with hoof parings, shavings, bits of metal.

Finally she dared to look up at the dim light filtering through the cobwebbed windows, saw on a crossbeam where new shoes were nailed — small, light ones for roadhorses, heavy ones for workhorses. At last she made herself look

72

right at the smithy, the silent, muscled man who, with one hand, held a horseshoe to the fire with tongs while working the bellows with the other.

Obviously at a ticklish point, Charles Glaudin ignored his observers. He pulled the glowing red shoe from the fire, held it aloft, squinted at it critically, thrust it back in the flame. The bellows blew the coals redder. Bernadette jumped a mile when, without even looking up, he asked in a rumbling, accented voice, "Master Pettee, what brings you here today?"

Trev started to open his mouth, but suddenly the blacksmith whisked the tongs from the flame, laid the shoe on the anvil and with powerful movements began to hammer it; nothing could be heard over the clanging. Orange sparks arced in the dark air. Trev hunched his shoulders impatiently.

Pushing the shoe into a tub of scummy water, Monsieur Glaudin was instantly hidden by a cloud of hissing steam which curled about the roof beams. The blacksmith reached down for the horse's leg, pinioned it between his knees, set the shoe against the upraised hoof. There was a dreadful, acrid smell; little wisps of smoke puffed from the hoof.

"Trev . . ." she murmured apprehensively.

"Don't hurt," Trev muttered. "It's like cutting toenails."

The smithy dropped the horse's leg with a thud.

"So you've brought the French girl from Montreal?" he asked.

Trev nodded.

"Welcome to my shop, mademoiselle." Charles Glaudin turned at last, a smile warming his broad, smudged face. She saw that he was not old and coarse, that the hair above his sooty forehead was yellow like his wife, Emilie's. Gravely wiping his hand on his leather apron, he took Bernadette's in greeting.

"Mr. Glaudin," Trev burst out, "remember when I told you about the slave petition? We want to stay here this morning and you can get your customers to sign for us."

"Of course I remember the slave petition," Glaudin replied, vastly polite. "Should I ask this pair to sign?"

In a flash Trev fished from his pocket the little bottle of ink and battered quill. The smithy turned to the man and boy whose horse he'd just shod, spoke to them in their own language.

After brief exchange, there were two beautiful, strangely writ signatures which she couldn't read. (And — alas! — a large smudge, which she prayed the federal congress would overlook.)

The door opened and a new group of workmen came in. Casting curious sidelong glances at her, they chattered incomprehensibly while one of them maneuvered his ox team into the shed.

Charles Glaudin motioned to Trev. "Master Trevelyan, take *her* to my wife."

"We're working together," Trev declared.

"Yes, perhaps," the smithy answered imperturbably. "Only not in here."

"But it's a good place to work; you have almost as much business as the general store. And they'll sign if you tell them to."

"That is so," Charles agreed. "So *you* may stay here for an hour and then fetch Mademoiselle Bernadette from Emilie's."

She should have known if she were foolish enough to linger in a smithy she'd be reproached for indecency. Would no one let her do *anything*?

"I'll go to Madame Glaudin's," she hastily promised a stormy Trev and slipped out the door. How she'd wanted to watch the oxen being shod, wanted to see them cradled in

74

the mammoth ox-sling, hitched up! Smoldering resentment burst into sulfurous rage. Why were the freest, most fascinating and important places forbade her sex? Furnaces, smithies, schools beyond children's ones? Everybody had to work too hard, but at least men got away to hunt and fish and could enter into the important life of town and church meetings. She twitched her skirts, then ran like the wind trying to escape from the huge, hateful knowledge. As she raced, in a crystal-clear illumination it came to her: in *her* life she was going to do interesting things no matter *what* anyone said. *Bountiful Lord, give me the courage to be what I'm going to be,* she prayed . . . and felt better.

An hour later Trev had captured an imposing list of names; there was only one space left. She hurriedly kissed the wobbly baby, then with Trev dashed after people on the road, stood by the general store hopefully.

With no success . . .

"Cook'll sign," Trev finally guaranteed as they rested beside the pond. "We'll go to my house."

"I've been at Mount Riga since morning; I've got to go home . . ."

"We're thirsty and need a drink," the boy replied crossly.

One more signature!

Fifteen minutes later she was racing Trev up the steps to the great mansion.

She followed him through an entry in which a beautiful staircase spiraled regally, wainscoted wood gleamed, her shoes mired in magnificent carpeting — if you ran you might even lose a shoe in it! She felt a sensuous urge to touch everything — velvet drapes, slippery sofa coverings, marble tops; most of all she wanted to study the dark paintings in their massive carved frames.

They were heading for the kitchen when suddenly a voice began from above. It grew in volume from loud to loudest as

75

an old man marched down the great staircase, a tall, bull-strong man with a white mane of hair which tried unsuccessfully to subdue the flaming face it encased.

"Pettee Trevelyan, where've you been? You've been gone for hours."

Trev looked as if he'd been ambushed. (So he *could* be afraid of someone, she observed slyly.)

"I've been getting a petition signed in the village."

"Petition? What petition?" demanded the man.

"It's *her* petition," Trev muttered ungallantly.

"Her? Who might *her* be?" The full glow of a volcanic red face scorched her; she sorted out jutting white brows, a bulbous nose, a short, bristling beard. The *Ironmaster*. It must be he, for he looked at her out of Trev's bold jet eyes.

"'Tis Bernadette Savard, the one who lives in Furnace Village with the Pastor," Trev's sulky voice explained.

"Ah, my young kin's mentioned you. Good day, Miss Savard. So you live with that clergyman, do you? I've heard of *him*, too."

She didn't like the tone he used when he spoke of Pastor McIves; it was one thing for her to mislike Pastor sometimes, but a different matter for others.

Having made a thorough canvass of her, the Ironmaster straightened. "Yes," he repeated, "I've heard of your minister. He's not to drag children up to meddle with my colliers, d'y' hear? Only a petticoated coward would hide behind children. Tell him to stay safe down in Furnace Village and not come up to Riga bothering us men."

Whatever could be said of Pastor McIves, he was *no* petticoated coward! Bernadette's chin came out, and there she was, glaring straight back into those hard-polished old button-eyes. "I could tell him what you've said, sir, but I don't think he'd pay you mind."

76

There was a startled snort. "Oh-ho, you've got flint in ye! Inconvenient for a lass to be pert."

They confronted each other, neither giving ground.

"If *you* don't tell your Pastor to stay away I'll roust him out of his pulpit and tell him myself." Then — a shade more respectful, she thought — he turned to his kin. "Been mischief-making again? Pray, what's the subject of this petition? To do away with school or give you more spending pennies?"

"It's to free slaves, sir."

"Free slaves!" the Ironmaster shouted. "Pettee Trevelyan, what have you been up to?"

"It's asking the Congress to abolish slaves in the federal district," she spoke up, feeling responsible for Trev.

"Abolish blacks? Well spoken, girl, I'd like to see 'em all abolished, every man jack of 'em. But it can't be done. We've got to have slaves, need 'em for sugar and rice and cotton. Where in thunder did you get such papers?"

"From Pastor McIves; he and some of his churchpeople are carrying them."

"I might have known. I've heard impractical nincompoops are rushing about New England agitating against the interests of business. Let me see it." The Ironmaster barked his order so unexpectedly that Bernadette handed over the petition without thinking.

The minute he snatched it, casting a brief, scornful look on it, she knew it'd end badly. His big, speckled hands abruptly tore the petition right in two; then he handed it back to her.

"Have 'em. My guttermen and molders won't be drawn into this, not on your life. We're having a hard enough time in the Riga iron industry as it is. Black men are made for slaves just as northern mechanics ought to do as they're told."

77

Trying not to let anger reduce her to tears, Bernadette clutched the mutilated page, appalled at the ragged part-signatures. Then an idea flashed over her. With flour and water paste *could* she mend it? *Maybe.*

"Now then, young miss, pay attention to me. You're a handsome girl. What in Judas' name do you want to run around doing things like this for? You ought to be prettying for beaux."

Blankly she looked up, saw that like so many lordly folk, once he'd had his way, he wished to be friends.

Not with her, he wouldn't.

"Pettee could bring you back another time. Wife — she's away right now — has ribands and baubles she never uses. Wouldn't you like a new riband for your hair?"

She shook her head, "I don't need your baubles and ribands."

Trev suddenly emitted a bellow of rage; just one short bawl came out before he fled. Breathlessly she found herself out on the front steps, the echo of a slammed door in her ears. Trev would certainly get thrashed for that exit; she just hoped it wouldn't happen in front of her.

Yet miraculously no one fetched Trev back; he just stood there, his face hid in the crook of his upraised arm.

"All that work for nothing," he finally gulped.

"Trev, I think I can mend the page," she confided.

He showed his surprised face to her, the soot runnelled by tears, and asked, "Do you?"

At her solemn nod he seized her hand. "I'll go as far as the pond with you."

This time he didn't suggest they poke around the water wheel, blast machinery, or wagon scales. "You go right down — fix the page before you get supper," he urged.

8

Sʜᴇ ʜᴀᴅɴ'ᴛ ᴇxᴘᴇᴄᴛᴇᴅ Trev to come down to Furnace Village the very next morning, but there he was on the back doorstep. They stole into the sunny backyard.

She handed him the petition. He frowned in concentration; then his face lost its anxious pucker.

"That's a capital job of mending! The names are all joined up! Wouldn't Uncle have a fit!"

She took it back, pleased.

"What'll we do with it now?" he asked.

"Send it straight to Congress. But I haven't the money to post it myself and I don't know if Congress'll pay to receive it."

"I'll take it to Mount Riga and mail it," Trev offered promptly. "I have the pennies."

She hesitated, afraid his uncle might find it; afraid above all of the proprietary gleam which flashed in Trev's face. Who knows? He might just keep it around to admire!

"No," she answered slowly, "I'll keep it here; you bring down the pennies."

"I want to take it up with me."

"No, Trev."

"Yes, Bernadette," he insisted, both of them half-laughing, determination springing up in the air between them, making Bernadette unloose her feet from her skirts the better to jump up.

He grabbed unsuccessfully for the page; she took to her

heels. "It's mine," she exalted, wanting to plague him for his imperious possessiveness.

He was slick as a weasel, not wasting *his* breath in taunting.

She flew toward the little horse shed but the minute she got inside knew she'd made a fatal mistake — there was no way out. She felt Trev's grasping hands brush her hair, dived downward on the straw thinking to elude him by scrambling on all fours back to the open door.

Ill-reasoned strategy! She sprawled headlong, felt a great weight on her back — Trev, fastening to her like a young bear cub . . .

She kept laughing, unable to stop from excitement, though mortification began to course through her as his boy's arms pinioned her shoulders and pushed her face to the splintery boards beneath the harsh straw. He kicked at her thrashing legs, barked her ankles.

"Trev!" she shouted indignantly. "Let me up!"

"Give me the paper!"

"Well, get off me then!" She tried to roll to one side with him latched to her.

As she turned, her eyes came to rest on a very familiar pair of large, blunt-toed black boots, both of them planted right beside her nose. She twisted her head up, saw a pair of black pants legs, long, tall. Apprehensively, her neck arching, her look arrived at a double-breasted long-tailed coat, a dark vest, a whalebone neckcloth she herself had just ironed.

Finally there was the horrified face of Pastor McIves peering down at her.

Abruptly, there was no scuffling boy weighing her down; instead, there was Trev suspended in midair, his legs going like pump handles, his face turning beet-red, his eyes furious black coals. But no more furious than the gray ones whose owner held him off and surveyed him as though he were a feckless hunting prize shot from the skies.

80

Robb McIves glanced down at her as she lay in shock; his expression told her her skirts were tumbled about her exposed legs, her hair was undone.

"Who is he?" Pastor asked thickly.

"Pettee Trevelyan of Mount Riga, sir," she answered, scrambling up, straw, skirts, hair, and — oh woe! — paper falling after her.

"So you're the Ironmaster's kin," Robb said, setting Trev down with a thump which jarred the boy's teeth. "You appear to be as willful as he is."

"It's all my fault," Bernadette wailed despairingly. "I was teasing him."

"I'll speak with you later, miss. What are you doing with my ward, Pettee Trevelyan?"

"We got the paper signed in Mount Riga, and I wanted to take it back up there for posting, but she ran away with it," Trev answered in the same sullen tone he'd used with his uncle.

"What paper?" Robb asked with dangerous evenness, holding his long arm out to her and snapping his fingers. Quickly, she scooped the petition off the floor and placed it in his outstretched hand. He never looked at her, only at the boy.

He glanced at the paper. "Who tore it?" he snapped.

"The Ironmaster," Bernadette answered low, seeing Trev wouldn't.

"Why?" Robb demanded.

"Because —"

"I'll beg you to be silent, Bernadette. It's this young rip I'm asking."

"Uncle doesn't want the slave to be free," Trev muttered.

"Oh, he doesn't, does he? And what right has he got to tear up papers signed by others who feel differently? What right, eh?" the Pastor pressed wrathfully.

"He has a right to say what his founders and fillers do," Trev finally flared back.

"Indeed? Owns them, does he? Tells them what they must think as well as do?"

"Yes, sir," Trev answered instantly. "They're his workmen; his company brought them from Europe. They wouldn't even *be* in Riga but for my uncle's iron company."

"More's the pity they should fall under the influence of an infidel, even though supposedly churched. You tell your uncle I expressly disapprove what he did with this petition. You tell him I don't approve *your* behavior, either."

What a broil! Bernadette thought frantically. What if these dreadful insults grew into a meeting? She couldn't bear to imagine the two men colliding, didn't believe Pastor realized what molten metal the old Ironmaster was made of, didn't believe the Ironmaster had any idea of Pastor's grit.

"My uncle don't approve of you, either," Trev burst out furiously, boldly ignoring the risk of a thrashing.

"No, I don't suppose he does; from what I hear, the Ironmaster'd not approve any interfering clergyman," Robb retorted drily, but with some semblance of returning self-control.

"I don't know about clergymen," said Trev, emboldened by the calmer tone. "It's just my uncle don't favor prissies."

Bernadette sucked in her breath. *Merciful Lord, let the words stop flowing! Pastor McIves would throttle him!*

But strangely, he didn't flare up again, only looked pinched and stern.

"You tell your uncle there's a *man* in the pulpit down in Furnace Village, a *man* first of all. And you stay away from Bernadette, do you hear?"

"Yes, sir," Trev answered, scuffing his shoe in the straw.

"You come near her again, I'll go straight up to Mount

Riga and have it out with your uncle. I've a mind to anyway."

The quiet in the shed was awful.

"Now get out of here," Robb ordered.

They watched Trev leave, Pastor with his hard face and she barely able to watch the humiliated boy.

"Go to your room," he told her, not looking at her.

She dashed upstairs, threw herself on her bed, hugged her pillow, burst into stormy tears.

All mixed up in her were terrible indignation at Pastor and helpless remorse for Trev. In astonishment she realized how much she'd come to care for Pettee Trevelyan, his wary, sidelong glance, his cautious hiding of his true self by wild bravado.

There was a bond, then, growing between her and Trev; Trev had begun to trust her, she'd begun to trust him.

Would this break their fragile connection?

Where have you gone to hide your hurt, Trev? What barn loft, what woods pool, what tree notch?

She rolled over, trying not to think of Trev out there without her.

Robb punished her for the stolen petition by bundling her off for the summer to Canterbury; farm work and the lack of village distraction would do her good, he said. He expected her back penitent, ready for the salvation experience. "Keep your journal every night without fail," he instructed.

It was no punishment to be back at Canterbury, but heartwarming instead. Rachel had lost none of her roundness, because Hester still nursed her; David joked they'd have to send Rachel to school to wean her. Cousin Paul, with his accustomed shy blush, promised to teach Bernadette to swim.

But hard work soon descended like a harness dropped squarely over her, cinched tight. Country marriage, she thought, was a sentence to a life term of hard labor.

With the adored baby tagging at her heels, Bernadette fired the flagstone fruit kiln to dry quince and drained whey from the cheese with a long quartering knife, holding Rachel back to prevent her scorching or drowning herself. When David brought the entrails of a freshly butchered hog and Bernadette and Hester picked the guts to extract lard, Rachel gleefully sneaked her fists into the slippery mess, made greasy fingerprints everywhere, but it was somehow small hardship to wash them up. Even when they dragged the feather ticks down the back stairs to wash them outside and Rachel scattered feathers all over the farmyard, strangely the downy mess only made Bernadette laugh.

Despite incessant work and the omnipresent baby, Hester and Bernadette had time and enthusiasm for talk.

A small antislavery society was forming right in Canterbury. Opposition was fearsome, but the group went bravely forward.

Bravery was needed elsewhere, too, Hester said. In Canaan, New Hampshire, citizens had whipped oxen to a boys' academy and dragged it into the swamp because it had opened its doors to two colored students. . . . Dr. Reuben Crandall was lodged in a Washington prison for circulating antislavery material; the district attorney, Francis Scott Key, had publicly declared he'd ask the death penalty for Crandall. . . . In Tennessee, Amos Dresser, a Lane seminarian, was seized for distributing abolition tracts and lashed twenty times; he barely escaped with his life. . . . Odious President Jackson said he'd like to see abolitionists drummed out of society like traitorous soldiers.

"Won't the petitions to Congress help?" Bernadette

wondered, scrubbing Paul's coveralls on the wood washboard.

"Oh, yes. Petitions are one of our chief ways of fighting back."

The *slap-slap* of wet cloth in steamy silence. "Pastor McIves doesn't think females should get petitions signed."

"Garrison believes in women in abolition," Hester replied firmly. "He believes they should hold fairs, organize lectures, carry petitions."

Bernadette wondered for a time, then decided in her own head that of course Theodore Weld would want women in abolition . . .

It was Pastor's mandate about her journal which finally soured her summer. Looking at it unopened on her table made her despondent, confused, anxious, rebellious. As the days hurried on and it stayed stubbornly blank, she longed to be done with it and just dash off *I am sinful, I am sinful* endlessly, monotonously, on every line in all those loathsome pages.

Her normal buoyancy shriveled, in half-asleep helpless torment she finally began simply to scribble in the journal — small designs, random, meaningless patterns, scratchings. Weary head propped in her hand, nodding so close to the candle she almost caught fire, she bent over the blazing white emptiness.

In trouble, drawing was always her solace.

What would she *draw?*

I'll capture the one who never comes to hard life.

With sweeping strokes she began to sketch, feeling instantly freed, transported. Under her deft fingers a person sprang into being. Face first — thin, fine-bred; high forehead; noble brows arched over large eyes she'd finish later;

aquiline, classical nose; bow lips curving. Light hair rolled above sloped shoulders . . .

But could such chivalrous beauty defy a rough mob? She knew she needed to put a tough hero in the eyes: farseeing, charismatic, commanding. But the eyes wouldn't come right; her gifts were taxed past her untrained capacity. Roused from torpor, she flipped the page and began again, terribly awake.

Four times she drew Weld. On the fourth page he shone out exactly as she *knew* he looked. Despite lack of technique, her primitive talent had created a romantic man, fair and delicate, yet saved from the sentimental by a deep, fiery gaze.

She stared in fascination.

What would it be like to know Brother Weld? She believed he'd make her feel good about herself, let her be alive and natural. *He* wouldn't ask her to live under the blight of sin or constantly test her submission. *He* would help her understand the strange web around her, understand why she longed for whole and freely-given love, not the dreadful stunted emotion which she sensed was Emma's in Salisbury — hurtful, smothering sacrifice followed by closeted nothingness.

"Frère Weld, que je vous aime," she wrote, unable to stop. Ardent French words poured out, uninhibited words of need, not the mannered words of veiled novels and stilted poetry.

After that she wrote to Weld sporadically, knowing ruin awaited her upon her return to Salisbury but helpless to restrain herself. These letters, in French, rushed mysteriously from her . . .

One night she went back to drawing. There was black Miriam Hosking; there was Trev, his whole figure springing over the page.

While she worked on Trev she was aware that she wanted to draw someone else but was mortally afraid to make the first stroke, was like the moth which circled in the candle flame at her elbow.

Eventually — like it — would she tumble in fascination into the very thing which sealed her fate? Spellbound, she stopped and watched as the moth was consumed — as she would be when Pastor McIves looked into her book.

When she began to draw again, these lines came hard. Later she counted the spoiled pages and a frightened breath caught her throat.

But at last it was he, just as overpoweringly he as though Pastor McIves had entered her room. She turned back the pages, looked at Weld. Jealously, she intuited that the drawing of Weld was a phantasma beside this real likeness of Robb McIves which throbbed and shouted with a crude, craggy energy.

After a time, she touched what she'd drawn, found the thick, shredded places roughed by her pen. Roughness went with Pastor, she thought, tracing in wonder the black hair, her fingers moving to brow and eyes, down the angle of cheek and jaw, up to the mouth. They ran back and forth over the lips, swollen and raised from the page.

She jerked her hand away.

Whatever made her want to feel his lips? she wondered in shock. She shut the journal with a thud, blew the candle out, crawled into bed, stretched taut.

In the few weeks she remained on the farm, she never dared open the journal again. She saw it resting there, dusted it, set it hurriedly back. She told herself she'd leave it behind when she left; then she decided she'd take it and toss it from the stagecoach.

But she wouldn't do either of these things, she finally knew in helpless certainty. She'd take the book back to Salisbury. When Pastor McIves asked to see it she'd have to hand it over to him just as it was.

It was her summer penance; the dire punishment which would come to her as result of its revelations would be her atonement for what Pastor required of her but she couldn't induce in herself.

All the way back on the coach, her sense of fatalism welled up so serenely she could even think of other things: how she'd learned to swim, even with water-soaked skirts; how she'd galloped with Paul on the half-broken colt down the streaking green pasture, come back to ride again — "Gritty," Paul had said.

She thought of Hester sewing coarse slave shoes in the evening by lamplight to help earn her way to Boston to an antislavery meeting; remembered Rachel, sly as a fox, poking her fingers into the yellow cheese making. She savored what had given her the most pleasure of all . . . cutting green rye, scalding and bleaching it, splitting the strands with her teeth, braiding them to make a straw bonnet for Rachel, a bonnet which enclosed the bright face but let the tender hair escape.

Long before she spied the village, she smelled the wood haze in the Salisbury air.

 9

SHE GOT BACK in October's burning beauty to find life awry at the parsonage.

Emma was bedfast. The young wife hardly waited till Bernadette was in the little house to call her upstairs.

"The very day you went away I was trying to tend the fire," a wan, pinch-faced Emma explained, "when all of a sudden I had a terrible chest pain. Though I don't remember it, I must have staggered to a chair where Mr. McIves found me. He sent for Dr. Turner and we learned my heart had suffered a congestion. I was carried straight to my bed and I've been in it all summer."

Heart? *Poor Emma! Poor Robb McIves!* Bernadette listened with shocked compassion. "But surely you'll mend."

"Doctor gives me nostrums, but my heart skips so many beats I'm afraid it'll stop altogether," Emma went on feebly. "My limbs won't support me from here to the window. The farmgirl moved right in with me; so Mr. McIves took your room."

As Bernadette glanced at the cluttered eave of Emma's room allotted to her, consternation struggled with sympathy. She went soberly downstairs to fix the evening meal.

She'd been so busy with Emma she'd hardly had time to pay attention to Pastor. Now, surveying him secretly by the light of the table lamp, she was appalled to note he looked positively gaunt. No wonder, she concluded feelingly, with his wife abed!

He caught her standing there studying him.

"Well, Bernadette, so you finished your Cotton Mather?"

"Yes, sir."

"We'll have Greek to catch up on, won't we?"

His heavy-spirited effort to be friendly made her feel funny; she wished she'd gone about her dishwashing instead of staring at him. In some ways at the parsonage she was starting out a stranger all over again.

As for him, he sat in the yellow lamp-glow stroking his jaw. "It's been a long summer," he murmured at last.

89

"It must have been, with Mrs. McIves ill."

A shadow crossed his face; he gave an imperceptible shrug. "Yes, that's true, her illness has been difficult. But I was thinking of something else . . ."

Juggling the dishes, she waited.

"There's a regular devil's brew in Salisbury, Bernadette," he burst out.

"Devil's brew?"

"If I'm going to tell you, put down the dishes," he remarked with the old testiness.

Carefully she put the dishes on the shelf, went to sit straight-backed, hands folded, across from him at the table.

"It's the church," he commenced. "I've known for some time many of my people disagreed about slavery but I was sure I could bring them around. I came back in June from the church national assembly in Pittsburgh, certain I could win over the world. I was with Weld at the assembly; it was magnificent, working with Theodore — we convinced a fourth of the delegates to support abolition. You can imagine how fired up I was to get home and save my people! But while I was gone, Otis Atchison told me, half the deacons met and rose up in arms, saying no matter how well I preached they'd not have a rabble-rousing fanatic in their pulpit. Seems they got the idea from reading this fellow Garrison that antislavery men want instant black emancipation and prompt race amalgamation."

Very quietly they both sat, she clasping, unclasping her hands.

"I know who my friends are in the church. It's my enemies I can't get hold of; they're a slippery business, like catching an eel barehanded. A rumor here, gossip there, an accusation repeated from one to another till no man knows who said it first. It's not the out-and-out troublemakers who don't hide,

90

it's ones like Achsah Miller I despair of — he goes behind my back and then denies it to my face. At best, one's friends never shout as loud as one's enemies," he finished despondently. "In the past few months I've fought for my right to speak, for my pulpit — even, perhaps, for my life as a churchman. By the way, Mrs. McIves is too delicate to know any of this; visitors don't mention it."

Longing to say something to comfort him, she thought suddenly of a tract Hester had given her, rose, fetched it from her cloak pocket, offered it simply.

Absently he opened it. She went to the neglected dishes, aware of his silent figure.

"*An Appeal to the Christian Women of the South,* by Angelina Grimké," he read out loud. "Who's Angelina Grimké?"

"I don't know; neither did Cousin Hester."

He turned pages rapidly while she wiped dishes.

"Hmmmmm," he finally finished.

She came back by his chair.

"I suppose it's a good enough tract," he commented. "It's even a telling thesis that southern women ought to persuade southern men against slavery. These same words by an antislavery *man* would deserve wide circulation."

What Hester had told her of Abolitionist women was strong in her; denial rose in her throat. But just as she was about to argue with him, he put his hand on his forehead, rubbed it wearily; then his head sank forward with fatigue.

She stood looking down at his hair, that dark, thick, crisp hair.

Pity filled her.

Would she dare comfort him by touching his hair?

She stood rooted.

He reached and found her hand, held it briefly, let it drop

and looked up at her, his expression grateful. "Never fear, I still have high hopes of winning my church; I'll not back off. I've missed you. I'm glad you're home."

Running, Trev kicked up the leaves; she dashed in his crackling wake. Everything about Trev was commotion; she was glad she'd screwed up her courage and marched to his grand front door. All summer she'd brooded about her part in Pastor's shaking Trev up. Was she the only villager who saw not wickedness but shy loneliness? Feelings flashed in her, were blurred in the need to pant up the slope.

They crested the ridge and looked triumphantly into the ravine. Down there, trees had been cleared to make a great bare circle. In the bare middle a towering mound of short logs had been piled; over these logs dirt and leaves had been thrown to form a thin cover. Beside the circle a druidlike collier's hut was built half-in the forest.

They looked down at a forty-foot-high charcoal hearth.

An old fellow in a stocking cap was beckoning them. In one hand he waved a lit faggot.

"Hurry, I'm late!"

"Wait! Don't start! I want *her* to light it." Trev grabbed her hand, hauled her so fast she nearly rolled like a barrel down the slope.

"Ah, miss, 'tis not often a Raggy man has a lass to light up." The old man spoke out of a soot-darkened face with yellow-white eyes.

Trev snatched the torch from the collier's hand, pushed it at her.

"Now, then, lad, keerful! She has marvelous long hair and a burnable cloak," the woodsman soothed, reclaiming the torch without rancor. "Please tie up your hair and take off your cape."

With hands so eager they shook, she bundled her hair into

92

her kerchief, unbuttoned her cape, shivered it carelessly to the ground. "What do I do?" burst out of her.

"Now, then, young master, follow but don't grab." The raggy collier led Bernadette to the house-high hearth and pointed to some leaves stuffed into log chinks. "Touch a fire," he ordered quietly.

She tipped the leaves, watched them catch fire, waited till this chink was well-started, moved to the next, held the torch steadily there.

"Takes an acre of hardwood forest for one day's furnace, miss; I've lost track of how many wagonloads of charcoal I've delivered to the shed," the raggy said in her ear.

Slowly they circled the pile of lumber, lighting, lighting, lighting . . .

"The dirt and the leaves make a slow burn, no wild flames; that would make ash, not char," the raggy explained. "I'll be weeks tending this one; that's why my hut's here."

"But it's getting too cold to live in the woods," she protested.

"That it is and too bitter after the end of November for coalin'. I'm late this year."

After she'd lit enough fires, she sat on a log, chin on fist, pensively watching the great mound. Wood smoke smelled so good — October-smell. Inside houses, hearth fires were starting; at windows by dusk there was lemon lamplight. Outside — bright, vaulting sky; beneath, trees like clusters of coral anemone under the wash of brilliant seas. She felt most alive in the fall; its spirit of wind and rustle, of odor, color, tuned to the exultation in her.

Her little mound fires were taking hold now, licking up the logs; white smoke puffed out. Still, she hated to think of all the trees cut down to be turned into black char to feed a stone maw. Trees whose leaves wouldn't grow crisp, turn yellow, turn scarlet, turn umber, turn brown, fall down in slow circles or roll on the forest floor before the wind. She thought of tree seeds she'd whimsically rescued, pulled out of barren places — pockets of rock, surface of water.

Was life all a planting, a burning down? she pondered. If true, would the planting grow faster than the fire?

Later, she and Trev sat by the mountain trace.

"Did Pastor McIves know you came to fetch me?" he asked.

"No."

He whistled softly. "If he were my guardian, I'd run off."

"Trev, look at me." He obeyed, unblinking. "I don't care what Pastor McIves thinks about you," she spoke slowly, yearning to reach his insides.

The boy just kept staring at her; she couldn't read him. Then he jumped up and threw a stone over the cliff. "It's a long way down; tell me if you hear it land."

"Someone might be down there."

"Some fierce old injun?" he asked scornfully; long ago she'd accepted his disappointment she wasn't an injun. "I'm going to climb out on that exposed root; bet we can see a long way down the cliff from it."

Grabbing a branch above them, they footed their way out on the slippery snag.

Yes, Trev brought out strange, hidden things in her, lured her with dangerous, forbidden adventures. Like what, un-breathing, she was doing right now.

Danger was out in the world. Forbidden to test herself, how would a girl know what she could or would do?

"Looks like it does from a forge top," he commented carefully; even Trev was afraid to talk for fear of jiggling the root.

"Oh, no! It's not smoky hellfire; it's soft little tops of trees for a bed!"

"Would you go up on a forge with me?"

Suddenly her arms were too taut above her head; dizzy green space was too empty beneath.

She slid to the safe end of the root; he crouched beside her.

"I'm afraid of a forge top, Trev," she admitted at last, very softly.

For a long time he didn't answer, just broke twigs and threw them over the edge.

"I thought so. I'm glad you finally told me." Then, by his next answer, she knew trust still flowed strong and sweet between them, even after the summer. "I'm glad we can tell each other."

Going home alone, she came to a place where she could look back to the ridge they'd climbed to get to the hearth. Trev had said, "You light this hearth; then when it smokes in the sky, it'll be yours."

Up against the sunset her very own smoke rose in lazy circles. Witching weather, she mused exultantly, and her coal hearth a witching thing. An early owl hooed; it broke her joyous spell, it sounded so lonely.

The whole world assumed a Halloween shape: the skullcap of the sky, the whiskered ridge of the hills, the smoke of her hearth rising out of the mouth of the draw, and later, as she pelted up Meadow Street, the winking eyes of Furnace Village's lights.

10

HER DRESS BODICE left little gaps between the buttons, showing her petticoat. But at least she didn't have pimples like Rosie Butts who picked the scabs in her hair with her quill so that they fell into Susie Coffin's inkwell, Bernadette thought, fastening up the stretched-tight alpaca.

No use to ruin her fine mood with despair; she didn't have time to mope tonight.

Tonight was the gala donation party when churchfolk eked out Pastor's salary, brought contributions to "tide him over the winter."

She gave a last slap-dash to her hair, ran downstairs to check out her table; her dry apple and pumpkin pies had, every one of them, come out well.

Robb carried ruffleless Emma downstairs; he wore a grim air as though this party were warfare. Well, he *was* fighting, his back sometimes to the wall. Heated conferences were never more rancorous, he said, than in Christ's imperfect earthly instrument, the strife-torn church. Yet Bernadette was constantly astonished at his dogged efforts to reconcile views and still save the right. She sensed Robb McIves, in his chastened mood, was finer in travail than triumph.

Annis came first, bubbling, of course, about next week's sugar-off party. Sugar-off party! Boiling maple syrup poured off long-handled iron spoons onto chunks of hard snow! Girls and boys all sticky, sucking delicious wax!

Soon there was hubbub everywhere; the little house bulged, wouldn't hold six more.

Wherever she rushed, she spotted friends and heard gossip: Aunt Lucy'd been led into truth by God at two in the morning, but she'd come right down and pounded on Pastor's door; Eddie Heath's cider press had broken down, but Pastor had rolled up his sleeves and helped him fix it before the juice could ferment. On the larger scene, William Lloyd Garrison had been caught by a dreadful mob and dragged through the streets of Boston like an animal; it was natural that southern states should post huge rewards for captured abolitionists, it was their right . . .

Achsah Miller, the whispering nonconfronter, was master-of-ceremonies. Achsah wasn't brave enough for big insults; instead, he took little digs — as he was doing now, Bernadette observed. Some folks, Achsah intoned in a way to make you instantly suspicious, didn't have an honest pastor like they did; why, he'd once heard of a pastor who'd planned to sell his matched steers but had left them out one winter's night so one of the tails had frozen and fallen off. "Know what that tricky pastor did? He wired that dry hide of tail to the stub and sold the pair for a fancy price . . ."

"He should have my pair," Otis hollered above the men's laughter. "My off-ox is too lazy to wink when a fly lights on his eyeball."

With all the uncouth talk of oxen tails, wan Emma asked to be carried upstairs. After that, Achsah began to show off the donations.

It didn't take long before Bernadette understood why Pastor had been grim about the donation party. Never had she seen such a jumble of castoffs! Only a few things were at all usable: a supply of strike-anywhere matches; a tin of sperm lamp oil; a few earthen jars of preserved fruit; a new swine-bristle broom from the Haines's fall butchering; a little cone of hard sugar for company; a whalebone jagging wheel for crimping pies; shoe-blacking made of grease and burnt straw for Pastor.

Castoffs? She couldn't decide whether to laugh or cry! A redware churn with a crack; a mechanical flytrap from Nat Dressler, the town's inveterate but unsuccessful inventor; a rusty cast-iron cherry-stoner; a copy of Sparks's *Life of Washington* with half the pages torn out; a dented pewter sausage-stuffer (when they kept no pigs); a calico apron with a medallion of President Jackson—well, she'd wear it inside out . . .

Annis whispered comfortingly, "The decent things are out in the kitchen with the committee." The Atchisons had brought a lot of those, Bernadette knew gratefully: bags of cornmeal, crocks of salt pork, huge hams . . .

While everyone waited for the committee to evaluate the donations and announce the sum — some churches even subracted the sum from the pastor's salary, but Otis wouldn't stand for that — people went back to their chattering. She and the Schultz twins were funning in the kitchen corner when Bernadette made a momentous discovery. Ida Schultz had bodice-button trouble, too! For a moment she could scarcely talk; it was so hard not to stare.

Would everyone soon be that way? she wondered, amazed.

Judging by Ida, maybe, maybe . . .

French, smart, orphan, colt — and *buxom,* too. The prospect of at least not looking a freak was too good to be true.

But, oh, the Lord giveth and taketh away, and He managed to loosen her anxiety up just a few seconds before He snatched off her new feeling of self-respect.

In a greased voice, Achsah Miller was reporting the inflated value of things when Robb put his head in the kitchen door and nodded for her to come out on the stoop. Otis was shivering out there, too.

"Somebody brought a terrible book to our party," Pastor began without preamble. "It's called *The True Story of Maria Monk.* Have you ever heard of it, Bernadette?"

"No, sir."

"Well, Otis tells me they're gossiping about this story all over the village. It's going around the country like wildfire, too."

98

"What is?"

"This supposedly true account of a Protestant girl who was lured into becoming a novice at a Catholic nunnery in Montreal. With the Mother Superior's connivance, the vile Catholic monks made Maria Monk's life dreadful."

"Spells out the Catholic corruption," Otis went on. "Spells out what's supposed to happen to decent Protestant girls in Romanized America."

"Bernadette, on your honor, did you *ever* see anything dishonorable in your Montreal convent school?" Robb asked in a dangerously even voice.

"Never," she answered, beginning to tremble from cold and upset. "I don't understand that book. And whatever it says, I believe it's lies."

There was a considering silence. Inside, a shout of laughter rose up; a few minutes ago it would have sounded so friendly to her with her new-found confidence. Now, with everyone apparently gossiping about Catholics and herself, it sounded awful.

"Well," Robb allowed, "I've just now soaked up a few of Maria Monk's pages and, concerned as I am at the spreading Catholic influence, I believe it's scurrilous bilge, too."

"It's not what *we* think; it's what folks are whispering." Otis shook his head. "She's just got to join the church to save her good name and dignify yours as her spiritual guardian."

"But she hasn't had the salvation experience; it doesn't come to her!" Robb cried.

"There, now," Otis soothed. "Folks used to get into the church graduallike, without a great moment. With all these evangelists about, it's hard to remember it *can* happen like a flower unfolding."

"Yes, yes, of course. I've shamefully neglected her spiritual

99

life these past troubled months. After the party, Bernadette, I want to see you in my study."

"Go fetch your diary," were his first words.

How had she ever lulled herself into thinking he'd forget? she asked herself, dragging up the steps.

Maybe the best thing was simply not to go back down there.

Then the summer mood of resignation came back mysteriously. Nothing for it but to take the journal from its hiding place and stolidly return with it to Pastor's study.

Pastor had turned up the lamp and was reading the *Antislavery Standard* when she entered the room. She laid the diary on his desk.

He folded the newspaper, reached for the book. She watched his strong hand reaching, ducked her head.

Pages turned. Silence grew.

"But a lot of it's writ in French!" he burst out indignantly.

She didn't dare look up.

"Bernadette! Who are the letters written to?"

"Mr. Weld, sir."

"Read me this letter in English," he ordered, his voice like a pistol shot as he shoved the journal at her.

She looked at the words. She couldn't read *those* words to *him.*

"Bernadette . . ." he warned, half rising from his chair.

Twice she worked to get out "Dear Brother Weld"; twice her voice failed. He leaned forward, his dark bulk threatening her.

"Tonight I look down from my window on the twenty-mile meadow in the moonlight. At its farthest end there's only a line of mist. If I could go beyond that mist, would I come to Ohio where my heart is? If I did, would you be waiting for me?"

"Go on," Robb's voice prodded.

"In Ohio, there's a wooded clearing and you've sat to rest yourself. That forest country's dark and green like the waters of a deep sea, but there's light enough for me to see you. You get up and your arms go around me. I'm safe, I'm yours entire —"

His guttural exclamation of disbelief brought a merciful pause to her words. " 'Yours entire'! Have you any conception of what that means? For shame! A young girl writing that!"

Helplessly she moved to the next lines, those lines of confiding love . . .

Robb sat rooted.

"But while I dream of meeting you," [she came to safer passage] "what really happens to me is so different. The bees have stung my face and one eye's swollen shut. Paul went to plow the new field and someone had to follow the panicky team with a shovel to smother the bees with dirt . . ."

"You never told me they made you do that," Robb half-shouted. "You wrote it to Brother Weld instead."

She nodded mutely.

"Don't go on. Spare me!" he exclaimed in fury. "It's clear what you've done; you've filled the journal meant to be an account of your coming to Christ with letters of tender sentiment for a man you've never laid eyes on . . ."

Under the lash of his outraged voice she shook her lowered head silently, struggling against bursting tears.

"Your view of Weld is utterly unreal," Robb declared.

101

"You think of him as completely different from what he is. Why, he's — " Then something held him back; she didn't know what.

"Pray, give me the journal," he snapped, "and let me search for *any* redeeming signs of God's power in your life."

But one unsettling revelation followed another as he came to the pictures she'd drawn. He didn't even ask her who it was; he seemed to know as he snorted at the beautiful Weld.

"Of course, I'm not so shocked I don't recognize talent," he muttered, half to himself. "What a bold, public talent drawing is, one utterly unsuited to a female. Except for a little teaching, females must keep their capacities rooted privately."

Wetting his thumb, he came, of course, to her final picture, that of himself, and stared in stunned recognition. She couldn't know — because he was speechless — how he marveled that her primitive lines lent themselves in perfect accidental mariage to the power of his face. Marveled that she'd so perfectly captured his features, so sensitively caught in his eyes the paradox he knew to be in himself: intensely a creature of this world of people, he yet lived within himself in some stubbornly private place and couldn't always get out.

Genius flashed in him. Then, *Girl!*

What a tragedy!

He looked up; for the first time, she dared look directly at him. Their glances caught, spoke mysteriously; his fell before her steady wonderment.

"I want you to join my church at next communion," he spoke quietly.

"But you can see, I'm not ready."

"You'll join the church anyway."

"No," she cried; then, with despairing honesty, "Pastor McIves, I don't want to join your church, no matter what's said of me."

102

"Bernadette," he went on more gently, "I must protect you. You must absolutely accept communion next month."

She twisted and turned in her chair, finally put her head in her hands and wept helplessly. Knowing she couldn't stay in this room with him, she rose and stumbled to the door.

He leaped up, kicked his chair aside, caught her at the door. His arms went around her, held her against him.

When he spoke, it was with gentle firmness. She must be his dear child and do as he said. He'd forgive her the ruined journal; they'd look no more into it. Instead, together they'd go over the articles of faith to prepare her for the elders' questions.

He drew out his handkerchief, tenderly dried her face.

Leaving, she wasn't sure whether or not she'd consented to do as he'd asked; dimly she felt she had not.

It was Annis who told her the truth the next day, told her it would help Pastor if Bernadette joined his church. If town gossips whispered she'd been seared by Catholic corruption, they'd have to applaud Pastor's canny strength in leading her out of the jaws of Rome.

"My father says if you joined the church it's the one thing everyone — even his enemies — would praise him for," Annis said. Then she fell unaccustomedly quiet. "Bernadette, *were* you seared by Catholic corruption?"

"Annis, do I act seared?"

"No, you act just like I do. You're my best friend. The other girls like you a lot. Still, I wouldn't know a seared person if I took hold of one, I expect."

"I'm not seared," Bernadette guaranteed darkly, jaw set.

With every cell, she was resisting Annis's words, fighting her old horror of Iron Gods and the prisoned world they created.

But Pastor McIves was no iron man, despite his Iron God.

Instead, he was a white-faced, driven, exhausted man, often too tired to eat — and often too troubled to sleep, as she knew by the twists and turns she heard through her wall at night.

Yes, he was short-tempered with her, demanding, cold. But underneath, there was something else, something she'd always understood.

He cared for her. He cared for her even if he somehow feared to show it. He cared enough for her to take her under his roof when she wasn't even his blood.

I'll join his church.

When her inner turmoil had subsided, she was quietly glad Annis had told her how she could help him, how she could repay his concern — flinty, unfathomable as it was.

God would forgive her lie, would understand its necessity.

But on the front bench with all the congregation watching her, with the other communicants, she found it impossible to swallow down the sour communion liquid. It kept wanting to turn and come up. She gulped convulsively; Christ's blood it was, she told herself in terror — she dared not vomit it.

Marching before him with the other communicants, she didn't look at Robb even though she knew his eyes sought hers in a special, questioning way.

She looked down instead, remembering with sudden, dizzying pain the High Mass words of the priest: *"In nomine Patris, et Filii, et Spiritus Sancti"* — "In the name of the Father, and of the Son, and of the Holy Ghost . . ."

And the choir's swelling response: *"Introibo ad altare Dei: ad Deum, Qui laetificat juventutem meam"* — "I will go unto the altar of God: unto God, Who giveth joy to my youth . . ."

🌿 11

MIDWINTER, 1836.

Not a bad winter, with other girls rounding out like herself and everyone nodding approval now she was out of the jaws of Rome and into their church.

She brushed the snow off her cloak and with bright eyes surveyed Mount Riga's lively general store. Her eyes lit on Trev, watching her.

"How'd you get here?"

"I came up with Pastor McIves," Bernadette explained, overjoyed to see dark Trev looking like a Montreal boy in his sheepskin coat and red stocking cap. "The road's nearly clear . . ."

"What'd you come to buy?" he asked bluntly.

Muslin, she explained; Emma's dowry sheets were wearing out.

Trev listened, thinking of something else. "Madame Glaudin'd scold me if I didn't bring you to her," he remarked in the offhand way he always had when trying to get around her.

"I have to meet Pastor McIves at the lower fork of the road in an hour," she warned. But it was worth the rush to be in the warmhearted papish kitchen — a little sloppy, a little noisy, but not stodgy, not dour. Emilie Glaudin, proper? Or, this noon, the husky blacksmith himself sitting by his kitchen hearth? She was overjoyed that *none* of them had a proper way or look!

The bird jumped out of the little Swiss clock; if she raced, she could be at the fork a few seconds before Pastor.

"How does your Pastor get on with his talk of the black man?" Charles Glaudin asked unexpectedly.

Could she answer that in a hurry? She hunted for words.

Before she found them, Charles answered himself. "Ah, well, I know how he gets on. He makes many enemies. Moreover, he doesn't even see the slavery right at his own doorstep."

"Slavery, here?"

"The choppers, miners, forgemen required to render the Ironmaster a serf's obedience. I mean to speak with your Pastor; we need outside friends up here. Friends who understand that there are more forms of bondage than the one in the American South."

"Charles," Emilie warned, "the child does not want to hear all that."

Trev rattled the door handle to turn off the tiresome French.

And she? She couldn't stand stock-still pondering this strange new matter Charles spoke of.

Hurry . . . "Adieu!" . . .

She ran across the blinding sheet of thin snow with Trev; he faded into the bushes before she got to the fork.

Pastor was sitting on his horse watching the busy forge traffic. He'd walk, he muttered, swinging her up to his saddle in tacit admission that she was no longer a little girl to cling behind him.

In the cold air, the forge noise was deafening. Its wheel screeched as plunging Wachocastinook Creek waters pushed against and revolved it. Bellows' snorts sundered the peaceful woods.

She remembered Trev had said he meant to visit the new top man up there.

The trail turned; trees hid the forge from her view. She grew aware of the sound of the hurtling stream and the whispering whiteness of the winter woods.

When the forge exploded, the noise it made was so violent she fell off the horse. As she tumbled she glimpsed Robb's turned-back, stunned face, eyes great with shock.

From the ground, on her knees, she saw a great column of fire shoot upwards above the shielding trees, saw huge rocks cannonading skyward along with the flames. Falling, they crashed against trees which cracked and broke; cinders were igniting the forest.

Unbelieving, Bernadette jerked Robb's sleeve and shrieked, "Trev!" But before she could make Robb understand, he started with great loping stride to run up the trail.

She chased after him.

An upturned charcoal van — its horse bolted — blocked the trail. She followed Robb through the underbrush, couldn't see the forge yet but felt and smelled it; the air was heavy and hot, and a terrible sound of burning filled her ears. Men were shouting frantically.

She came to the little road which led to the forge cupola, knew she mustn't go on that broken bridge but must seek the lower trail to the furnace base. She clambered downward, fell headlong over a rock, picked herself up, stumbled on.

"Pastor!" she shouted. "Trev's up there!"

Strange hands grabbed her from behind, hauled her to higher ground. The rocks she stood among radiated heat.

"Stay there!" a rough voice warned in her ear; she had only an eerie glimpse of a sooty visage before the figure bolted away. Coughing, she climbed onto a haze-circled rock.

Trev, what's happened to you? she asked over and over in panic, hardly taking in the ruin which lay below her, the desperate men digging, prying, the lost horse emerging from a cloud, the central fire shrinking from scarlet sheet to livid mound.

Impatient with her desolate immobility, she scurried up to the road. But the road was teaming confusion — carts and rein-tangled mules, workers streaming down from nearby forges, men shouting for stream water, Mount Riga women and children beginning to arrive fearfully.

A group of horsemen thundered down on her. In its midst was the Ironmaster.

"Trev!" she shouted in desperation to the Ironmaster, but he didn't hear; he flung himself off his horse, clambered over the stone-strewn bridge toward the cupola. His mount, left riderless, reared, plunged, ran off down the trail.

She began to weep from her own impotence. *Pastor McIves!* He must speak to the Ironmaster . . . But she couldn't find Robb anyplace, though she traversed the trail, up, then down.

The Ironmaster was climbing on to the road again. "My nephew was coming here today," he was insisting.

"He was up there when the explosion came," she yelled, but again the Ironmaster was swept away, not hearing.

"Pastor McIves!" she shrieked, running up the trail again.

Far away, down in the smoky woods, she heard a faint, drawn-out "Bern—na—dette!"

"Here! Here!" she shouted. *Where was he?* She started toward the distant voice, clawing her way over rocks and growth.

On her hands and knees, she looked up and saw him stumbling toward her.

He carried something.

She stood up, tipping from uncertain footing.

Red cap, sheepskin coat. Holy, beneficent Lord, Robb McIves carried Pettee Trevelyan! *But dead?* was the next terrible question she asked herself, watching the powerful man climb laboriously up the rough ground with his burden.

"He's dead?" her voice asked.

"Of course not," Robb panted. "A falling rock must have struck him. But there are others dead."

"Where did you find him?"

"This young simpleton? Down by the stream — what he was doing there I can't tell you. He was lying right near the wheel, and I got him away before it burnt out and crashed; otherwise, its timbers might have killed him."

"His great-uncle's looking for him."

"His great-uncle had best be tending his blown-up forge," Robb answered grimly. "But where is he?"

"He was up on the road," she breathed, trying to keep up. Trev didn't look dead, his face looked calm and sleeping, his feet bobbled as Pastor hurried with him.

On the trace, Robb plunged into the milling crowd, Salisburians now adding their numbers and confusion to the Mount Rigans'. She could hardly follow in his wake.

"Find Master Pettee!" a voice suddenly yelled in her ear. "This man's got his young one."

"It's the Pastor from Furnace Village," she heard another cry.

In all the jostle she couldn't see the Ironmaster till he was right in front of them; she peered around Pastor's arm.

The two men confronted each other.

"The boy was struck by a branch or stone," Robb explained loudly over the crowd noise. "I've felt his head; it has a knot."

"It's a great thing you've done for me," the Ironmaster exclaimed. "You're McIves, the Furnace Village pastor, aren't ye?"

"I am."

Even in his intense relief, Bernadette thought, the Ironmaster's eyes on Pastor were appraising.

109

The Ironmaster reached out his arms for Trev; she thought Pastor delivered the boy as though he were a sack of grain.

"There are some who need a minister," Robb commented, moving away without another word.

In a calmer place, he turned to her; it was then she saw the jagged tear in the shoulder of his greatcoat and the burned spots where cinders had devoured it — saw how black and singed his face was, thought of great Lucifer, who had stood in majesty beside the Lord before the fiery fall . . .

Robb McIves was why Trev was alive . . .

"Find my horse and get on home, Bernadette," Robb ordered. "I'll stay here with the injured. When I'm not needed with them I'll help fight what's left of the fire."

It was nine that night — with a cold gale brewing — when he came home at last.

"I heard him jump off his horse, clatter up the church steps, pound on the door. When I opened up he was blowing great clouds of breath into the air.

" 'Good morning, Pastor McIves,' he said, 'I've come to pay my respects, thank ye for the rescue of my ward.'

"Of course I asked, 'How is he?'

" 'Entirely recovered,' the Ironmaster answered. 'The doctor called Trev's injury a small concussion. A day or so in bed and he will be fit as a fiddle.'

" 'What about the injured men?' I asked next.

" 'One alive but one unfortunately dead. Too badly burned to live, they said.' They lost four men, Bernadette."

She looked up from scouring the splintery kitchen floor, sat back on her heels, fascinated by Pastor's recital.

"He told me the destruction of the forge had left them in awkward circumstances; some of their navy deliveries will be late. Said if only the Almighty had warned him, he could

110

have made plans accordingly and saved a great deal of delay and expense."

"How did he seem to you?" she asked curiously.

"Well, he's hard, determined, practical. But there's something hale and likable underneath the red old shell, too."

She waited in silence.

"So then the Ironmaster fished in his pocket and pulled out this little packet his wife had gathered for you."

A sudden memory of Robb sitting on his horse looking up at the Ironmaster's grand mansion flashed in her.

" 'Wife's now without children, ye know,' the Ironmaster went on. 'She'd love to know your fine, dear girl, deck her out; meanwhile, you and I could sit by the fire and draw a draught.' Weather permitting, we'll visit Mount Riga next week," Robb finished his tale abruptly.

Suddenly remembering the Ironmaster's gift for her, Pastor handed it over. A bit of cream lace, six pewter buttons, a hairnet — fine things beyond Pastor's ability to provide, but none so fine as to insult him, she realized.

"There'll come a time I'll talk of my views, Bernadette, come a time to strike for the Lord when the anvil's hot . . ."

Later when she and Trev compared notes about the great meeting, Trev told her he'd overheard Uncle tell Aunt Pettee he'd found Pastor more interesting than he'd suspected, said he was "tough and virile." Said Pastor's eyes could probe right to a man's core and as for what they'd do to a bunch of weak-minded women, why, those silly creatures would be helpless before them. How in thunder, the Ironmaster had asked his wife, had McIves ever got into a business filled by males in petticoats? He looks to me, Uncle had added, like he'd make a first-rate iron man . . .

"I think, Trev," Bernadette observed cannily, "your Uncle

found someone stronger than he'd thought and my Pastor found someone kinder."

"There's something more." Trev was skeptical. "Does Pastor know the Glaudins?"

"The Glaudins!" she exclaimed in surprise. "No, why?"

But if Trev had some connection he'd meant to make, he clapped his mouth shut and wouldn't say another word.

❧ 12

No time in her life was ever like that spent in Furnace Village, no person ever like Trev. Annis finally gave up being jealous when Bernadette and he skinned off together; shrugging philosophically, she said, "Well, I reckon you need each other because you're orphans . . ." (Orphans, Bernadette had finally come to realize, were a class of their own — suspect because no one knew exactly what their blood was or if it were bad. If you had a family and were wild or stupid or criminal, you had the comfortable excuse that you took after some auntie or grandpa; but if you were an orphan, you had nobody to blame but yourself.)

While Pastor worked in his study, made his church and reform rounds, huddled with his new friend the Ironmaster, and Emma slept away her afternoons, Bernadette and her orphan friend Trev stole off to wander the three smoking villages in the high ring of Taconic peaks.

Whether or not because they were orphans, Trev brought out joy, abandonment, gave her the unique, non-girl chance of stretching her muscles in racing, climbing, scrambling, poking about, wading — of watching outside herself instead of being primly self-conscious; he even got her used to not noticing stares around mines and forges. In a word, Trev gave her a wider space, not a pallid, shut-in girl box.

Yet there began to be times when things happened between her and Trev, as though there were a lot waiting to come up, waiting, perhaps, to consume what was beautiful and free between them.

The first time she had some sense of it was when they'd paused in a sunny field. He was mad because he hadn't been able to catch her. He had finally tripped her; then, like children, they'd pummeled each other briefly. He was the first to stretch out on the grass. He wouldn't stay long that way, not Trev; so she'd dropped down on one knee beside him, was observing that — unlike other colors of things — ridges of hills got bluer the farther they marched. She stifled the continuous deep-down need for water or oil paints. Color! Oh, what a marvel coloring things would be!

Suddenly he said, "I'll be grown like that Pastor someday. Then life won't be so muzzy for you."

In surprise she'd glanced down, saw he was looking intently up at her, and there *was* something naked in those black eyes, something which made her laugh uneasily and reply, "Oh, Trev, when you're as old as Pastor you'll have forgot me."

"I suppose you're right," he'd agreed calmly, sitting up, making her comfortable again.

Or there was the time she'd gone poling with him on his pond raft. She'd tucked her front skirts in her pantaloon top so she'd have no water stains to explain and was just grabbing the pole to shove away when she saw his eyes were fastened on her underpants. He wasn't even guilty about his fascination but reached and touched the cloth at her ankle.

"How do you know they'll stay up?"

113

"They will."

"But everything might just fall down," he'd grinned in his dreadful way.

"Trev, I'm not going to pole you off the bank if you don't help," she'd answered indignantly; at that he'd grabbed his pole and pushed like a tartar, and the next hour who cared about pantaloons, petticoats, and skirts? Not she, not he.

But the uneasiest time, the time with the most consequence, was when they had tramped across Farmer Treadup's back meadow and come on one of his stallions. They'd just climbed the fence and were about to thud to the ground when, on the rise above, both noticed the Treadup horse silhouetted against the bright sky.

Her eye had been caught by a long, skinny emergence of strange and huge proportions from the stallion's underbelly. The appendage grew and grew and grew, plunging evenly downward until it nearly touched the ground.

"Ding bust!" Trev breathed beside her. "Where's the mare? I don't see the mare anywhere."

She'd jumped frantically to the ground, heard Trev follow, heard him exclaim, "If he pokes that in her, it'll come out her gullet! Bernadette, where are you going?"

"I have to go home."

"All right," he'd answered absently, "but I'm going to stay around."

The very worst thing *that* did was spoil her imaginings of Weld. For a time, she was somehow afraid even to think of Weld; she went straight to sleep at night, indulging herself in no delicious Weld fantasies.

Once, soon after, she even had a strange nightmare. Weld was facing a mob. But when he crossed his arms, she saw to her horror his hands were hoofs.

For a few weeks she was downright uncomfortable with

114

Trev, and she never again went across the Treadup's back meadow.

But about these times she finally puzzled herself out, forgot them. Trev was careless, that's why he had so much fun.

Two could be as careless as one.

Besides, Trev — as a boy-person — was, after all, only at the edges of her feelings. At her center she was shaken by one far different from him.

She watched Robb raise the ax, bring it down with a splintering thud on the gummy stump, toss the split pieces to the log pile. Before he'd gone out, he'd told her that the famous old cleric Lyman Beecher, in moods of black despair, took to his cellar and shoveled sand from one pile to another.

Snatching her from Rome had helped unify things for a time but soon his church seethed again . . .

Although the main fighting was clearly over abolition, it seemed as if Pastor was in dutch everywhere. Old Lights claimed he was a New Light, some church members sniggered at his Cold Water Army, others couldn't care less about his support of frontier missions, still others thought it was shocking that he didn't stand for the Sabbath shutdown of stages and canalboats. Then there were those look-under-the-bed ladies still trying to force him to preach anti-Catholic sermons based on Maria Monk's scandalous story, which he refused to believe.

It had got so, Robb had confided to her, he couldn't even get his elders to agree on repairing the leaky church windowsills!

Rubbing her hands on her General Jackson apron, Bernadette went to the kitchen door, flashed him a smile, stooped beside him to pick up sticks of splintered wood. "Soup's heating for supper."

She carried six loads to the shed, came back in the house, called him to supper shortly. She saw him chunk the ax into the chopping log, go to the well, immerse his whole head in the bucket, stand in the wind, running his hands through his hair, studying the spare, dark branches scraping the steely sky. Was he remembering his unusual last night's confidence to her? "If I could only pray! But ever since the second child died and Emma took sick, my prayers do well enough for the public but seem to enfeeble me. Still, for all the buffets and loneliness, I believe I do as I should."

The kitchen was aromatic in the late afternoon light. She moved swiftly, juggling kettles, set down the compote before him for his ladling. Emma was asleep; she'd take her supper up later.

"There'll be almost enough wood chopped to finish the winter," she commented cheerfully, sitting down beside him, knowing she smelled of flour, beef juice, stove fire — not knowing how comforting to him the homely smells were, not knowing how the hanging lamp threw fascinating shadows on her.

"I don't care if we have wood for the rest of the winter or not," he said all of a sudden.

She put down her fork, looked straight at him as though he'd taken leave of his senses. "Why?" she asked baldly.

"Weld asked me to join the National Antislavery Society as an abolition agent."

She stared, struggling to comprehend.

"The officers of the society have decided they're going to find seventy revivalists to travel the land and preach for the slave. Seventy men made up the first Christian band, you know."

Softly, urgently, she asked, "Will Mr. Weld be one of them?"

116

He looked annoyed. "No. But he'll help train the Seventy."

"*Would* you leave Furnace Village?" she finally asked.

"If I had my druthers, I'd leave it tonight."

Instinctively, she'd always known he longed to be Weld, mobbed scores of times, subject to fists, rocks, tar rails, but always moving on, striking the light of truth, blazing a fiery trail. She also knew intuitively how much harder in a way it was to be rooted. At first in Furnace Village there'd been a cell of eager converts to Abolition, but soon for every one of them, ten opposed churchmen seemed to have sprung up. Weld himself, she felt, would be the first to admit how much harder it was to keep a fire going than blow it into life.

Robb got up to prowl. "Well, when Theo's letter first came, my impulse was to cry, 'Amen, brother, I'm coming!' But consider what difficulties there'd be. The traveling allowance for the Seventy'll be eight dollars a week; for bread and roof they'll be largely dependent on the good will of those to whom they preach. It was for no foolish reason Weld vowed long ago abolition was *his* wife."

She was silent, head ducked, trying to think of Weld married only to abolition; her gesture didn't escape him.

"No," he sighed, "I have to stay here, it's my duty; I've started something I must finish. Still, God alone — and possibly you and Otis — knows how hard it is for me," he smiled bleakly.

He came back and sat down, picked up the two-tined fork and ran it across the bird's-eye tablecloth; they both watched the hard little lines flow from his fork.

"The Seventy'll work on a gigantic petition drive, a campaign intended to swamp the government, take advantage of the mass stirring Weld's got going in New York and Ohio."

Silently she scraped and stacked the plates, took them to the wash table.

Forgotten, Emma called.

Bernadette gasped, rushed from the dish tub to the stove, reached over Robb's shoulder for the steeping teapot.

He seized her reaching hand, seemed to waver strangely, then closed her fingers over the pot handle.

She swung up the tray of dishes and passed swiftly through the door, leaving him alone in the room.

Leaving him alone to agonize over Emma, whom he'd married passionately, expecting to create a perfect wife, and hence a perfect union. Leaving him scourged by the baffling knowledge that no man could apparently *make* a wife; she must have strength in herself for her own being. Leaving him anguished that from guilt over his mysterious failure with glass-blown Emma he sometimes couldn't feel love anymore, only this tension-made flesh-urge that had shockingly seized him just now.

He got up angrily, banged into his study. Inner battles, quieted by the exertions of the ax, began to rage once more in him.

At the Glaudins' this afternoon she'd heard the Ironmaster had summarily let go all the workers at the blown-up forge.

"What will they do?" she'd asked Emilie, knowing most were company-imported foreigners and oughtn't by rights be stranded in a world they didn't understand.

"Some of us will feed them as long as we can," Emilie had answered carefully; then, in a burst, "Charles says the power of life and death some hold over others is a sin, for what is starving but dying?"

So now Bernadette sat out in the hall waiting for Robb and the Ironmaster to finish their pipes, listening sharp, trying to catch the Ironmaster's every word. Trying to piece together in her own mind whether Joseph Pettee was as callous a monster as Emilie said, or as hopeful of having his anvil heated for the Lord as Robb predicted, or as deserving of the offhand, uncritical affection Tev showed him. To Trev — except when in the throes of a usually deserved thrashing — Uncle was "jolly."

He didn't sound very jolly at the moment, she thought, hitching her chair closer to the door.

"My ancestors," he was growling, "go back to the Puritans and none were squarer with the Gospels. Where's all this evangelistic reform tweedledum coming from? Take this antislavery nonsense. It has implications — beyond the offense to property rights — I can't endure."

"What implications, sir?"

"All kinds, but the main one's simple: consider a slave a real man and free him, what's he then? He's another worker, that's what, except infected by his new-got independence and ready to spread its fever. Team him with our northern laborer, there's a hobble! You know the Workingmen's Party would break the country up! Mark my words, we'd be ruined if black and white workers ever got together."

"Among Abolitionists it's hardly even discussed. I suspect blacks and workers wouldn't get on at all."

"Oh, no? Take a look how they get on as seamen; my naval friends tell me right now one in six on our sailing ships are niggers."

"That's a very small group, sir; I don't find that fact alarming."

"You're not alarmed, McIves, because you haven't the practical problems businessmen face — we're the ones keep the country marching. Here at Riga we're in trouble and can't tolerate begging, unruly founders, miners, teamsters, fillers. I meet an annual payroll of $150,000; that's quite enough, considering how handicapped we are in getting our products to tidewater, the fact that the forest is running thin, and now coming out of Britain there's a hot-blast smelt that uses coal for fuel and makes more iron to boot. If this method — along with railroads for easy transport — becomes general, Riga's finished; every city'll boast its own ironworks. Don't talk to me of antislavery — I've got enough adversities right here to hone my character."

The pipes and the talk appeared to run out together; the men came into the hall.

The Ironmaster looked her up and down, then said in an expansive voice he'd be glad to find a husky young artisan for her when it was husband time.

The shock of it made her drop her fringed reticule. When she stooped to pick it up, her hairnet slipped back and let down her hair; when she rose, her crispin fell off.

Would it be like this all her life? One awkwardness compounding another? And she was not just embarrassed this time, but humiliated! The Ironmaster speaking of her as though she were farmer's stock . . .

As for Pastor, the friendliness in his face shriveled up; as he explained curtly, Bernadette was being trained to have her own female seminary.

The Ironmaster looked astonished, then boomed, "Pity she's to be crammed with learning and baled away for a bluestocking. Hardly seems the thing to do with the rosy girl!"

Pastor's goodbye was more of a grunt than a farewell.

Plodding downward, she ventured to ask how he was getting on with the Ironmaster.

"The fact," Robb answered thoughtfully, "that he gets so heated now is a good sign. He's already admitted there's no defense for a condition like slavery he'd so hate for himself. Still," Robb added, "his life flows by in a round of industry concerns; it's natural he should have such a flinty obsession with practical matters."

"Will you change his mind?" she asked curiously.

"More likely his soul," Robb answered with his old stout self-assurance. "Some day he'll slow down long enough to cast out the spirit of slavery from his heart, then lend his aid . . ."

Trev told her, grinning, that the Ironmaster had banged the door shut after that visit, sworn, "Old clootie! I was only offering to market the girl! No point in a good product if it don't sell. That Pastor's a deuced proud fellow. And ambitious, riddled with it! Yet his stubborn beliefs — especially this antislavery phantasm — will lead him to ruin. I can understand his love of himself, but his devotion to an idiot idea is beyond a sensible man's comprehension."

Then, Trev said, the Ironmaster had wandered into the library, found Pastor's forgotten pipe sitting on a table, picked it up, rubbed it thoughtfully, smiled, "Been a long time since anyone's dared stand up to me, though. Forgot how I used to love a fight — fists or words."

He'd turned, Trev said, grabbed Trev by the collar, shaken him, teased, "Where do you sneak with the girl?"

"To the Glaudins', mostly," Trev said he'd lied.

"To the black-smith's house, eh? McIves ever fetch her from there?"

"I don't think so."

"That's a wily Frenchman on the lookout for earnest and willing friends," the Ironmaster had mused, more to himself than to Trev. "Well, it isn't the first time men like that have infested us."

At the end, Uncle Joseph had turned his full attention on Trev, looked him in the eye, said, "It's vexing, the things a man has to keep track of. But that's what it is to be master of forges, furnaces, ore hills, char sheds, even villages, boy. I've been a long time at it, had a life to be proud of. Hard work, loyalty, rectitude. When your turn comes, don't forget what I'm saying to you, you young scamp."

It wasn't, Bernadette decided, as easy as she'd figured to tally the Ironmaster.

❦ 13

"You get to ride on a train before I do! Goldang!" Trev had sworn — he was an expert on American as well as Lith cuss words.

She couldn't believe it was true, even now after they'd crawled into their seats. The little rail car lurched, its timbers cracking. Bernadette glanced over her shoulder, saw Emma had been thrown from her propped position and now leaned like a tilted poker against her husband. Her eyes fluttered open; they were not glazed with invalid's prostration but bright with rage.

She's so angry at him for trying to help her get well, she'd die just to get even, Bernadette sensed, pondering for the hundredth time the dark tension that vibrated between husband and wife.

In the afternoon light, the sooty train window revealed narrow box houses, rutted Hartford streets; a drooping dray horse played statue in front of a shoe factory.

Emma groaned. It sounded less like misery than reproach,

Bernadette thought, remembering the fuss of getting her here.

When Robb had announced he was taking her to a fine New York heart doctor, Emma had turned from feeble Emma to insubordinate Emma. A foreign doctor, Emma had let fly, could not *possibly* appreciate her critical condition the way old Dr. Turner did. When Robb had obdurately stood against that argument, Emma had resorted to another.

"I'll die on a train; they're dangerous!"

"Dangerous?" Robb asked, obviously surprised by her new tack. "What do you know about trains?"

"A lot of things Papa said. There's no signal system — they just pass a staff from one train to another; they unscrew the lid sometimes before the force is out of the boilers . . ."

"Indeed," Robb murmured, "I didn't know Papa had made you an expert on trains."

"The snakeheads come right through the cars, too."

"For heaven's sake, Emma, what are snakeheads?"

"They're the iron strips that cap the wood rails. They come loose, puncture the floors right under your feet. And the trains get derailed."

"Then I expect the men passengers simply lift the cars back on the track — that is, what track isn't curling up through the floors," Robb had answered with unexpected whimsy.

His light-mindedness brought out Emma's last vengeful thrust: "Well, Mr. McIves, at least *you* ought to be the first to admit it's against God's will to go fifteen miles an hour."

"As for God's will in the matter of speed" was the husband's dry retort, "I suspect He can accommodate to hurry, having given man the genius to invent it. We'll go to the city doctor by train."

New York, Bernadette sighed, or at least she tried to, tried to get an honest-to-goodness breath past the new whalebone corset and india-rubber garters Annis's mother had given her.

New York. Maybe it meant a terrifying new doctor to Emma; certainly to Robb it meant the meetings to train the Seventy Abolition Evangels. But to her? Well, New York could be summed up in one short word: *Weld*.

Theodore Weld was in charge of the Seventy's training. Surely she couldn't be a fortnight in the same city with him and not meet him. She shivered, moved restlessly.

The harsh clang of the bell picked up tempo — faster, louder . . . With a grinding jolt, the carriage bucked forward. Bernadette shut her eyes in terror but curiosity wouldn't let them stay that way. At the dizzying and immoral speed of fifteen miles an hour, the city of Hartford began to lurch past her window. She put on her mitts; she didn't like the feel of wet palms.

Soon the town gave way to chill November bogs. The cars clattered onto a spidery bridge, daringly shuddered over it to safety. The spire of a village church rose above woods. The train traveled down the main street; when it stopped to take in wood and water, children gathered beneath Bernadette's window to gaze open-mouthed up at her.

Embarrassed, she turned her attention back to the innards of their ladies' car (sprinkled with gentlemen in tall beavers taking care of their females and offspring), grew aware of sizzly retorts — the sound of men spitting tobacco at the red-hot stove.

It *was* like an oven, Bernadette thought, untying her bonnet ribbons. Emma hissed; wearily Bernadette yanked the ribbons tight under her chin again. *Proper.* Proper and parboiled, that's what.

Light leached from the skies as afternoon waned, and the

view out her window, already obscured by trails of white wood smoke, dimmed.

But as dusk fell, something more fascinating than endless aisles of spindly trees enchanted her: sparks flew past in countless clouds. As the tracks curved ahead, she watched the fire which danced in a cloud above the engine's high smokestack.

How right for her to be riding this fiery fierce thing, this thing which devoured the dividing miles between her and the one who'd awakened her heart!

It cost more than Pastor could afford of the funds borrowed from Otis Atchison, but they rested at a New Haven ordinary. While Emma slept, Bernadette and Pastor ran up the fine, tree-lined street to his theological seminary. He pointed out Yale's spires behind the lace of the leafless elms, explained quietly he'd known the heights of hope here, followed by the deeps of despond. She thought his expression of intense remembered suffering made his face the most beautiful she'd ever seen. But when he realized she was studying him, he walked away with a harsh, closed face.

The next morning, mist was rolling from the ground when Robb carried Emma across the wharf to the Long Island packet, an enormous, floating box with double decks and huge side-wheel.

Robb deposited his wife on a cot in the cabin for women and children, stood up, gave Bernadette a curt salute and turned on his heels. This time it was up to her, his disappearing back said.

The huge side-wheel plash-plashed as the big box shuddered off. Bernadette sat on the bottom of the cot trying to assess Emma's hysterical warning: they'd drown — the Sound was rough, and steam packets blew up, caught fire, ran on shoals.

"I'm nauseated," Emma moaned. "I told him I couldn't

125

stand up to rough weather." Bernadette gave Emma laudanum drops, and soon she slept, snoring evenly.

A troop of children burst in from the deck; Bernadette
sniffed the fragrant air which trailed them.

Suddenly it was too much, this being shut up in a rackety
box.

Where *was* that open deck?

Guilt lent wings to her feet.

Bursting into a deserted world, she knew why the children
had smelled so chill: the sweet, pure air was an arctic gale.

She ran to the rail, leaned out.

Crystal-blue sky bathed her in icy radiance. Everywhere
she looked there was nothing but glittering sameness — no
outcropping of land parted the water's spangled surface, not
a single cloud rent the stretched sky. She was alone in a
world of shimmering space; impulsively, she held her hands
out as though she could capture a cupful. Her turned-up
face was numbed by wild air.

A sea gull looped into sight, dipping, skimming, crying its
ravenous cry. As suddenly, she was the gull, its open sky her
home, its broad sea hers.

Something marvelous was going to happen to her, she felt
it overpoweringly.

When she went back inside, Pastor sat by his wife;
Bernadette expected to get a tongue-lashing for leaving
Emma. But he only glanced up as she bundled her dishev-
eled hair, returned to reading his book.

Eventually they came into a river channel. She heard
names: Hog's Back, Frying Pan . . .

A lighthouse slipped past, then a large building which one
of the ladies nearby said in a hushed voice was the madhouse.
Bernadette saw a man running along the ground, his
pounding legs keeping time with the pounding of their
engines. They left him under the madhouse wall shouting,

126

dancing, pleading. A moment of fear. But even that quickly slid away.

They entered what must be bay.

Pastor rescued her.

"Emma," he said, "you'll be all right if Bernadette and I go outside to watch the city, won't you?"

Emma sniffed piteously, but Robb picked up Bernadette's cloak, pushed her firmly to the door.

On a vast, low-lying plain this mightiest of America's cities stretched before them, this place of three hundred thousand people, of three hundred teeming avenues, uncounted dirty alleys, this place which flaunted great hotels, public buildings and parks, but reserved for its heartbeat its marketplace. This coming-in place — the whole world was coming in here . . .

After the unbelievable spread of the city, what caught Bernadette's astonished eyes next was the teeming harbor. Sleek sloops — sails belled out — dipped and rose; a half-dozen ferryboats huffed toward wharves which bristled like leafless forests with tied-up sailing ships.

"Old Trinity Church spire." Robb broke her stunned absorption; she glanced where he pointed. "Been a sailor's landmark for years. It and Grace are the society churches. I wish I could name you all of the church towers."

She couldn't admit she didn't give a fig for which church was which, simply observed that there were dozens of steeples piercing the low-lying lines of brick row buildings, square Dutch houses set among trees in brown yards.

"The fire last winter gutted the city from the Battery up to Wall Street." Robb's arm arched from left to right. "Burnt three days; wiped out seven hundred shops, houses, ware-houses. Baltimore and Philadelphia sent a thousand men to help but they got stranded by ice in Perth Amboy."

The packet shuddered and jerked, backed and filled; then

127

a jumble of rickety wharves, piled high with goods, caged them in.

This, then, was where her bright hopes lay.

A sudden, shrinking fear convulsed her, crowded her abruptly against Robb McIves's bulk. He steadied her, asked was she sick; his look cleared when she shook her head.

Chandlers' shops, provisioners, wood houses painted white, sharp red, pale gray, with dark green venetian blinds and rows of outhouses in back.

In their hired hack, Bernadette noticed Emma didn't slump; she even seemed to peek out the window.

"I'd like to walk the Battery," the wife suddenly sighed, "even if it's no longer society. Clara Currie said I should get to Stewart's or Bonfanti's . . . they're such elegant stores. But I suppose my health won't permit . . ."

Refuse grinding under its wheels, the carriage bumped over cobblestones, fell into a mudhole, eased into the ragged traffic which Robb said was headed for Broadway.

Signs of building were everywhere — impressive tall, narrow buildings, some four stories high. Bernadette understood why New York had burnt down when Robb pointed out a fire lookout tower, a ludicrous little wood hut on stilts sitting on a corner.

Hackneys, two-wheeled gigs, wagons hustled them. Bernadette had never seen an omnibus before; straining horses pulled high, clumsy, gaudy omnibuses with names painted on them like *Mercy Warren, DeWitt Clinton, John Hancock.* A tall coach without hammercloth or footboard bowled past, driven by a barrel-chested black man.

"No livery," Emma sniffed.

Bernadette and Robb turned, stared at her in astonishment; she *was* looking . . .

"They abolished slavery in New York ten years ago, Emma," Robb reminded.

128

"Well, blacks should wear livery anyhow." Then, after a plaintive silence, "I can't make out, Bernadette, if sleeves are full at the shoulder or farther down. Bonnet crowns look lower, but are brims round or oval?"

"I don't know, I'll look," Bernadette promised hastily, hunting out the few visible women — here a great turbaned Negress, there a young woman threading her way past beef quarters crowding the sidewalk outside a meat shop . . .

But what had her bonnet brim been, round or oval?

"We're into Broadway Street now, Emma, can you see?" Robb inquired.

"Yes, I can see," Emma admitted peevishly. "But the wealthy are moving out of lower Manhattan, building houses up north."

"Oh, are they?" Robb asked in genuine curiosity. "I didn't know."

"Just look at that man!" his wife exclaimed next, peering back over her shoulder. "He's got a beard, Mr. McIves. It's an outrage to let oneself grow so . . ."

"Hairy," Robb finished bluntly. "They say that in the cities children hoot at them on the streets. Well, we've no uncouth types like that in Salisbury — not yet, anyway."

"Bernadette, I believe skirts are getting wider; they must wear half a dozen . . . petticoats."

"Emma, did you see when we passed City Hall?" Robb demanded sternly.

How exciting — the huge columned hotels, the shops with their small crowded windows, the conveyances, the walkers hurrying! *Brother Weld, cher frère Théodore,* which are you in this surge? That one striding along with the high-collared cape? That slender, fair one with the neat-combed beard? Why did Emma and Robb deplore beards? Bernadette asked herself rebelliously.

Before she was half-ready, they turned off enchanting

129

Broadway to quieter regions, seeking Chambers Street and their boardinghouse. Sedate two-story houses here; stray pigs rooting in the gutter.

But by nighttime in the cheap garret room, with Robb rattling around next door and Emma moaning beside her, with the diversion of new sights worn off, Benadette was anxious, assailed by gusts of reality which for months her girl's need had stifled.

What if he isn't pleased by me, what if he doesn't even like me?

What if he likes me but doesn't wish to love me? Once he vowed he'd not love anyone till abolition was won.

A tatterdemalion policeman, carrying a whale-oil lamp, rattle, and skinny stick, took up his stand at their boardinghouse corner and bawled the hour . . .

"Nine of the clock. All's well . . . all's we—lll . . ."

But how can he not love me when I love him?

"All's well . . . all's well . . ."

Below her attic window, a sandman's cart crunched to a stop at the boardinghouse across the street; the sandman shoveled sand furiously into a big barrel, then rolled it around back of the house. Sand for the kitchen floor.

Bonnet rims were oval and mutton-leg sleeves were in . . .

A band of thin, tough, hairy pigs, led by a black-spotted sow, rooted in the gutter with savage urgency, passed on toward Broadway and flusher scavenging.

Bells clanged. Bernadette flew up out of the rocker, scanned rooftops anxiously, found no smoke. As the crash of wheels and clatter of hoofs ebbed away, she sat down, disappointed not to have glimpsed the fire engine so as to describe it for Trev.

Was Pastor talking to Weld right now?

She stopped knitting, leaned her head back, closed her eyes.

> There is a dangerous silence in that hour . . .
> And Julia sate with Juan, half embraced . . .

Lord Byron had writ those lines, the dark poet forbidden decent women (but sneaked by Annis from her oldest sister). Bernadette sensed Byron everywhere: in Emma's petulant advice ("Look frail, faint a lot"), in ladies' magazines where the rage was for listlessness — girls drank vinegar for pallor, took belladonna to enlarge their pupils. And it wasn't just women: love-blighted young men suffered from unspeakable Byronic urges. Byron — who had thought of himself as a lost demon . . .

"These crazy, self-pitying young," Pastor had once muttered, "are drinking too much."

She began to knit again.

Emma turned over; she had had a restless night.

"Don't leave her," Robb had ordered, going down the boardinghouse steps while Bernadette stood in the doorway. Why could some sally headlong into life, while some must stay shut up behind? she had asked herself.

Now, sitting in her chair, she wondered abruptly if she might stay two whole weeks in New York and never see Weld.

Her chair stopped creaking as she faced the enormity of that possibility, then creaked again with her resolution. Never mind, she'd meet Theodore Weld. If worst came to worst, she'd simply find a roomer to sit with Emma, and follow Robb McIves to the church.

A serving girl in a coarse dress banged out to a farm wagon with a big pitcher, dipped milk from a huge crock. The serving girl vanished; Bernadette fished for and picked up the stitch she'd dropped.

Emma opened her eyes, looked around in confusion.

"Where's Mr. McIves?"

"Gone to the church with the Abolitionists."

"My gown's soaked from being hot," Emma complained.

Bernadette rummaged in the carpetbag, found a fresh gown, took off Emma's soiled one, put it in the basin, poured in the last bit of soft soap.

"He had a funny thing he used," Emma said.

"Who?"

"That Dr. Thorndyke. He didn't just listen with his ear to my chest, he had a little hollow wood thing he put at his ear and listened through. He called it a *stethy-scopp*, if I heard right. He said the heart was a muscle and it grew irritable if it wasn't used. He said the leeches and bed rest Dr. Turner employs aren't any use. *His* patients take cold baths, take walks; eventually some of them run . . ."

"But it sounds as if they get well!"

There was no sound from the bed; Bernadette looked up. Emma was lying there, the tears running down her face. She wasn't making any sound at all, just crying silently.

"I don't want to take cold baths or walk, and it's not proper to run."

"Don't you want to get well? I should want to do *anything* just to get well."

"If I do what the new doctor says, it'll kill me."

"But I don't see why." There was suddenly something in the air, some ominous hovering on the edge of mystery.

"At first I cried," Emma continued tonelessly. "Finally I didn't feel anything — what was happening to me was happening to someone else. That was three days into it, after Mr. McIves had begun to walk in the fields because of my begging to die, after Dr. Turner said it wasn't his habit to interfere with a confinement . . ."

Confinement. That means having a baby.

132

What *was* Emma talking about?

Bernadette hardly dared to breathe; her needles, crossed before her, suspended there.

"It was born dead, that first one. I was split and drained, and nearly dead, too, but Mr. McIves, well, he prayed me back to life."

"I see." Bernadette let out her breath.

"But then right away there was another one; Mr. McIves said I must. I saw that one, it was a lovely big boy, round and sweet; its head was covered with peach fuzz. It looked all right; I don't know why it died — nobody told me. Mr. McIves stooped over that one, he took his finger and ran it all over the roundness and the silky head, and his tears fell right down on it . . ."

"Yes, ma'am," Bernadette swallowed hard.

"The only thing," Emma spoke distinctly, "that makes me feel good are Dr. Turner's drops. I'd like them, please."

Hurrying awkwardly, Bernadette measured out the drops in a cup, put her hand under Emma's head, said softly, "Drink this . . ."

Putting the bottle back, she saw, thunderstruck, that it was empty.

Emma's eyes opened; they were bright but didn't seem to see.

"If I get out of bed, I'll die in another childbirth. But if I lie here, that's death, too. You don't know how brave I am — in the morning I wake before you do and I think of this box I lie in, all alone, all by myself, and there's a pressure around my head and I shake."

Bernadette recognized the dread signs; Emma was growing distraught.

I have to find an apothecary shop, the young girl realized. Thank God, tied in her handkerchief were shillings saved from what Uncle Marcus had sent.

133

"Mrs. McIves, can you be still while I go for more medicine? I'll give you a really big dose; you'll fall asleep."

Emma's teeth chattered. "I can wait," she promised, "but hurry. It's terrible suffering."

Bernadette threw on her cloak, ran down stairs, asked the whereabouts of the nearest drug shop.

On Broadway she collided with a maid carrying a bucket of water; angry Irish words trailed her. She dodged a street vendor of oyster stew, a roaming shoe salesman.

"If I get out of bed, I'll die in another childbirth."

Emma didn't want to get well because then she'd have to have another baby. Yet why couldn't Emma be allowed not to have another baby? Why did getting well and having a baby go in lock step?

Pastor had a part in this, of course, that part which went with unversed tittering at school, with Annis's saying that the second weaver at Wolcott's was a disgrace — seventeen kids he had, which meant he'd done *it* seventeen times. Decent men only did *it* five or six times in married life; you could tell by the number of their kids.

It.

More mystery after all.

She flew down the basement steps to the apothecary shop, waited in a frenzy while the white-haired old man puttered among his jars. At last, bottle in hand, she tore up into the street.

When Bernadette got back, Emma was lying quietly. After the second dose, she turned on her side, face to the wall.

Bernadette, standing beside the bed, admitted to herself how often she'd resented, even despised Emma McIves. Yet the enormity of Emma's plight washing through her now left only a strong, sweet undertow of compassion.

134

All-alone Emma McIves, I'll take good care of you; I'll be a friend to you . . .

Then, quite without bidding, a guilty but overpowering feeling backwashed her.

Emma's and Pastor's life was theirs, not hers. Theirs must be a terribly special life; Emma's troubles must be special indeed.

I'm Bernadette Savard. Something different waits for me.

❀ 14

SHE AND ROBB came late into the crowded church, clambered over a row of gentlemen's boots which up-ended or turned pigeon-toed as they squeezed by.

Robb settled himself restlessly, wild with impatience at not being up front in the thick of the antislavery training.

"That's Henry Stanton speaking," Pastor whispered. "He helped recruit the Seventy."

Henry Stanton. Bernadette studied the lithe, sharp-faced young man, remembered Robb once telling her Weld had held Stanton's dying young brother in his arms at Lane Seminary.

"Is *he* up there?" she asked; nobody up front seemed to fit the right description.

"Weld?" He craned his neck, shook his head. "Not at the moment."

If her palms had been stuck together on the train, it was nothing to what they were now.

Stanton was explaining the method the Seventy must employ when arriving in a town. Stanton minced no words: the going would be tough. Agents must be unflinching, stand up in an atmosphere of brute violence, hecklers, drummers, abusers — but despite threat, be pacifists. By the second or third night enough curious men of a more decent stripe would probably come by to discover the source of the agent's courage. At that point, real converting to antislavery could begin . . .

Robb leaned toward her abruptly. "I've got to talk to Garrison." He extricated himself, moved out to the aisle, found an empty space in a front pew. She watched Pastor talk intently with a slight, bald person; all she could see was the glint of spectacles as the man turned in profile.

She couldn't just sit here waiting alone; she'd fidget to death. She flipped open her journal, scrambled for her pencil.

A colorful crowd of men it was, she thought, eying them.

Forgetting the anguish of waiting, she began to draw a big, red-faced man in a loud plaid cape who sat rubbing his beefy chin. Her fingers raced, sketching his odd Scottish flamboyance.

The Lane Seminary debates were being discussed now by energetic young enthusiasts. Could the one who was talking possibly be the one called Amos Dresser who'd been flogged, then chased out of Tennessee? She had a hard time drawing him.

There was a hushed moment when a newcomer entered; briefly, she was sure he was Weld because he was tall and slimly romantic. But no one treated him the way she was sure they'd treat Weld, and besides, he was dark-eyed and swarthy. But he made a good drawing subject . . .

Robb made a short statement quoting a man named

136

Beriah Green: " 'The chill hoar frost will be upon us. . . . Waves of persecution will dash against our souls. . . . Let us fasten ourselves to the throne of God as with hooks of steel.' . . ."

She liked those vivid words, paused in her sketching to write as Robb spoke.

In late morning came the need for a recess in this charged place with its hurried air of high excitement.

She sat by herself, waiting, waiting . . .

No one noticed her; after all, she was just a young girl in a dim corner who'd only been allowed to come because she'd asked the landlady to watch over Emma and thus Pastor had been without an excuse.

"Sister, isn't that remarkable!" A voice spoke softly behind her. "It's a drawing of John Greenleaf Whittier as plain as anything!"

She jumped a mile, her hand covered the journal page; apprehensively, she looked over her shoulder.

Into a long, angular face, patrician, unpretty, a managing look about the thin mouth. But fair-skinned with handsome dark blue eyes alive with curiosity — and, yes, appraising amusement.

This interesting face caged by an enormous Quaker horse-blinder bonnet; how awful to cage that looking-out face in blinders, was Bernadette's instant reaction. There was a second Quaker female beside her, older, fatter, blander; not such a tragedy to cage *that* face.

"Would you like to step outside with my sister and me?" the first woman asked. "Since we're the only females here, perhaps we should get acquainted."

Bernadette stumbled up. Naturally, her reticule fell on the floor, then her journal. She scrambled under the pew, feeling every whalebone stay digging at her, recovered her property, followed the tall woman and her stouter sister outside.

It was clammy in the shadows of the little church courtyard, but the women in gray began to pace briskly; Bernadette followed in circumspect confusion.

"We're Sarah and Angelina Grimké," that composed voice trailed the pair. "Who are you?"

"I'm Bernadette Savard, ma'am, ward to Pastor McIves of Furnace Village, Connecticut."

"Bernadette Savard. That's a French name, isn't it?"

"Yes, ma'am."

"Grimké's French, too. Our father's people were Huguenot."

"A French name makes things hard," Bernadette observed quietly.

"Hard?" The voice was surprised. "On the contrary, dear child, ever since the days of Lafayette many Americans have thought it very desirable to be French."

"They *have?*" she asked, a whole different perspective from that of Maria Monk suddenly widening in her. "I guess I never realized. I didn't know there was *anything* good I could say about being French."

"You've every reason for pride," the stouter one added firmly. "But where are your parents now?"

"My father was a Frenchman, my mother American. Both of them died so my great-uncle brought me down from Montreal to Ohio. I'm living with his friend, Pastor McIves, in order to get better schooling."

Grimké, Bernadette's memory prodded. Then it came to her in a rush. Of course! From Canterbury she'd once brought a booklet called *Appeal to the Christian Women of the South*, signed by one of these women. She'd shown the tract to Pastor and he'd said a woman shouldn't have writ it.

"But I've read it!" burst out of her.

The younger woman turned, smiling. "What did it say?"

138

she teased lightly, those glinting blue eyes telling Bernadette *she* was the author, *she* was Angelina.

"It said southern women can't make laws against slavery but must persuade their men to. It said southern women should free any slaves they own personally. It said southern women must petition southern legislatures. I thought it was a *grand* appeal."

Both women stopped in their tracks, wheeled to face her. Now the tall Angelina made a surprised gesture which brought Bernadette close. "What an earnest young girl you are! How old are you?"

"Fifteen."

"I don't care for babies and often not for older children. But *fifteen* and you care so much about slaves?"

"I was in Canterbury when Miss Crandall's black school was wrecked. One of her girls was my best friend."

"Where did you learn to draw?"

"Draw? I was never taught; I just draw when I can't help it. I know I shouldn't."

"Why not?" Angelina Grimké waited, eyes fastened intently on her.

"I guess," Bernadette floundered, "females shouldn't . . ."

"Oh?" was the cool rejoinder. "Who told you that?"

"My Ohio country teacher; Pastor McIves; my academy teacher, Miss Miller. But the nuns in Montreal," Bernadette brightened, "liked me to draw. Of course, I was just a child then."

"Heaven bless the nuns of Montreal," Angelina Grimké drawled dryly. "Come sit down; let's see what else you've done." She had such a pleasant way of taking command.

So they sat together on a stone bench, Bernadette at the end beside Angelina.

"Why, sister, it's Thome! Isn't it a marvelous likeness! And there's Charles Stuart in his tartan. He used to be in the

139

British army; it was he who converted Theodore Weld to antislavery."

But they couldn't make out Amos Dresser; Bernadette *knew* she hadn't got him right.

"Wouldn't it be glorious," Angelina murmured to Sarah, "if tracts could have drawings! People who can't manage reading *will* look at pictures."

"Someday," Miss Sarah confided to Bernadette, "we mean to write a book called *Slavery As It Is*, Angelina and I. Just think, if someone could fill it with drawings of slaves living and working — "

"*Good* drawings," Angelina amended sternly. "Of course, Sarah, she's so talented she ought to be trained . . ."

"What artist would take her?" Sarah asked bleakly. "I've never heard of any who would take a woman."

"Well," Miss Angelina finally sighed, "at least no one can deprive her of her natural God-given talent. Imagine drawings for *Slavery As It Is* — of the markets, the field hands' huts, the coffles, the workhouse . . ."

All of them sat still for a moment, the women caught up in the marvel of drawn slaves, Bernadette caught up in it and them, but in other things, too.

"I didn't draw Mr. Weld. Is he here?"

"No, not this morning. I don't know why; he's always here."

"Perhaps he's finally resting his throat," Sarah Grimké nodded like a wise old aunt, the kind of aunt who sets great store by people's aches and pains.

"All three of us French and all Abolitionists," Angelina mused. "Why, it's as if we were of the same family."

"I haven't any real family," Bernadette confided, all her shame at that primal lack rushing out at last.

Silence. Then again came that calm, not-to-be-argued-with voice.

140

"In a way Sarah and I are orphans, too, Bernadette. You see, we left our family and can't go back because the Charleston police have put a price on our heads for writing against slavery. Sarah left first; I came later. Now we're Quaker converts and live in Philadelphia."

"Besides, from time to time in their lives, everyone's an orphan," Miss Sarah reflected.

"Ah, sister, in the spirit," Angelina smiled quietly.

"I've never known anyone from the South," Bernadette observed. "What was it like?"

So, in voices that often blended, they told her. High-born, urbane father, the Judge; elegant Mama; black Mauma, who was also Mama; Sarah, the oldest; Angelina, the thirteenth child (and Sarah's appointed godchild). The smattering of female education and, when Sarah asked to be a lawyer, the severe denial — "Preposterous! The only public place allowed women is church," the Judge had declared.

In summer the family's great Beaufort plantation, and once, on a neighbor's gate, the impaled head of a runaway slave.

Sarah, alone, nursing her father at his deathbed in New Jersey, meeting Quaker Abolitionists on the boat going home, realizing she couldn't stay in slave-owning Charleston, fleeing to Philadelphia.

Left behind in the Charleston family, the eighteen-year-old Angelina growing up different from the self-abnegating Sarah, growing up a fighter, soon dominating the fatherless household. Nina, Sarah implied indulgently on that cold stone bench, had always done as she thought best and expected others to let her . . .

"It's time," Angelina interrupted, "to go inside. Maybe Brother Weld's here by now."

But he wasn't, and soon Bernadette was sent back to Chambers Street, sent back to sit in the rocking chair with

141

her turbulent thoughts: Weld, the fascinating Angelina, drawing slaves — a welter of rocking chair thoughts.

Dusk was falling when she heard the door clapper, heard a distant voice calling, "Little lady in number seven, lit — tle la — dy! Someone wants to see the young pastor; you'd better speak with him," the landlady explained as Bernadette came down on the landing.

A man sat in half-profile, gazing out the window; his appearance stopped her in her tracks.

A face to frighten children — the dark, merciless face of a pirate! Whoever was this to be seeking Pastor? A convict, perhaps? Robb was sometimes hunted out by such people. But in New York?

She made an agitated movement, one toward flight. The stranger turned, looked straight at her.

She got a full view of his piercing eyes; coarse, porcupine hair; swart, rough skin, blue from careless evening beard; thin, off-center nose. Above one somber eye ran a disfiguring depression; heavy lines were carved around the razor-thin mouth.

"Miss Bernadette?" he asked, rising. Too stunned he knew her name to comprehend the pleasant light which transfused his expression into one of ugly sweetness, she saw only that when he got up he exposed a mussy shirt front, unbrushed coat, unblacked boots.

With an inhibited lurch, he came toward her.

"Yes, I'm Bernadette Savard," she swallowed. "You wish to see Pastor McIves?"

"He visited us today, but when I looked for him, he'd left."

Could this be an Abolitionist, this man who'd apparently been with the Seventy? Surely *he* couldn't be one of the sainted evangels, this repulsive man of middle years!

142

"He's expected back soon. But Mrs. McIves is ill and I mustn't leave her alone."

"I shan't be able to wait," the stranger replied, frowning. "Just tell Brother McIves I came by to see him."

He seemed not to know how to extract himself; she waited uneasily. Concluding he'd finished his business with her, she started back up the hall steps.

But his name! She hadn't got his name.

She turned back reluctantly. "I need to know who calls," she was saying when Robb McIves let himself into the hall from the street.

He glanced into the parlor; his eyes lit up with affectionate surprise.

"Theodore!" he exclaimed, arms extended. "How good to see you! I wasn't able to get close to you!"

"Every minute was taken," the visitor replied. "I was telling your ward I had hoped to have a private word with you."

At the mention of her, both men turned and looked at Bernadette. Disinterested, Theodore Weld saw only a girl half-poised on the step, a girl with an unfathomable expression of dawning horror.

But, recalling the moon-faced Galahad of her journal, in Robb's face sardonic understanding leaped, a look which said he should have got them together sooner, the sooner to dispel her infantile vapors.

She pelted up the stairs.

Outside Emma's bedroom, she leaned her head against the door, her emotions in chaos.

Tante Cécile, Uncle Marcus, Hester Fry letting her be taken away? She'd reconciled herself . . .

But Weld lost to her?

I'm only fifteen but I'll never get over it, not for the rest of my life.

143

I've built my whole self around Weld.
He's been hope itself to me.

Terrifyingly, the dreams dissolving in her seemed to be washing away her sense of herself.

After a time she fished for her handkerchief, mopped her glistening face and went in to Emma.

✿ 15

SHE SAT in numb wonder, listening to that strange Weld up there. She needed to die because there was nothing much left in her that wanted to live.

Then it seemed to her she'd probably go into a decline instead. Girls did that, took to their beds for love.

Well, that meant she'd be like Emma, she concluded, filled with foreboding. A bedfast wraith living out her life nursing a secret tragedy.

The thought of being like Emma began to stir the hardy optimism which always lay deep in her.

I won't be like Emma, was her first fighting whisper on the way up from despair. *I won't be a shut-away thing.*

She began, little by little, to absorb again what was going on around her . . .

The ninth day of the great training for those destined to lead the most sweeping reform movement America had ever seen.

Late, Bernadette slid into the pew beside Robb, saw Weld had already risen to the speaker's table.

144

He stood there, his face drawn and hollow-cheeked, his expression frozen.

Why, he looked on the verge of collapse!

His face straining inhumanly, he opened his mouth; nothing happened. With a strangled expression, Weld tried again.

Everyone waited, some leaning tensely forward; everywhere, faces were shocked.

A pitiful, ragged sound emerged; she pieced together the fact that Weld's talk would be on Hebrew servitude.

As his voice grew more forceful, she asked herself, panic subsiding, what would the antislavery movement do without Weld? She heard a hushed comment behind her: "He's up before dawn, works on his lectures till three in the morning . . . and after years of dangerous abolitionizing . . ."

But as his speech flowed reassuringly, her feelings slipped willy-nilly into personal reflections.

She remembered once looking in her wavy little mirror, asking herself who she was, why she was. It had come to her on that long-ago summer evening that love was partly a search for self-recognition, too; she now sensed that she'd been too intent hunting her own self to see the object of her "love" clearly, that real love would not be possible until she could perceive who the other really was.

Now, in this crowded November room, she couldn't bear to think of those misspent, moonstruck summer evenings when she'd loved this ugly man so different from her imaginings. Well, Robb McIves had hinted at her monumental misconception; she wished he'd allowed himself the disloyalty of telling her *all* about Weld. She reflected honestly that if he'd wanted to, she might have resisted hearing.

Hubbub of voices, scrape of feet and chairs.

Garrison — dapper, slight, gray — approached with Miss

145

Angelina and Sarah Grimké in tow. "Brother McIves, we've heard another great Weld lesson, haven't we? Did you know he will be preparing these two fine ladies to speak to small groups of northern women on the slavery issue?"

With Robb's face blowing up a blizzard, Garrison continued suavely, "He expects to train them in oratory. Their appeal should be powerful, they themselves having owned slaves."

"When we were little," Sarah Grimké admitted quietly, "it was customary for a well-off child to have a slave."

"Teach *women* oratory?" Robb finally managed.

"That's the plan," Garrison replied cheerfully.

Later, alone with Angelina Grimké out in the little church courtyard, Bernadette asked, "Will you *really* make speeches?"

"Yes."

Enough astonishing things had happened to her in New York City to make her head swivel permanently. "But won't you be terribly afraid?"

"Yes."

"Ladies never speak up in public; I've never heard of them making speeches."

"I know. Still, Brother Weld feels that as southerners Sarah and I have something special to share."

"Pastor'd forbid women doing that. But I guess I'm not surprised Mr. Weld feels differently; I thought he'd let women into antislavery. In everything else he's . . . different from what I expected, though."

"How did you think he'd be?" Miss Angelina asked softly.

"I heard so much about him — he's Pastor's best friend — so I thought about him a lot. But I thought he'd be younger — more like Pastor. I thought since he'd converted

146

so many people he'd be . . ." In shame, she couldn't go on.

"Younger, more attractive," that inexorable voice supplied.

"Yes, ma'am."

"And now, even though he's the 'Lion of the Tribe of Abolition,' you're very disappointed."

Bernadette fought back her tears, looked up, confessed, "At first I could hardly stand the way he was. But I'll get used to it, I suppose."

"Bernadette, when these meetings are over will you write me?"

With cool people, when their rare warmth shone out, why, that *was* something special! Angelina understood about her foolish feeling for Weld, didn't deride her. Relief overwhelmed Bernadette.

"Oh, yes!" She faced those knowing eyes. "I'd like to hear what it's like for women to speechify."

Sarah arrived just in time to catch the last. "Truth to tell, child," she allowed, "we're terrified. But Nina's leading the way."

Bernadette smiled to herself, figured it *would* be Nina leading. After all, hadn't she learned this week that young Angelina had set herself against her whole Charleston family's highborn customs and religion, tried to convert her powerful, slaveholding brothers and orthodox sisters and mother to abolition, not allowed slaves to wait on her, nor anyone else if she could help it? Didn't flee Charleston for Philadelphia but finally defiantly marched out?

Later that afternoon, listening to the eloquent Weld, Bernadette gradually grew aware that something strange was happening in her. Her self-hate was breaking apart, seemed to be flowing into Weld's passion.

147

She began at last to feel his real nobility — not the nobility of chivalric perfection, but that of bleak, selfless, suffering care.

These last tormenting days she'd shriveled at the absurdity of making a coarse, indifferent, aging pirate personal to herself.

Now she seemed to feel her mistake differently; she'd wanted for herself what belonged in a different way to everyone, this universal Brother Weld.

She momentarily folded her dream to rest within the wings of reality.

Somehow, by understanding her, Angelina had begun this healing . . . this folding.

I'll never be fifteen again, Bernadette thought. But, shedding a top layer of shame, she was glad to be fifteen this once; she would somehow remember fifteen, for all its confusing and foolish pain, as beautiful.

In this room, in this soft, growing dusk, lived Weld. Lived Robb McIves. Sat Angelina nearby

Lived she, herself, Bernadette.

Myself. What a comforting sound that had.

Whatever was Emma McIves's doctor doing here? Bernadette asked herself as one of the church's side doors flew open. She and Pastor reached the door at the same moment.

"I've brought Mrs. McIves with me in my phaeton," Dr. Thorndyke said brusquely. "I'll tell you right off, McIves, I can't do anything for her; she's determined my way will undo her. If I were you, I'd take her home because she's hysteric. And whatever else I did, I'd get that laudanum bottle away from her. If this goes on much longer, she won't be able to exist without it."

Robb's face blanched. There flashed before Bernadette

the vision of herself running up Broadway to the apothecary shop.

"I can give you a really big dose; you'll fall asleep." . . .

It wasn't until Bernadette got outside the church that she remembered she hadn't bade farewell to Angelina Grimké. She started to rush back but Pastor grabbed her, swept her along with him.

She never went back to the church of the Abolition Evangels. She had to stay with Emma, hold her until the seizures passed. Bernadette determined never again to yield to Emma's importunities for laudanum. *Fight, Emma, fight. I'll fight with you.* And Emma finally started the fight.

Bernadette heard from Robb, in undertones, the details of the final days spent preparing men to convert Americans to the most unpopular cause in their history.

On November 27, it was over. Robb hurried back to the boardinghouse; Bernadette dressed Emma and he carried her to the cab.

"Miss Angelina Grimké," he remarked absently, "said I was to tell you she missed you."

 16

Though Emma was coming through the crisis, Bernadette concluded ruefully that Furnace Village seemed a world of fires, as many of them smoking in Pastor's life as smoked on the sooty skylines.

One of the secure things in her life had come to be Robb and the Ironmaster sitting toe to toe by the Riga fireplace, locked in pipe-clouded debate.

Until the day that Pastor appeared at Emilie Glaudin's door.

"Is Trev here?" He peered in. "Come quick, boy!"

They streamed after Robb toward the great house and pounded up the steps, Glaudin breathing like an ox in a sling. (Where had Glaudin come from anyway? she wondered, distracted.)

Trev pushed the door open, catapulted through.

Mrs. Pettee, two housemaids, and the stableman stood in the drawing room. All Bernadette could see for their bending backs clustered about the chair were the Ironmaster's feet and legs propped on his gout stool.

Then she saw past. The Ironmaster's face was drawn up on one side and white as snow; where had the ruddy life gone? A dusting of pipe ash spread across his waistcoat, which pulsed with his labored breathing.

"Shock," Mrs. Pettee was murmuring, kneading her hands. "He had a little once, nothing like this. He got well . . ."

"Trev, fetch the doctor!" Robb commanded. "Glaudin, you and I must get him upstairs."

They lifted him, the weighty Ironmaster making his gurgling sounds, while Bernadette cleared the maids from the steps, steered the frantic Mrs. Pettee so she wouldn't trip up the heavily laden pair.

In the cluttered bedchamber with its massive, curtained high bed, Bernadette yanked down the counterpane. Robb and Glaudin lifted the Ironmaster up to his resting place.

A door banged below, the house shuddered, they heard a man's voice. The doctor.

Despite herself, she stood there and stared at the Ironmaster's ravaged face.

As she did so, she became aware someone else across the bed was staring, too.

His feelings naked to all, kind Glaudin, the hospitable smith, studied the Ironmaster. Was this how the mighty met defeat? his look asked.

With a triumphant look, he answered himself: Defeat, then, was no different for the mighty than the lowly.

The world with its puzzlements was suddenly too much for her. She turned on her heel, went out, walked down the mountain, needing to be by herself.

Robb remained faithfully beside that big bed, giving up any thought of contest in the simple act of friendship. Trev was awfully quiet for a time; then as his uncle improved, he began to be Trev again.

Like this afternoon when he just wouldn't stop pestering her about her train ride.

"Let's go up in the Dawson's haymow," he urged, "out of the wind. We can dig down, you can tell me about the steamer. Uncle says when the packets race on the Hudson, the captains tie the safety valves down, that's what explodes the boilers. But then I don't suppose you saw the boilers . . ."

She climbed the rickety barn ladder above him. "No, only the cabins and decks. Packets scare me worse than trains, Trev. I like trains — you can feel the tracks underneath. On packets there's just wavy water underneath; sometimes we couldn't see any land."

"No land at *all?*" he asked incredulously.

"No," she shook her head. "*Zut!* It's cold up here; even the hay crackles cold."

151

"You'll soon warm up. Do this." The hay flew as he stooped and made a hole for himself, like a dog scratching for a bone; he settled down in the nest, began to pull grass around him energetically.

For a while her teeth chattered so much and she was so busy with Trev's nagging about boilers and valves, she couldn't relax. Finally she leaned her head back, peered into the far-up rafters where gently scolding pigeons huddled, watched a knife of light from the window sliver the sifting shadows.

Her thoughts drifted off to her latest letter from Angelina Grimké and how hard it was for her learning to speechify under a harsh taskmaster like Weld . . .

She came to to Trev's repeating, "Well, why don't we?"

"Why don't we *what?*"

"Jump from the mow to the hay wagon. It's a long way down; it'll be jolly. You can sit here all night but I'm going to jump."

The dry grass exploded as Bernadette shot up, plowed through the hay to the edge of the mow, now, in early winter, piled almost to the barn ceiling. Far below, the little hay wagon was loaded, a fork sticking up.

"Trev, that's too far!"

"Here I go!" Trev shouted, took six running steps, leaped off, down, down! landed in the middle of the wagon. His cap flew off, he looked up. She thought he was grinning. "Miss the fork!" he shouted; of course, he knew she would do it.

She inhaled, held her nose for the dive, sailed out, feet pumping, skirts belling. When, when?

She lit on the straw, Trev grabbed her, and they went down in a laughing tumble.

But instead of jumping right up, he just lay there, holding her. His eyes were so near he looked like a long-nosed

Cyclops. He moved his head back, ordered quietly, "Say 'Zut!' "

"Zut!" she whispered.

"Say it again." This time he put his fingers on her lips, feeling them move.

"Again."

She could feel his breath on her face; his fingers were alive with feeling.

Suddenly she kissed them.

His eyes went wide in the dusk of the wagon; he jerked his hand away; then, still staring, he kissed her cheek. Softly, with touching boy-curiosity.

Things stirred powerfully in her, made her leap up, straighten her coat. What crazy thing were they doing? Whatever had impelled that kiss out of her, now she wished she hadn't done it. What *was* the matter with her? First Weld, now this. Something lay deep in her, some threatened storm of real feeling.

Sick of her own mystery, she climbed briskly off the wagon, marched for the open door, glanced back, saw in relief that, after a brief disappearance, Trev was following her cheerily.

"We're going to Christmas night, ain't we?"

Pastor had chosen this Yuletide to prove that primitive Christians never celebrated Christmas. After prayer meeting Christmas Eve, she and Trev planned to skin down and crowd in to marvel at the pagan candles and gilt star on the Episcopal altar.

"If Pastor thinks Mrs. McIves is well enough to stay after prayer meeting, I can sneak off," Bernadette replied. Then, "What were you doing back there in the barn a minute ago?"

"Oh," Trev said casually, "before we went up in the mow, I let the boar in with the sow. I had to get him back in his pen before we left."

153

"Trev!"

"Maybe come spring," he grinned, "Farmer Dawson'll get a surprise — maybe a lot of them."

Since her journal was her own now, her questions flowed into its pages at last, in avid search of meaning.

Last night she'd finally written: "This is what I think about sin. If you really want the truth, the Father of your own spirit won't let you go without it. If what you believe leads you to honor Him, to love His people and want to do good for them, I don't think this is a sinful life."

Then, with a strong flourish of the pen, "I'm not going to let myself be badgered about sin anymore. I'm going to stand up for what I believe. Women can stand up, too."

 17

SHE BLEW OUT SOFTLY; she could see her breath. After three hours of sitting, the congregation still hadn't warmed up the sanctuary. She nudged the foot-warmer nearer, wished she could take her shoes off, plump her stocking feet right on its steamy comfort.

Her stockings, like her mittens, had holes in them; pulling an index finger into one mitten's woolly cage, she concluded that ragged-beyond-repair mittens didn't show if you made your fingers behave.

"Too many are boiling mad, Robb," Otis Atchison had observed soberly at last night's donation party, looking over the junk. "I never thought I'd live to see the day when I'd

154

advise you to go easy on antislavery, but I'm advising it now, for your sake . . ."

She jerked her thoughts back to the church. Here she was, fretting about foot-warmers and holey mittens when Pastor was struggling alone up there in the pulpit. He'd written a magnificent antislavery sermon and, as he'd passionately answered Otis Atchison's warning, he was going to deliver it come hell or high water.

Right now, as he was finishing it up, the silence in the sanctuary was thick enough to slice.

From under her eyelashes Bernadette studied a nearby abolition critic. Sitting in wired discomfort, Justin Snedecor looked as though he'd twang with rage if she tweaked him.

" '. . . Remember them that are in bonds, as bound with them; and them which suffer adversity, as being yourselves also in the body,' " Robb pleaded, shutting up the big Bible, sermon done.

He bowed his head in a call to prayer. "Oh, God," he began, "Thou art a righteous God; to enslave even one of Thy children does unspeakable violence to Thy Image in man . . ."

Suddenly she couldn't stand that all-alone voice; she raised her head to be with him.

A lock of dark hair fell across his bowed forehead; his hands gripped the lectern edge — she could feel in her own bones how hard he was gripping. She wished he'd raise his closed eyes and look at her; she wanted him to know that except for one disloyal minute of ice-cold feet, for three hours she'd never deserted him.

Her dark, unpraying gaze, filled with emotion, fixed on him until his face faded into a shimmering oval . . .

The church was emptied of its uneasy people, the grimly satisfied ignoring the grimly outraged, while those torn in the middle hurried off, tight-lipped and out-of-sorts.

155

She moved to the front of the church, stood aside while Glaudin — who sometimes came down the mountain to sit in the church balcony — spoke confidentially to Robb. Pastor was drawn, sweating from exhaustion; she wished Glaudin would let him go home.

"Skip on without me," he nodded, not looking her way.

She hurried up the road, turned off at the shortcut. On all sides, the town's soft, spacious meadows lay shriveled with frost into lumpy brown tussocks.

She rounded a curve in the shortcut, saw a group of farm wagons drawn up in a line. Homeward-wending people. But why had they stopped?

She came quickly abreast of the end wagon. Where was the driver, the host of children? Up ahead?

Yet each wagon seemed as empty as the last, even the lead one.

She walked past it, automatically reached out a hand to smooth the horse's withers. Glancing to the ground under the horse, she saw the circle of shoes before she looked up over the horse's head and saw their wearers.

Achsah Miller, his brother, Moses; their friend, Timothy Jones, he of the bull neck and meaty bulk; David Treadup who farmed at the foot of Mount Riga; Justin Snedecor, his bright eyes on her, ready to let go like a spring released . . .

What were they doing standing in a group, no families anywhere? And in this lonely shortcut place, past the town, but not yet to Salisbury?

No one responded to her wide-eyed greeting; the men faced her in flinty silence, wagon whips in hand.

"Run along, girl," David Treadup warned evenly.

She ran, all right.

Raced back to the churchyard, found no Robb; rushed into the sanctuary — empty; raced up to Main Street — no sign of him; ran to the Atchison's — found only the bound

156

girl; went to several other houses of sympathizers, one of whom had just got home but hadn't seen Pastor.

Bad things were happening all over the country to Abolitionists.

Maybe he wouldn't take the cutoff. Maybe she was just imagining.

After all, nobody's said a thing.

She slowed from a run to a trot, slowed from a trot to fast walk, puffing.

She'd just been overexcited, anxious from the pre-Sunday tension of waiting, the long, strained hours in church.

I can certainly get funny ideas, she half-murmured in rueful relief, head shaking. She'd skin home, find he'd arrived safely . . .

She started up the cutoff once again, trudged up the hill, looked absently downward, expecting to see the trail empty.

The wagons were still there!

She saw like a nightmare come true what she'd instinctively feared: a circle of men, Pastor facing them, coat off, hands behind him.

Then she saw an arm raised, a whip curving . . .

"Pastor!" she screamed, rushing pell-mell toward him, everything blurring as she ran, hardly hearing Robb McIves shouting, "Bernadette, go away!"

She paid no attention, ran right up to him.

Stopped and for the first time heard behind her the sound of galloping horses striking flint from the frozen ground. Heard Otis's rescuing bellow, realized Robb's enemies were scrambling up on their wagons, realized she and Robb were surrounded by a tangle of turning spokes, thumping wagon bed boards, grinding wheel rims, snorting horses.

One wagon gone, another, another . . .

She scarcely noticed his fleeing enemies, his rescuing friends; all she could see was his standing there with his hands

157

bound behind him, with an expression of mute, shut-eyed silence that said he couldn't endure her to see him this way.

His greatcoat and coat were off, his shirt torn. She reached, tried to hold up the tatters to cover him, couldn't collect them all, simply put her arms around him and hugged him close to her.

He shivered once, violently.

"Here now!" Otis exclaimed, coming up.

She let go but Robb's eyes stayed closed. Otis cut loose his tied hands; they swung from behind him, fell by his side. His head sank on his chest. The wind blew his hair across his white face.

Bernadette picked up his trampled coat and overcoat; Mr. Davis took them from her.

Then they got Robb up in the chaise, Otis and the others with their horrified faces; she stumbled after his rescuers.

At home she slipped upstairs to Emma, lied to her that an emergency meeting had been called to reconsider buying a stove for the church. When she got back to the parlor Robb was sitting in a chair with his greatcoat still around him; he was speaking hoarsely to the cluster of men and carefully didn't look at her.

"First thing David Treadup said to me was that they wanted me out of the church.

" 'You'll not get me from my church this way,' I flared.

"Timothy Jones laid on the first whip; it struck my greatcoat but the tail of the whip flicked my cheek and I flinched.

"I tell you, waves of scarlet anger seared clean through me when I jerked back. God help me, but I discovered in that moment I'm no pacifist; I lunged for Jones. So then hands were laid on me, my coat was torn off. I struggled to fend off the hands.

158

" 'Before God,' I remember yelling, 'no man'll buggy-whip me.'

"My arms were grabbed, my hands forced behind me; when they bound my hands I knew I'd be helpless.

"I can't tell you what made me stop struggling — prayer, I hope. Anyway, I remember saying to myself, 'Lord, let me stand up and let myself be beaten and not cringe and not cry.' . . . And," his voice softening a shade, "it's funny, but the next thing I did was worry how my best shirt'd be cut to ribbons and I'd have such a hard time getting another . . .

"Well, at least they were men enough finally to suggest turning me around so they could stripe me decently on the back. Just as Jones was about to come forward, turn me, I heard Bernadette's voice shrieking. Bernadette here at a time like this, I thought despairingly, Bernadette come into this male brutality, come where I was helpless to shield her. So I shouted for her to go away, but she wouldn't. Then I heard the rest of you shouting, realized in my dimness you were scaring them off . . ."

His voice played out, he put his head down, shook it like a confused dog.

"He's going to faint," Seth Shelton exclaimed.

"Here, into the study," Otis commanded.

They got him under the arms, half-dragged him; just before the door closed, Otis called, "Girl, get water and unguent and a clean shirt."

Upstairs, Bernadette found his shirt, his wash basin, put soap in it and a towel over the soap.

She tapped downstairs, detoured through the people in the parlor, rapped on the study door.

Otis, in the middle of a sentence, opened the door wide, unthinkingly exposing Pastor. Pastor sat on the couch, his head in his hands, his ripped wool undergarment hanging off him.

159

She handed the basin and salve to Otis, who came to his senses, grabbed them, slammed the door shut. But in that confused second she'd seen what she was afraid to see — the red welts which encircled Pastor's chest, the columns of welts on his shoulders and arms.

She stood there by the closed door. *Gladly would I wash the hurting flesh. Gently would I rub the salve along the welts.*

Would bandages be needed? Did he bleed?

Only his heart, only Pastor's heart. Her bandages would be of no use for it.

She moved to the kitchen window, looked blindly out, recalled the image of him standing by the road, head up, his shirt sleeves blowing in the wind. He'd shouted "Go away!" so that she wouldn't see what was happening to him. When she'd gone up to him to hold the shirt cloth, his face had borne suffering past her bearing; he'd shut his eyes, saying nothing.

Ever since she'd come to his house and he'd told her of Weld she'd been living in a dream. She'd lived believing she loved someone who was real, but he'd turned out not to be, that Theodore Weld of her longing.

And all the while she held to that dream, nurturing it by lonely imaginings, a real love waited to show itself to her.

The French letters? All written for Robb McIves, of course. The drawings? How exciting to conjure up Weld! But it was Robb's picture she couldn't ever look at again.

She loved him; that was the mystery in her. She thought she'd loved him, probably as long ago as when the forge blew up and he'd found Trev.

With finality she at last plummeted out of the lingering world of adolescent fantasy into a tough, beautiful world where real folk lived.

She was in love with a man, a *real* man.

160

Weld had been a giant to her. But if people were giants to you, you looked always from the eyes of a child.

She sensed she'd be torn up by her realization later.

But not now.

Now it was a great welling up, a great quiet wholeness in her.

It was like communion with an old friend who'd long lived in her, unrecognized.

Of course he'd never love her back. Yet at this moment, whether her love was returned or not wasn't its essence. Its essence was all her real feeling for real Robb McIves.

"Bernadette!" a faint voice fretted.

Emma McIves needed to be fed; Bernadette felt strangely practical and able to face her true life, the only one she'd been living all this time, the only one she really had to live.

 18

IF TREV had only told her at the beginning, he'd never have got them in such a mess.

The way Bernadette later pieced it together, it'd happened like this:

Hunting Bernadette, Trev had gone into their yard; from her window Emma had spied him, asked him to come in the empty house.

Reluctantly he'd let himself in the kitchen, looked sharp for the hall door. It was quiet down here; empty houses gave him the creeps, especially when they might have a daft woman hidden in them.

He'd jumped when he looked up the high, narrow steps and saw her standing at the top. Emma half-leaned as though she couldn't support herself. He said her face was really white, but her eyes were blazing blue.

"How old are you?" she'd asked.

"Thirteen."

"You're not very tall, are you? Not nearly as tall as Bernadette, I mean."

"I'm not as old," he'd muttered. "Besides, I'm getting my growth late."

All at once she'd seemed to sway. *Don't let her faint*, he'd implored — Aunt fainted and it was a terrible nuisance.

But she'd caught herself.

"You're fond of Bernadette, aren't you?"

He'd felt the flush rise to his hairline. A fellow didn't have to answer a question like that; so he'd stared rudely back, lips tight.

"Come here, Master Trevelyan," she'd commanded suddenly.

But he'd hung stubbornly to the step where he was.

"Very well, I only wanted to see you better," she'd complained. "I was improving at Christmas, but now I don't see many people, even Mr. McIves. Bernadette's the only one who cares enough to spend a little time with me."

Poor Bernadette, he'd thought in silent sympathy.

"If you were only older . . ." she'd said, looking at him in a way which started a strange tingling at the base of his neck. Daft woman; she was daft.

"I have to go home now, ma'am." But he'd stood there, rooted by a hint of something extraordinary to come.

"You'll be very rich," she'd whispered. "No, you'd never marry Bernadette; men don't always marry what they crave . . ."

She wasn't saying anything sensible after all. What did she

162

mean? Of course he'd marry Bernadette; he couldn't imagine marrying any other girl. The urge to leave had grown uncontrollable. Trev had turned, struck the bottom step when she'd fairly screamed, "No, you can't go yet! I have an errand you must run for me."

"But I'm late," he'd lied.

"Good, kind young boy, I need medicine right away. Here are coins; run to Dr. Turner's office and ask him for the kind of medicine I used to have. He'll know. Hurry!"

He'd stooped to pick up the little rain of metal that fell around him, looked incredulously up at her.

"Bring the bottle to the top of the stairs and put it there."

"Bernadette could get it for you."

"Oh, no, I need it now; I might die without it. And Bernadette mustn't know of it — she'd never forgive herself she hadn't been here when I needed medicine."

But hang! He hadn't wanted to do her old errand! Still he'd now got possession of her money and supposed he'd have to run to Dr. Turner's. And she'd even asked him to come by again in another fortnight and carelessly he'd promised to, just in order to escape.

After he'd sneaked the wrapped-up bottle to the top of the stairs (there wasn't a sound in the house), he'd started soberly home.

Marrying, craving? Naturally, a fellow had to crave a wife, or he wouldn't bother with one. Craving without marrying? He'd tested out the phrase, feeling illumination dancing just out of reach.

What did it all have to do with Bernadette?

He was chasing bumblebees in a thistle patch, catching them in his chip hat, swinging them round and round so that when he let them go they flew off in a drunken zigzag, when Bernadette had come skimming down the road with a basket on her arm. He'd looked in and seen a bunch of whippoorwill shoes and wild pink lady-slippers, grabbed the spring flowers, flung them in the air, raced to trample the ones that scattered in the path.

She'd glared at him, put down her basket and come at him, got in one good dutch rub before he beat her off with his strong, unsentimental fists.

Mrs. Shatterbrain would have to get her own medicine after this, he'd thought, as Bernadette tried to pummel him.

The way girls fought was funny, it really was. He'd roared with laughter, dodging her.

The Ironmaster stirred, made a throaty growl, then the white-maned, florid face on the pillow lapsed back into sleep.

Across the counterpane from Bernadette, Robb leaned back in his chair, rubbing his chin with thoughtful finger.

He tossed the letter across to her; she read quickly.

Brother Weld was gratified to learn that since the horse-whipping, a strong new conciliatory tide was running for Robb and abolition in the Furnace Village church. Men were sometimes shocked into sanity by their excesses, Weld observed, and this appeared to be what was happening with the coming over to Robb of a number of church members horrified at the recent barbarity.

Weld said he liked work at the National Antislavery Society office in New York, found a certain excitement in it even after abolitionizing. His nearly destroyed voice, he reported, was mending.

But his main job these days was coaching the Misses Grimké to be public speakers. He was proud to report their meetings had now grown too large for session rooms and had moved into church sanctuaries.

Oh, the outraged Philadelphia Quakers were giving the sisters all kinds of trouble. "As I see it," Weld observed dryly, "the country Quakers are a hardy antislavery force but the rich city Quakers have grown stale and soft."

Angelina, Weld wrote, was preparing a strong statement against northern race prejudice — upsetting talk for abolition, but new and courageous.

Weld had a favor to ask Robb. Garrison had invited the sisters to speak in New England. Trouble would brew, Weld wrote, because not only would the sisters come up there as the first female public speakers, the first females to speak against slavery, but now the first women to speak to men who were, in growing numbers, joining their audiences. "I well know on all these counts New England's clergy will be shocked. Could you see yourself as at least vouching for their dedication and sincerity?"

"Will you speak for them?" Bernadette asked.

He shook his head emphatically. "I think Weld's losing his mind. These women of his could split the abolition movement wide open."

The Ironmaster gave a snore, then a snort, and woke up.

"I dreamt I was a lad," he growled. "Queer. As we grow old we more and more become what we were at the beginning. Of late I've hoped I was as a lad what I want to become."

The Lord had felled the Ironmaster and set him at last to reviewing his life. Robb found reason for optimism in Furnace Village and Riga, too.

Later, outside, he walked with a springy step. He didn't even break stride when she put straight and hot to him the question of why he wouldn't support the Grimkés. He was about to give her an adamant answer, then stopped, misliking her young eyes studying him as though he were a strange insect under glass.

Women, he thought irritably, were barely to be understood. But he was in full flood, success rising, too busy now to brood; he didn't even brood about Emma lately. He

165

dropped like a stone into his late-night bed, didn't even have to try, like Weld, to run off in the early morning the agitations of his flesh. .

🌿 19

SHE SAT on the stone wall in the spring sunshine and waited for Trev. The land oozed soft with seed and rainworms working through loosening sod. A lamb not yet sooty from the charcoal hearths bounced on springy legs, then, alarmed by its own acrobatics, ran and hid by its mother. Bernadette ached for a set of watercolors.

She poked her shoe at a rock in the mud and watched a curling grub surprised into the light. After wintertime, she mused, people looked like they'd climbed out from under rocks, too: on the first bright days they went around blinking and grubby. The warmth made her sleepy; she'd been up till midnight last night helping Robb fold tracts.

For a time the urgency with which they'd folded had dispelled her uneasy new sense of him. Then it'd begun to change. There at the kitchen table she'd first begun to notice his hands as he picked up the tracts, folded once, folded twice. Big, determined hands, long-fingered . . .

Well, if Trev was *never* going to come, she might as well lie back and settle herself; she wriggled, trying to get the rocky lump out of her back. Sun softened her upturned winter face . . .

Last night when he'd lit his pipe there was a flickering flash of firelight on his forehead and cheeks. She saw, was afraid

166

to see, those lips which held the pipestem. The remembered realization of how beautiful they felt, raised ruggedly on the page. Behind them the teeth clenched tight.

His puffing made a soft, sucking rhythm.

I'm falling asleep. Fought her eyelids, lost.

Other acute awarenesses, too: scratchy shoulder of everyday coat, tobacco drift, blue-black sheen of bent, dark head.

A dream of Weld seeped into her somnolence — her old dream of the fair, chivalric, incorporeal Weld in dancelike slow motion. The world of Weld — no tormenting complexity because no reality.

The real world with Robb McIves: he'd asked her to read the French Bible; touched her hair, then snatched his hand away and galloped up the trace; leaped up, kicked aside his chair, put his arms around her, said she must be his dear child and join his church . . .

She didn't know whatever had made her say it last night; she wished she'd bit off her tongue, instead. Even half-asleep, she twisted in a paroxysm of embarrassment.

"Mrs. McIves might get well if she didn't have to have a child," she'd blurted out, determined to say what she was afraid Emma dared not.

He'd stopped folding, stopped puffing, stared in disbelief at her. Then a horror-mask had slid over his face and out of it he'd snapped, "Never speak to me again of such a thing."

She tried to rouse from her nightmare of recall . . .

"Bernadette, wake up! You're going to fall!"

She blinked blearily, sat up, "Where in the world have you been?"

"Hunting arrowheads. I got a pocketful. Beauties, too."

"Pettee Trevelyan, you have barrels of arrowheads. Where do you put them all?"

"Only a couple of boxes," he defended.

In his other bulging pocket she could see little chunks of

167

iron ore. Trev could never resist picking them up: they contained flakes of real silver.

Bernadette and Trev slogged across the meadow. She couldn't remember when he hadn't pestered her about going up to a forge top. Finally it'd got so bad, she'd given up putting it off.

Forge top.

It always looked like a hell up there.

Lately she'd grown more aware of the poor men who, dried and shriveled by heat, had to live twelve hours a day in that heavy smoke, breathing the gases. Going about in Riga with permanently soot-streaked skin in permanently soot-stiffened coveralls. Looking at the world from mind-dulled eyes; on off-times, carousing a lot, drinking like fish. When she'd been a child, the men of Riga had looked wild, carefree, and colorful; now in their work-worn helplessness she saw tragedy.

It was good, Emilie said, they had country to hunt in, streams to fish in, places to go in nature where they could be made men again. If coal came in, the forges would move to the cities and then the forgemen would finally become less than men, just work beasts.

"The top man's Antanas." Trev skinned under a rail gate.

"Will it blow up?" she half-teased.

"No, it won't," he answered, stung. "Antanas has been top man longer than I can remember."

The huge stone pyramid reared like a rocky embattlement as they came up on the road and fell in behind a charcoal van piled with flaring baskets. Naturally Trev twaddled with the drayman while she darted after, holding her bunched skirts.

They turned sharply onto the narrow wagon bridge and climbed. Acrid, gray smoke soon enveloped them. *Phew! How could anyone work in this air?* She coughed.

"Hold your hand to your mouth," Trev ordered; he was a

short ghost beside her, dodging a horse loaded with saddle-bags of limestone.

Now they were surrounded by a real traffic jam. Two wagon vans, one coming, one going; another horse, a man running. To make iron, she knew by heart, was a continuous feeding of the ravenous tunnel head — every twenty-four hours, fillers dumped into the charge four hundred bushels of charcoal, over four tons of ore, a mix of limestone; this charge produced over two tons of iron and spawned two and a half tons of slag.

Down below, the enormous leather bellows chuffed like a maddened bull . . .

Now they could see the figure of old Antanas, top man, wielding his long-handled flare. He plunged it downward out of sight.

"Come on!" Trev said; they dashed from the shelter of a van and sashayed right up to the maw.

She looked down into a yawning bright mass of glowing, winking, heaving stuff. Its hot breath belched up and seared her face.

"It's like a stew!" she yelled.

"Hell and damnation!" Trev shouted back. "It ain't just kitchen cooking!"

Flames suddenly leaped up through the suffocating air. They jumped back, stumbled over Antanas who had just then turned from helping a filler.

She didn't have to know Lith to understand what Antanas shouted at Trev. Expulsion was in his round bulging eyes, in the arm he pointed wrathfully toward the wagon bridge.

They darted off.

"I *know* it's dangerous up here; I *know* if Antanas don't mix right it could blow everybody to kingdom come. He don't have to yell those things to me."

169

"With all that unloading, we were in the way, Trev."

"I've been in the way *lots* of times before. He sent us down because you're a girl."

"I didn't want to stay all that long anyway. It *is* like a little hell up there."

"Well, if it weren't like that, how'd they get the iron made? You like your new cookstove, don't you?"

She had to admit she did; it saved scorching her arms and face at the hearth, it saved torrid kitchens in the summer, it cooked evenly, steadily.

They came down into the main road and got a clear, unsmoked look at themselves. Each was soot-smudged; and no good to rub, that just made it smear.

"Anyway, I don't suppose there's a girl in Litchfield County been up on a cupola," he flopped down by the road. "See, you were afraid, but you did it. That's nervy."

"Ummmm."

"Bernadette, when I own a furnace you can come up and look at the fires all day. Don't you *hate* being shooed off because you're a girl?"

"Yes," she admitted quietly. Hated it deeply, darkly, until sometimes it was a great seething in her.

But there was one bittersweet old compensation: without being a girl she couldn't love Robb McIves. The same pulsating Weld-core was in her, but now covered with the relentless and exciting rind of actual and proximate experience.

"I have to go home," she told Trev abruptly. Her psychic space was crowding up, making her burst. *I want to get away from Furnace Village. I want to get away from the warring things in me.*

Charcoal burning on the hills would be like Martial-red stars come night.

Robb McIves looked up in surprise when she burst into the kitchen.

"Bernadette, where in the world have you been? You're sooty."

She fought down in herself the small Bernadette who'd have answered obediently to his accusing tone; there were things in her now which weren't part of that girl's life. He sat there, Emma's man; she stood here, a woman growing.

"I'm going back to Ohio," she announced. "I want to go as soon as Uncle Marcus sends the money."

"What foolishness is this?" he asked, getting up from the table. "You know you haven't finished at Miss Miller's and I still have things I need to teach you."

"I want to go home."

"Why?" he asked, obviously surprised by her deadly tone.

"It's time for me to go back."

"What will you do in Ohio?"

"I don't know . . ." she began to flounder.

"Well, you can't," he answered crossly. "Your cousin Hester expects you in Canterbury this summer and you've another year with Miss Miller and me. Besides, Mrs. McIves needs you. For that matter, so do I."

"No," she answered.

"Bernadette, I can't argue now; I'll talk about it with you later, truly I will. You know how much work I have waiting for me at the church this evening. The tracts weren't all distributed. Now tie up your hair and start cooking."

But she just stood there, her jaw set, her eyes dark and inexorable. "If I can't go now, when can I then?"

"By a year from this spring. Your uncle and cousin both agree you should spend another winter with us. Bernadette, *do* fix the food."

She turned away. *A year from this spring.* Could she live in this house with him another year?

She scooped her hair up into its net, took the General Jackson apron and pulled it over her. Water was needed, and fire. Which first? The fire, of course. She shook down the stove.

She'd be indifferent, distant, protect her secret self by quickly coming and going from his study, by hard housework, by escaping with Annis and Trev — by distracting Emma who fretted for companionship.

She blew on the coals. They leaped to life under her breath.

 20

ANNIS DUMPED *The Heart of Midlothian* into Bernadette's skirt pocket where it promptly tore half the stitches out. In a panic, Bernadette grabbed her knee so that the stolen novel wouldn't fall right at Miss Miller's feet. It was kind of hard walking out the door scooched over; she pretended to be hunting a tear.

Stolen romances, she thought wistfully, weren't nearly as delicious since she'd stopped adoring Weld. Novels of love troubled her now.

At home she dragged the braided kitchen rug out into the yard and beat it lustily. All winter she'd kept after that pesky rug but it'd got dirty anyhow.

She heard Robb's horse clop to the shed, kept whacking.

"I was talking with Brother Atchison this afternoon. He plans to take you and Annis to the Canterbury farm by way of Talcott Mountain."

"So he said, sir."

"Bernadette, stop beating that rug, I want to talk with you. You're lucky Otis is taking you to Talcott Mountain, it's the most beautiful spot in all Connecticut."

"Yes, sir," she answered, laying the board carefully on the grass, looking up at him at last. But it hurt to look at his face, relaxed, kind, friendly — so she studied the shadow he cast on the grass as he moved hither and yon, ruminating.

"I'm going, too," he announced cheerfully. "How would you like to go to North Brookfield, too?" Then, seeing her puzzled expression, he explained, "There's a Congregational Conference being held in North Brookfield where an important statement's to be made on how New England churches should deal with Abolitionists. I'm hopeful it'll be in sympathy with us."

Visions of riding with him in the intimate closeness of a stagecoach through the unfurling June countryside flickered hurtfully in her.

She was silent.

"You don't seem overjoyed," he remarked dryly. "In any case, I've decided to take you to North Brookfield."

He went off; she went back to her whacking.

Be anxious about intimacy in a stagecoach with *him?*
She should have saved her fantasies.

The fight began when Otis and Robb fell to talking about the "crisis" in the abolition movement.

"If Weld doesn't recall them there'll be a flood of New England criticism nobody can dam up" was Robb's comment that brought her back from scenery-watching.

"Makes a circus of abolition, it does, two hussies speaking in public to men," Otis responded.

Grimkés, Bernadette knew instantly. In her pocket crackled Miss Angelina's latest letter.

The men said the sisters were carving up the New England

abolition movement and repelling potential converts, Garrison was an impractical ninny to sponsor them, and the clergy right to turn thumbs down on them as they had in Danvers, where the Grimkés had been forced to hire a hall. In not paying mind to Robb's appeals to recall them, Theo had taken final leave of his senses.

I'm going to get mad and argue, she knew fatally, saying she had an entirely opposite understanding of the situation. At Lynn, the sisters had spoken to a thousand people; Boston had received them warmly — because of Garrison, Boston was used to speaking women.

So of course the men shouted then about things she didn't know anything of: Garrison's idiot no-government theory which urged folks not to vote or believe in the Constitution; Garrison's pacifism in martial New England; a publicity-hound named Henry Wright who'd attached himself to the sisters and was infecting them with all kinds of outlandish ideas . . .

Garrison, Wright, a confusion of issues, things she couldn't know about — Robb's anger firing steamy feelings in her. These complications contending in her with the simple brave fact of Angelina and Sarah . . .

So of course she did what she least wanted to do: she burst into furious tears.

"Now, now," Otis clucked soothingly as Annis woke up in alarm. "There, there, chickie. You needn't get so worked up about something you know nothing about, nor ought to. The Grimkés are just meddlesome old maids who've taken a perverse liking to ye; you've no responsibility to defend their being so forward and foolish."

"I *want* to defend them," Bernadette bawled into her handkerchief.

"The trouble is," Robb's cold tone was very different from Otis's consoling one, "Bernadette's spirit needs quelling. I've

174

tried to bend her because I've known her best interests lay that way. But often she . . . oh, she seems to escape my intent."

"Well, now," Otis temporized, "I believe in mindful, pious women but they don't have to have a broke spirit. Just think of a mare — a lively mare's twice the good and pleasure of a witless plodder."

Bernadette crouched rebelliously by Aunt Atchison's Simsbury bedroom window, watching the stormy night sky, a sky to fit her mood.

What had *really* caused the latest abolition furor? She *knew* what graveled Robb most even if he hadn't said so. Angelina Grimké had introduced a shocking new cause — *the women's question,* as she called it.

"I've begun," she'd written Bernadette, "to speak on the rights of women. Before three hundred women I've just said, 'Cast off restraint in the company of men; begin to look on yourselves as responsible moral beings.'"

The Grimkés daring New England! Bernadette loved the hardy bravery of two itinerate women lecturers traveling from village to village in all kinds of rough carts, all kinds of blown weather, meeting all kinds of unmeetable schedules. No time to rest, only time to bolt meals. And now the first high excitement, the first challenge, first sense of liberation worn off. Now the pain of ubiquitous hatred and physical drudgery.

"But at least," Angelina had concluded, "we've proved we can speak intelligently and hold crowds."

The moon erupted from a black cloud for an imperious gold moment.

Well, Bernadette sighed, her chin in her hands on the windowsill, what did a man want of a woman anyway?

175

She slammed down the window against the storm-covered moon, pattered to bed.

How could you love someone you didn't understand, someone who didn't even like you? she swore as she yanked down the quilt.

Well, how could you?

She hauled the quilt straight up over her head, lay curled in a vengeful ball in the darkness.

"It's going to storm!" Annis wailed from the window.

Bernadette bounded out of bed, surveyed the gray clouds churning in the sky.

But cheery Otis would suffer no mention of thunderheads as they set out in Aunt Atchison's buggy. Their road had just climbed out of a rocky dip, washed bare of surface, when he reined in the horse and pointed dramatically.

Half-rising, peering, Bernadette made out a blunt mountain shaved by rocky cliffs. On its humped summit sat two buildings which seemed to have been born there, a weathered stone castle and a chimneylike tower.

"Cost old Daniel Wadsworth $175,000 to build that tower," Otis observed with satisfaction. "Visitors to Connecticut are always took here, especially from the old world, where they think they've a corner on castles."

Robb bounded out, tied up the horse; he wore the look of an eager boy just unloosed from a spool of care. The coil of her own apprehension since yesterday's quarrel unwound in her, seeing him look like that.

"Scamper on, gels," Otis urged, putting his hand to his paunch; Otis always had to follow his stomach around.

She and Annis flew up the woods path; an hour later, they clambered up to the rough foundations of the stone-and-timber mountain house with its high medieval windows.

"Let's not stay here — it's just a big house. Let's go right

176

on up to the tower," Annis teased as the men emerged from the woods, Otis waddling, Robb striding, coat over his shoulder, big, graceful.

He waved, smiled. Why did he smile so little? she wondered.

The men trimmed Annis's sails just long enough to poke around.

"It's a pity we didn't think to bring a pencil and paper," Robb said unexpectedly. "You could sketch this for me."

For a moment Bernadette was too astonished to answer. Then she stammered, "But I made myself a booklet. I brought it with me."

"Good" was his decided reply, one which left her trying to fathom his wild inconsistency. Now, apparently, because he wanted a sketch, it was all right for a female to draw.

"This isn't interesting," Annis pouted. "I'm going to climb the tower, Pa."

All four trudged up the rough steps. From slits in the tower's thick hexagonal walls, they caught splendid little views, slices of woods and sky; they climbed on, urged by the promise of wider splendor.

"It's great to get away from the smell of the tannery," Otis puffed. "I'm enjoying this fancy-loose, footfree stuff."

"Footloose and fancy-free, Pa," Annis laughed.

"Well, whichever," her father breathed. "Just so it gets me quick to the top."

Everyone laughed, Robb most of all; she uncorked, exhilarated to be with him in his fine mood.

Come into the dull light, she forgot everyone as she raced to the parapet. Miles of sapphire Connecticut stretched before her, unknowable peaks and chains, unknown chasms in between. She peered over the stone wall, gasped; frighteningly far below, a small lake was held in the dark clasp of the woods.

Wanting to be apart from the buoyant voices of Annis and Otis raised in gymnastic victory, she stood mute — looking, absorbing, washed by feeling . . .

Suddenly, hands grasped her shoulders. In blind instinct, she turned her cheek to nuzzle those speaking hands.

Robb McIves murmured in her ear, " 'Blessed of the Lord be his land . . . and for the chief things of the ancient mountains.' Moses stood on the hilltop and looked into the Promised Land but never reached it, Bernadette."

In his voice she heard the same rapture she was experiencing, and something else, a pleading. Was he trying to tell her that he, like Moses, had never reached home? Or was it that the timeless span before them made him feel his own little term was too short?

Whatever he was trying to say, his hands tightened; she turned, looked up to read him. His gray-eagle look held her eyes in a breathless, wordless tension.

"That's the Farmington Valley; yonder's the Connecticut," Otis explained smoothly, coming up.

She was let go abruptly, ejected from the utter safety of his grasp to the lonely reaches of her own space.

When Otis began to tell Robb about the tower's construction, what immense structural problems the Hartford builder had faced, she drifted off impatiently.

Annis knew to leave Bernadette be as she wandered from place to place catching here a different cloud shape, there a different angle of land, a different color of hill. Unsubdued by the immensity of the skyscape, Otis was describing with gusto nearby Simsbury's old colonial prison, which up till ten years ago had quartered prisoners underground in the copper mines.

Bernadette was intently sketching lines of hills when Robb came, sat on the wall she leaned against, dangled his long legs into space.

Behind them Otis rested on a boulder, Annis scavenged for pebbles for her whatnot shelf.

Robb watched silently.

Bernadette took her thumb, smudged the soft pencil lead, blending hills together.

"Where did you learn to do that?"

She looked up, smiled, shrugged. "It just came to me. Without it, pencil lines don't flow together well enough."

"Here, let me."

She handed the little sketchbook to him. Laboriously he took his big thumb and ran it over what she'd drawn. They grinned. "My thumb isn't magic like yours."

Heads together, they laughed deliciously at what a mess he'd made.

Simply, in gentle intimacy, he put his smudged thumb on the end of her nose.

"That's nay so fetching," Otis observed.

"All the same, she's pretty," Robb answered quietly, staring at her.

"But ye'll be not so pretty if ye tumble off that wall. I've felt a splat of rain; we'd best be going down. I wouldn't want the horse to take a fright and bolt."

They ran for the tower steps. "You go on ahead and take care of the horse, Robb. Annis'll bring up the rear with her Pa."

Mountain water flowing, fast-growing muddy trail.

Robb and Bernadette slipped and slid down together, something loosened between them. Free, free . . .

Wet growth slapped against her face as she plunged after him; her hair was plastered to her face in rivulets. His shirt was stuck to his shoulders and his skin showed through, but who could care?

He stopped; she nearly tumbled into him. A gully filling

with runoff cut across the trail. There was no way around it; it stretched left and right.

He leaped across.

Then he seemed to remember that Bernadette couldn't get over without his help; he anchored one foot behind, spanned the gully.

"Come," he urged, looking back where she hesitated. He reached out, started to lift her across.

Pulled off the ground, she threw her arms helplessly about his neck, her feet dangling.

The whole length of her pressed against him, electrifying her, stopping him in midair.

Their faces close, her breath on his neck, her wide eyes looking up at him, her lips opened in surprise.

He straddled the coursing stream, held her to him, the water pouring off both of them, but not off the cheeks pressed tight.

"Little one, what must I do with myself?" he sighed, then put her on her feet on the other bank.

Their bodies had come apart as though peeled; she felt him everywhere on her. A dreadful silence afflicted them; they looked intently at one another, looked away. She felt in a trance.

Otis Atchison's faraway "Halloo!" on the hidden path broke the spell. Curtly Robb nodded the direction they must take; they ran — this time not in a joyous way but far apart, as though nothing had happened, nothing had ever happened.

In the buggy he was stiff, remote; the frown lines between his eyebrows returned. And there was never once a look for her.

That night, shaken, unable to sleep, she tried to fathom what had been lurking beneath the rushing surface of the last few hours.

180

She was his ward. He loved her as a man whould love what he protected.

"Little one, what must I do with myself?" Could a father have said that, holding a child?

Instinct told her he'd shockingly forgot himself in a way no father would.

Sensing the dark tangle of Robb with Emma, she fought off her fear of the old mystification.

Man-and-woman love?

Some part of it, perhaps.

The part she misunderstood most of all. The part she sensed, without promises to go with it, might not be the best part at all.

"The whole Massachusetts church must be here," Annis grumbled as they toiled to the gallery and squeezed themselves into a bench.

Bernadette peered down at a heaving black sea; that many ministers looked suffocatingly funereal to her until she began to observe their very alive coming and going, their animated political confabbing, pew to pew.

Where was he? She spotted him and watched intently, wondering if Robb McIves had lain awake as she had last night.

A minister waited in the pulpit for attention while quiet spread reluctantly across the humming church floor.

The Quadrennial Conference of the Massachusetts General Association of Congregational Ministers, North Brookfield, July 1837.

Opening service.

Lengthy prayers for communal success.

Dull organizational pieties.

Hot, creeping spaces of time.

At last the Pastoral Letter on abolition was announced

181

and the balcony woke up; from miles around, these Massachusetts folk had come to hear a pronouncement on the subject of William Lloyd Garrison's unsettling criticism of their slave-tolerating church.

Otis settled confidently into his seat. "They'll accept abolition, can't claim the right for anything else. Be some red-faced pastors down there, mark my words."

The letter began with a bang. After its second sentence, Bernadette knew Otis was going to turn out to be dead wrong; these agitated Massachusetts churchmen would *not* come over to abolition. Indeed, Reverend Nehemiah Adams, composer of the letter, soon defined Abolitionists as wrongdoers seeking to make the church a place of disputation and abolition agents as unwelcome men who would swarm boldly into church services with disruptive messages.

She watched Robb sit unmoving under this rain of brutal hostility; beside her, the amazed Otis jerked around as though he were about to have a seizure. "Well, I never!" he kept muttering; or, "It's a crime!"

The speaker flowed on indignantly. With the Massachusetts Congregational churches in turmoil from abolition and deep-dyed disrespect for its ministry, another revolt had just raised its head.

"Women!" the speaker shouted.

Women, encouraged by irresponsible men, women so far forgetting themselves as to itinerate in the form of public lecturers! Such goings-on could only open the way for the rapid, widespread, and permanent injury of the female character; indeed, national degeneracy and ruin threatened.

A second minister now paced up and down the sanctuary aisle, looking from side to side with a bellicose air.

"Next he'll shake his fist at us," Otis declared, unbelieving. "Who is he?"

"Shh, Pa," Annis implored.

182

"The appropriate duties and influence of women are clearly stated in the New Testament," the speaker bawled. "The power of woman is her dependence, flowing from the consciousness of that weakness which God has given her for her protection.

"We appreciate the unostentatious prayers of women in advancing the cause of religion at home and abroad; in Sabbath schools; in leading religious inquirers to the pastors for instruction; and in all such associated efforts as become the modesty of her sex . . . but if the vine, whose strength and beauty is to lean on the trelliswork and half conceal its cluster, thinks to assume . . . independence . . . it will not only cease to bear fruit, but fall in shame and dishonor into the dust . . ."

Bernadette forgot her headache, forgot abolition, forgot Robb McIves. It grew clear to her.

Unwittingly, she'd come all this way to Massachusetts to hear an attack on the Grimkés!

Pure, molten, dangerous emotion erupted, born of what was fed up in her. Vine to trellis? If there was one thing she'd never be, she made up her mind, it was vine to some slatty trellis!

She struggled to her feet.

"Bernadette!" Annis exclaimed, "What are you doing?"

"I'm leaving."

"I agree, let's go," Otis sputtered; he rose fussily to make his exit with her while bewildered Annis fumbled for her gloves.

Bernadette shoved past the listeners on the bench, followed Otis who hurried out like a stout ship in full sail.

"After what he said on abolition I couldn't pay any mind to what he said on women," Otis fumed, clumping through the vestibule to the accompaniment of Annis's frantic "Hush!" "Mayhap the one who wrote the Letter was right on

183

speechifying females, but he's dead wrong on Abolitionists. What a hoke, from first to last! I misliked that gamecock patrolling the aisles, too! A man don't have to be browbeaten, even by the cloth."

The rest of the torrid afternoon, she and Annis sat on the porch watching passersby.

"What are you stewing about, Nad? Sir Walter Scott would say you look full of dark passion."

"I'm deciding I'm going to do what I *want* to do."

"Good heavens, what's that?"

Annis's starkly simple question brought her up short.

What *did* she want to do? How *did* she want to make real this bursting indignation erupting out of her?

The answer must have been lying in her ever since she'd heard of it.

"How wonderful," Miss Angelina had said, "if someone could draw slavery as it is."

Slavery As It Is. Angelina and Sarah Grimké meant someday to write that book.

I want to know the real world; I want to do what I know how to do best.

I want to put myself to the test.

I want a noble life.

I'll draw for abolition.

The decision was like a great sigh; tight knots in her untied invisibly.

Suddenly she felt so good; she felt as though she could lick her weight in wildcats.

I'll tell Angelina right away.

But even noble lives had basic needs.

"I'm starved," she moaned. "Aren't they *ever* going to ring the supper bell?"

184

🌿 21

Summer, 1837.

The living was always so skinny in the Furnace Village parsonage, scare talk of financial panic in the country passed right over Bernadette.

But at the affluent Canterbury farm, things were different, for it seemed the more money you had, the more you noticed its shrinkage. David Fry wore a preoccupied look and said if things were in bad shape in the city, the countryside would be next. That's why he hardly noticed when Hester decided to send Bernadette up to Pepperill for a few weeks to help David's always pregnant, constantly delivering sister. All David asked was, did Bernadette have the coin for the fare and could they find someone respectable for her to travel with? When Hester nodded "Yes," he was satisfied.

The real reason Hester was sending Bernadette to Pepperill was because Angelina Grimké would be speaking there.

After months of longing to hear Angelina, Bernadette would get her wish . . .

Sometimes, Hester chuckled, you had to help longing along.

Breathless and dusty from the hike into town, she found the right barn. Horses, wagons, gigs were tied up in the farmyard; people were still disappearing by twos and threes into the door. She ran, thrusting her head through her bonnet ribbons.

At the barn entrance she hesitated, amazed. In the dim, dust-filtered recesses sat a crowd of people on makeshift benches, boards laid on kegs, boxes. It struck her forcibly that, rude as the place was — straw on the floor, an old table and kitchen chairs for platform furniture — there was a defiant power in it. It smelled of dust, animals, people, and something else; then she saw that pungent evergreen branches had been piled along the walls and leaned in the shadowy corners. Clambering around chattering people, she was suddenly glad the Pepperill churches had shut Miss Angelina Grimké out. This place — down here with the people — was better!

She'd no sooner sat down, leaned out of line to peek at who was around her, when she spied a hand waving at her.

A shock of recognition swept over her.

Miriam Hosking, her black friend from Canterbury!

Bernadette hurtled herself out of her seat, and Miriam came scrambling toward her; they collided rather than met. By a lightning glance, both knew all was still well between them, those walls truly down which had once taken two strangers a long time to breech. After three years, they hardly even had to exchange greetings.

"Let's go sit in the back," Miriam urged. Once there, they sat shoulder to shoulder, not speaking, simply luxuriating. Miriam had never been a hugging type — as befit the granddaughter of a Foulah princess — but they'd enjoyed a deal of laughing and confiding, Bernadette remembered blissfully.

"Where did you go after Miss Crandall's school was wrecked? I didn't know where to write."

"I went home to Providence; then last June I came to Boston to be housemaid for Mrs. Forbes. She visits her brother in Pepperill every summer."

"Housemaid! But you were going home to teach school!"

Miriam gave her the old, hooded, disdainful glance, the look that'd been so hard to fathom. "I never expected I'd eat by teaching; I'm a good housemaid — Mrs. Forbes couldn't get on without me. Still, after listening to you, I'd like to go to Oberlin, too. I'm glad to know there's an institute that'll take blacks. You've grown," Miriam observed quietly. "I knew when you got yourself all in one piece you'd come out pretty."

Lately a lot of people were calling her "pretty." After the falling-over-her-feet years, Bernadette couldn't convince herself they were actually talking about *her*.

"You still look the same peppery way to me," she grinned.

"Oh, I'll always be chirky," Miriam grinned back. "This troublesome nigger'll see to that."

An accidental meeting with a true old friend, a chance to hear Angelina Grimké! The place bloomed exultantly for Bernadette.

Just then Sarah and Angelina Grimké were hustled in by what appeared to be a very nervous clergyman. Bernadette smiled; there were the familiar caps, there was Angelina's peering-out face. The women quietly sat down at the speakers' table. Gracelessly, the scowling cleric plumped himself near the door and surveyed the quietening audience; clearly he was taking a census.

Almost by instinct, Bernadette flipped open her sketchbook.

The crabby minister rose, opened the meeting with a prayer.

The churches of the town being unavailable because of feeling against speechifying females, a friend to the sisters had provided this barn, he informed the Lord. Turned out the cleric would have absented himself had he not felt duty-bound to reprimand his fellow Pepperill Christians, remind his wayward children that in coming here they just might need correction and improvement . . .

With that, the sour fellow strode haughtily to the door, paused and in his most majestic voice delivered his personal benediction: "I'd as soon rob a hen roost as encourage these women to lecture."

Stunned silence; embarrassed tittering. Miss Angelina rose to her feet.

"My dear friends in Christ," she began, in a voice with no hint of a quaver, "the discussion of the rights of the slave has opened the way for the discussion of other rights, and the ultimate result will most certainly be the breaking of every yoke . . ."

Bernadette's stilled fingers sketched again, catching Angelina, catching Sarah hunched over, her expression mournful.

In two hours of proud listening, Bernadette realized Angelina could cast a spell different from but no less potent than Weld's.

When the lecture was over, she and Miriam pressed up with the others.

Angelina reached for Bernadette in astonished pleasure, exclaiming disappointedly in her next breath, "But we have to move on right away!" Close up, Angelina looked white; there were blue circles under her eyes which told Bernadette poignantly what it meant in the flesh to "itinerate."

But for a marvelous moment she and Angelina stood alone at the barn door.

"You've brought your sketchbook."

Bernadette flipped to the right pages, waited, watching like a hawk. "It was hard," she murmured, "I really wanted just to copy down your speech."

Angelina shook her head. "My child, far better you sketched!"

"You see, I want to help with your book. I want to go to the South, draw slavery."

"But it wouldn't be safe!" Angelina exclaimed, aghast.

"Why not? Who'd know I was an Abolitionist?"

"Dear girl, you're not yet sixteen! Who'd go with you?"

"I couldn't go for another year; I'd find someone by then. Maybe I could find someone at Oberlin."

"I really don't know," Angelina murmured; but by the look on her face, Bernadette knew how much she was tempted. "You'd have to ask your Uncle Marcus, Pastor McIves."

"Not Pastor McIves," Bernadette replied firmly. "By the time I went, I wouldn't be living with him anyway."

Angelina's eyes sparkled in understanding. "Let me consider this, see if I can think of any suitable, safe means. It's true, no one would suspect a young girl."

The people waiting for Angelina couldn't be held back another moment.

Their time had been sadly fleeting, but at least she'd got to hear a wonderful, speechifying woman and feel her quick embrace, Bernadette thought, going out into the bright afternoon with Miriam.

Sticky little Jamie, one of her numerous boy charges, was waiting for her outside the barn door and wouldn't be quiet until the three of them had scuffed by the store to buy him bull's-eyes. Cheeks bulging blissfully, Jamie trailed after Miriam and her down to the creek.

She and Miriam sat on the bank and talked while the little boy waded in the shallow water.

Years were compressed into scant hours. Bernadette told Miriam about Emma and Robb McIves (but not all about them), Annis, Trev, the Ironmaster, Miss Miller's, how she and Angelina had become friends. Not much on Weld — that girl's fantasy quiet in her.

One arm dangling a tree limb, Miriam told how she'd spent a year in Providence teaching in her black church. Hard times in her father's comb business had forced her to go to Mrs. Forbes.

Miriam's voice stopped, the stream splashed, Jamie talked to himself. What things there were in life, Bernadette pondered, sensing how squeezed dry of the juice of hope Miriam was right now.

She got up, came to stand beside her.

"You're going to Oberlin," Bernadette answered quietly. "I know you, Miriam. How many girls would ever have got to Miss Crandall's?"

Miriam, face peering under her arm, brightening . . .

"Miriam, if we both got to Oberlin at the same time, you'd be the closest person I'd know there."

Miriam's white-palmed fist ran down the willow slip. "At first. But you're so full of spit and ginger it wouldn't take you long to know a *whole* lot more," she opined.

"I don't care about that," Bernadette answered impatiently. "I'd want a good *old* friend."

"For what?" Miriam asked curiously.

"You like my drawing, don't you?"

"I always thought it was a miracle a body could make a pencil do that," Miriam laughed.

"Angelina Grimké's going to write a book called *Slavery As It Is*. I want to illustrate it for her. I have to go south."

Miriam was very silent, hanging on that tree. "Do you now?" she finally asked softly, her face inward with thought. "And you need somebody to go along?"

"Yes."

"And that somebody could be me?"

"Yes."

On Miriam's face a dawning. "I could go as a maid, as your slave-maid."

190

"Kentucky's just across the river from Ohio."

They both stared at each other with the first grins of excited conspiracy.

Miriam let go the tree limb; together they stooped by the bank.

Jamie clambered up, bawling. "I dropped my last bull's-eye in the water. It's all muddy . . ."

Before she and Miriam parted, like boys they shook on their solemn plan.

With Jamie tagging along, she walked home, struck by the reality of a world where nappy fields stretched; Miss Angelina, a woman, spoke up bravely; she and her dear old friend Miriam made exhilarating promises.

There was so much to look forward to . . .

Trust. The word flowed into her mind.

There was nothing to mistrust from Robb McIves.

She missed him; all summer she'd missed him terribly.

She was what there was to mistrust; she'd change. Just because she loved him didn't mean she'd have to withdraw in hateful coldness.

Polarities of guilt and want could be reconciled halfway at trust.

October'd come. She and he'd be real friends again.

"Hurry, Jamie!" she urged.

Brookline, Massachusetts
October 16, 1837

Dear Bernadette,

I write hurriedly for Angelina; I can't write very long. Angelina has nearly died of typhoid fever brought on by exposure and exhaustion. After hovering between life and death, she mends.

191

We expected to be rebuffed by the generality; but we didn't foresee that letters written against us by New England churchmen would make everything increasingly difficult — we are abused by ministers to their people, shut out of churches, our meeting notices torn down . . .

Still, at Lowell and Worcester there were a thousand people each. Should we live, by year's end they say we will have spoke to fifty thousand people.

Most difficult of all is our now writing and speaking for women. Many abolition brothers stand against us; most, like Theodore Weld, upbraid us furiously and say if we *will* make an issue of women we can expect warfare.

But Weld sees more clearly than most the ultimate right of it — he asks only that we save the issue. First wake up the nation to lift millions of slaves from the dust, make them men; then it will be an easy matter to transform millions of women from babies to women, he says. Before she fell ill, Weld and Angelina quarreled savagely by letters, trying to hammer out the right of it, explain themselves to each other. Angelina replies that the time to assert a right is when that right is denied.

Last night she was able to talk to me a little. We talked of your drawing for *Slavery As It Is*.

She whispered to me, "Should we encourage her to go south?"

Then, before I could answer, she sighed, "Yes." She was quiet awhile and finally murmured, "What pain it is." But before she fell asleep she told me very distinctly, "We can't risk Bernadette."

So you see, in a more settled state of mind, we will consider it.

192

Dear child, bondage is against the will of God —
bondage in all its forms.

Christ keep you,
Sarah Grimké

 22

INSIDE THE LITTLE HOUSE, goods were heaped in the middle
of the floor — bedding, cabinet, crocks, pots.

Her eye was immediately drawn to the one beautiful thing
there — a hooded wood cradle, every dark, satin inch of it
carved.

A kerchiefed Lith woman came in from the back room,
two little boys clinging to her homespun skirts; behind her
trailed a sturdy girl of seven or eight, as frightened-looking as
her brothers.

Unable to speak with them, not knowing their language,
Bernadette peered out the window to the road, where a
tipped-down cart, its shafts resting on the ground, stood
waiting.

"Charles says if the tools won't fit they must give up the
little commode," Emilie bustled in.

"What will they do?"

"Try to stay alive," Emilie answered simply, wrapping a
pitcher and plate in a quilt. "And if there's no work, go on to

Hopewell by spring — though I don't know how they will get another cart. Glaudin borrowed this one; he has to take it back the next time he goes to Hartford. In Hartford . . . in the cities, because of the panic, people are starving."

One of the Lith men from the blown-up forge was having to leave Riga at last; Holley and Coffing wouldn't relent, wouldn't find room for the forgemen.

Two silent foreign men came in from the road and began to lift and carry; the mother stood watching dumbly.

Bernadette stooped; one child stepped bravely from the maternal shelter and walked into her arms. She held him; he lay back looking up with unblinking eyes, rubbed her cheek with his finger . . . soon the eyes smiled.

Shapes piled up on the cart under the old ticking Emilie had brought, outlines of boxes, spearlike points of legs, hoes and axes, stiff handles upright. Beside the road now sat, in immense dignity, the carved cradle; where would they pack it?

Charles stuck his head in the door. Like a sleepwalker, the woman walked out of the room and across the yard, not looking back. Bernadette followed the silent troop, carrying the little boy.

The Lith wife turned to her husband, pointed to the cradle. Words followed, Charles joined in, the men huddled. A knot of fear began to tie up Bernadette's insides.

The mother plodded up beside the cart, put her hand helplessly on its side; her little ones reattached themselves to her.

The cradle sat by the road.

"They'll take it?" Bernadette asked Emilie urgently.

But Emilie was distracted. "How can you tie the quilt down and leave the cooking pot free?" she was scolding Charles.

194

Neighboring doors were opening; people drifted out to watch with still intensity.

The family dog with its feathery black tail pawed the little girl importunately, barking to frolic. The little girl stooped and petted the dog's head, hiding her face.

Finally the father stepped between the cart handles, stooped, gripped them; slowly, with an inhuman effort, he strained upright. The cart creaked, the load shifted dramatically backwards, the men rushed to stop it; it settled itself.

The Lith man waited silently between the traces like an animal. The Lith woman stood beside the cart, staring at his back.

Bernadette, finding the tortured silence unbearable, started to drag the cradle into the ruts. "They have to take it," she implored.

"No, no, dear girl, you only make it harder," Emilie stooped beside her, trying to pull her off the load; Bernadette's body set the cradle to rocking.

Unhearing, unseeing, the man began to pull his enormous burden; the girl stepped bravely along, trying to keep from tangling with her dog. The little procession passed the first house, the second; at the fifth house, the road curved and the family vanished.

"Charles, whistle for the dog" Emilie exclaimed. "Josefa knows it must be left."

The smithy rushed down the road, disappeared briefly, came back dragging the struggling animal by the scruff of its neck.

With her palm, Bernadette rubbed the cradle's wood leaves, stems, flowers. Then there was nothing to do but get up.

Families.

Families were everything. Families needed a cradle —

especially one like this magnificent old friend of generations.

Looking up, Bernadette noticed tears in Emilie's eyes, too.

"Well, now, they can use a box or drawer."

"I'll take the dog." Bernadette's voice brooked no argument.

She led the dog down the mountain, tied it in the shed, went into the house to Robb McIves's study, rapped on his door.

One look at his annoyed face reminded her he was working on a sermon, a very important one dealing with the recent mob killing of Elijah Lovejoy as he defended his abolition press in Alton, Illinois.

"What is it?" Robb asked, sitting down at his desk, his body tense with impatience. She steeled herself.

"You told me Charles Glaudin had begged you to speak to the Ironmaster on behalf of the forgemen of the blown-up furnace. Have you?"

"No, I've not spoken to the Ironmaster. He's been mortally ill, or has that fact escaped you?"

She ignored his sarcasm. "A Lith family left today. They could only take a few things; they even had to leave behind the family cradle from the old country."

"Well, a cradle's bulky," he answered roughly. "No tragedy in that."

"They're walking to Hartford with the man pulling a handcart and his woman and three little children on foot."

He was silent, his jaw set.

"Emilie Glaudin says people are starving in the cities because of the panic. The Lith man may have to pull the cart all the way to Pennsylvania hunting work."

After staring at her for an eternity, he finally spoke. "Bernadette, it's awkward for me to upset the Ironmaster right now. Twice he's hinted he's considering building a

196

church in New York if he can find the right man for its pulpit."

"The Ironmaster build a *church?*" she exclaimed incredulously.

"A church is a good steady investment for a businessman," Robb replied stiffly. "The Ironmaster feels gratitude to God for his recovery and is charitable enough to say I helped by being a faithful friend — says he is indebted to me. Naturally, I've never talked of debt, never wanted more than to persuade his views . . ."

"Do you think you *have* persuaded his views?"

He shifted uneasily. "As a matter of fact, now that he's recovering, he seems to be backsliding. Says he wants an armistice on abolition, for instance."

"Well, does this church have anything to do with you?"

His look was level. "As a matter of fact, Bernadette, despite abolition, I believe it does."

"Has he said?"

"No. But then he likes a game, the Ironmaster does; he's used to playing with people's lives. But I wouldn't be honest if I didn't tell you that if he invests in a church I feel I will be under his direct consideration for its minister."

"A church in New York," she repeated wonderingly. Then the full import of it struck her, and with it came the spontaneous, vigorous joy, the unmixed joy they'd known in freer days. Her face broke into a broad smile; she jumped up, dropping her mittens, tramping on them as she rushed toward him.

Something in his still look stopped her in her tracks, made her mindful of what was proper between them. Flustered, she retreated, sat down, looking at him, nonetheless, from excited eyes.

"But of course he'll ask you! Who'd be better?"

"That's why complying with your request that I speak to the Ironmaster on behalf of the forge families right now would create a distinct awkwardness."

Her balloon was skinned; her happiness went flat in a rush. "Oh, of course," she foundered, understanding.

"Well," he said after a bit, after it'd had time to sink in, "*would* you have me speak for the forgemen now, Bernadette?"

She sat there thinking of the empty cradle, the animal-man pulling the cart, the girl who didn't dare pat the dog for fear she'd cry, the child with his sky-blue gaze. Right now on the road to Hartford it'd be blowing cold . . .

"Perhaps the Ironmaster wouldn't be too angry at you," she ventured helplessly.

"Come now, Bernadette, you know how resentful it'd make him. He tolerates no meddling in his business."

"But it's cruel to send the families away!" she cried.

"The forge blew up; what was to be done? They're free men."

Instinct instructed her. "I don't know how free they are," she stammered. "What's happening to them, they can't in any way help."

"What happens to all of us, we can't in any way help; only God has that dispensation over our lives."

But God had made some far more helpless and unequal than others, Bernadette realized. She dared to answer quietly, "Then God will see you have your church, if He so intends."

She saw he was struck speechless by her words, saw him sit back and look hard at her. She knew what he must be thinking: she'd risk his future for the Lith forgemen — that certainly showed no tender regard for him . . .

When he spoke, it was harshly. "But of course, you're

right to remind me. It's my duty to speak to the Ironmaster; I will at the right time."

How dryly he said it!

"But should you?" she asked in anguished reconsidering.

"You remind me I should; as you've also clearly reminded me, we don't live in God's world for our own benefit."

She couldn't contain herself; she stooped down on one knee by his chair, determined not to succumb to her childhood awe of him. Succumbed anyway. "I don't want you to lose the chance of the church, but it was terrible what just happened at Mount Riga," she pleaded.

"Bernadette," he ordered, "trust me to work it out. Now go away; I want to finish my sermon."

She sprang up, her skirt swishing. Cut down, he was sending her off. Nevertheless, she stopped at the door, turned to him; what came out of her was simple, unangry dignity. "If the church *is* yours, no one deserves it more."

The dog howled mournfully from the shed.

Since early morning, people had been gathering at Mount Riga village center, many of the men in strange caps and embroidered jackets, the women in layered peasant skirts and bright kerchiefs. Many shaded their eyes from time to time, appraising the sun scudding in and out of winter clouds.

As for Trev, he *wouldn't* stop following the mangy tame bear that'd been brought up for the anchor-testing festivities. Bernadette alternated between searching out Trev and watching the Ironmaster's house where he and his guests — Pastor among them — lingered over their cups.

The front door of the Pettee mansion opened at last and gentlemen began to drift down the steps by twos and threes. In a moment, as though at a spoken command to form ranks, they started in a group down the road toward the crowd.

199

The Ironmaster, with his shock of white hair, bright red face, high dress stock, and rich brocade coat, stood out from the rest, but it wasn't he whom she sought — yes, there was Robb McIves, bare-headed, wearing an austere black suit, plain white stock, his appearance in sharp contrast to that of the Ironmaster, or the naval officers in their dashing caps and rank-marked uniforms.

As the men approached, the hurdy-gurdy's foreign tune whirred, the player's hands moving with furious speed. Mount Rigans, infected by his contagious merriment, sent up a ragged "Huzzah!" as the dignitaries mixed in with the crowd.

"Get over!" Trev ordered. "You're standing right where the wagons bring the anchors."

They hustled to a safer spot.

For the hundredth time, she inspected the base and top of the hundred-foot iron tripod which, like a grotesque three-legged spider, straddled the village square. Several wagons now stopped where she'd been standing, each carrying a huge black anchor whose claws projected over the wagon sides at bizarre angles.

"Uncle makes a speech," Trev drawled, "then after *he* makes a speech, one of the admirals makes one, and then a captain says exactly what the admiral already said, and then one of Uncle's business friends from New York or New Bedford talks. It's tiresome," the boy finished in disgust, looking longingly around for the bear.

"But Trev, I want to hear," Bernadette scolded. Ordinarily she enjoyed Trev's racketing, but today she wanted to concentrate on this strange, grand celebration.

"Well, they *do* just honeyfogle each other; you'll see."

She had to admit Trev was right. The Ironmaster praised the navy and described (Trev said he did it every year) how the three-ton anchors for the *Constitution* and *Constellation* had been sent down the mountain behind a six-yoke ox team and the cart wheels had been chained to trees to prevent skidding on the rocky inclines. The navy men, two of them, went all the way back to 1812 and claimed their frigates couldn't sail without Holley and Coffing ordinance irons. Then a banker from New Haven spoke of Mount Riga chains going with whaling ships to the Brazil Banks and the Sea of Kamchatka and said he expected a business upturn any day. At this remark, the crowd clapped, and by mistake the hurdy-gurdy man played a few dashing bars before he was shushed. Everyone laughed.

The Ironmaster's voice boomed out, calling for the first anchor.

Bernadette watched mesmerized as men jumped forward to hoist the anchor from the wagon bed and buckle it up. In a moment, oxen were straining on the pulley; the great anchor — dangling from its enormous chain — rose from the ground and slowly crept into the air between the giant spider's legs.

"Let her fall!" the Ironmaster barked.

With a breathtaking rattle the great anchor plummeted downward.

Hands on her ears, she felt, rather than heard, the anchor strike the hard earth with an enormous thud. The ground under her quivered from shock.

"Did it crack?" Trev breathed.

Men crowded around to inspect the fallen monster. One raised a hand, made a sign.

"It's all right!" Trev exclaimed in relief. "See? The admiral's coming forward to put the navy's stamp on it."

A congratulatory buzz rose from the crowd; workmen shook hands.

Chains clanged again; a second anchor rose, hung silhouetted against the pale sky, shot down.

"It's the only way they can test them," Trev explained, as the second anchor was approved. "Sometimes they crack; we'll see one crack yet, though Uncle's hoping this'll be a good year."

Afterwards she was glad for Trev's warning; it cushioned her against disappointment over the fifth anchor cracking and having to be dragged away like a crippled disgrace.

After a time, with anchors rising and falling, Trev disappeared; she finally found herself wondering what was going on right now in the mansion's basement kitchen. The spit must be turning, the cook and cook's helper, elbow deep in flour, baking for the evening's reception in honor of the deputation of officials — those same men who right now detached themselves from the crowd and started back toward the Ironmaster's house.

The crowd thinned, heading for its own celebrations.

She gave up finding Trev, skinned back to the big house where she was to spend the night. For several hours, she flew from second floor to basement, between cook and mistress, maid and coachman, deaf in her excitement to the grumblings of all. Trev, of course, got under foot; the last great explosion was over exactly how the cook's helper was to progress with her pastries if the young master ate them as fast as she could fix them.

Men congregated in the drawing room; she glimpsed them as she hurried through the hall, heard hearty laughter, the clink of glasses.

She banged the bedchamber door. Everything was done; Mrs. Pettee's skirts dutifully twitched so she could go down and greet guests, men with their women this time. Nearby business associates, Holley and Coffing managers and masters were joining the city iron-buyers and navy officers.

202

After washing, Bernadette stood shamelessly before the long mirror in her full-sleeved chemise, corset, three petticoats, and pulled the dress over her head. The Pettees had given it to her for the party and it brought up from deep in her all her love of fine French clothes. Paris gold the dress was, bought cloth of cashmere as soft as dandelion down; the smooth-fitted waist buttoned down the front with precious jet buttons. It had a very low neckline which Mrs. Pettee's dressmaker had filled with a tucker.

She held out the skirt. It certainly hadn't been made with an eye to saving goods; no edge of petticoat showed as she twirled. Her slippers were silk; she stood poking out first one toe, then another, preening delightedly. Following Mrs. Pettee's directions, she carefully, tongue out, took the long braids hanging over her shoulders and covered each ear with a rich coil. Little wisps at her forehead and the nape of her neck insisted on curling out; she slammed the brush down in disgust — never would she be a faultlessly put-together lady.

As she started carefully downstairs, she suddenly realized Miss Miller's stiff little school parties hadn't prepared her for anything this grand. It was all very well to be decked out in an unbelievable dress, but how ought she to act in it? She hadn't the faintest idea; filled with consternation, she stopped right there on the steps.

Just then Trev bounded out of the dining room where men were seated at the table eating and explained, "But Bernadette, you're not to come down here; this is for the men. Didn't Aunt tell you the ladies were in the ballroom?"

She was certainly off to a *bad* beginning. But at least she had a direction in which to flee.

The ladies, it seemed, ate dinner afoot. In the vast, candlelit room, strange women wandered everywhere talking with a great bobbing of heads and clacket of tongues, reminding Bernadette that a British lady had just scornfully called American women roaring mice. She wandered hopefully past one group — intense discussion of a new dyspepsia pill; lingered within earshot of another — the manners of the young were being deplored; eavesdropped on a trio extolling the wisdom of a book of sermons by a popular Hartford minister.

Awkwardly, she found a small splay-legged gold chair against the wall, sat down, folded her hands, wondered how Emilie and Charles Glaudin were celebrating the anchor-testing. Trev had said the men would join the women later; something in Trev's voice made her suspect that there wouldn't be a stampede.

A maid hurried in with platters heaped high with ham, turkey, hung beef, and Mrs. Pettee's pickled peaches. Several younger women drifted to the table, filled their plates, came to sit near her, balancing their food on their laps, exclaiming how unhungry they were all the while they ate. There seemed to be no girls at this party. She longed for Annis.

Then Mrs. Pettee discovered her and with cries of joy presented her to some of the older ladies. But shortly she left off doing that and whispered to Bernadette to pass the trays of cakes; they must absolutely be finished upstairs by the time the gentlemen got up from their dinners.

The first gentlemen to filter into the ballroom were two young officers on the admiral's staff and right behind them, a hurrying, sun-dark young New Bedford captain.

Bernadette couldn't believe what happened next. All of a sudden — after longing for a friend — she found herself with too many.

"Miss Savard, is it?"

"Ah, then, French! Miss Savard, may I have the next dance?"

"Go along, Jack, she was about to promise me . . ."

Where was Bernadette Savard, that coltish, gape-buttoned

girl? Finally, shyly triumphant, she *had* to believe that girl was no more, had metamorphosed into someone more pleasing; it was there in the young officers' eyes, in the surveying looks on matrons' faces, in Trev's surprised stare, his banging the door and going off in disgust.

She felt a sudden firm hand on her elbow, and a voice said to the surprised officers, "Sirs, she's my ward and not permitted to dance."

As neatly as though he were wielding a knife, Robb McIves cut her out of the center of frivolity and maneuvered her out of the ballroom.

She was trying to sort out the mixture of relief and resentment she felt when he said there in the shadowed hallway, "Bernadette, the Ironmaster and his friends have just asked me to New York City to be examined for the new church."

"I knew it!" she exulted, her mind instantly fled from fiddles, candlelight on glossy floors, swarming officers. Looking at him with proud intensity, she tried not to dance up and down like a child.

"If it's not an offer, certainly it's a very good challenge of one, Bernadette. Later I'll speak with the Ironmaster about the forgemen," he spoke baldly.

"Oh." With one meaningless, small word her shining face dimmed and with it their moment of triumphant intimacy.

"I've got to go down to Emma; it's late and time you were abed."

"Yes," was her dull reply.

The silence that fell between them was awkward.

"Good night, Bernadette."

"Good night, Pastor McIves."

Out in the stable, Robb saddled the nag with fingers so furious they fumbled. Couldn't she grasp that he'd be going to New York to push forward, with vastly greater effectiveness, the moral reforms in which they both believed?

For her to be disappointed that he hadn't, at this crucial juncture, spoken for the forgemen was unreasonable, disloyal.

All the way down the mountain he thought about loyalty and women.

She wasn't loyal to him.

Wasn't she?

Perhaps more loyal than any other, she with her different expectations of him — for who didn't yearn to be loosed from the shackles of his own weak egotistical self, enlarged into a better whole by the vision of another?

If she could see what *he* might be, she'd beg of him an equal comprehension of *her*.

Yet apparently he didn't know how to discern a woman.

Was incomprehension, with its mutual and meager, its blind and slavish expectations, what had made the hopeless wound between him and Emma, the scar he'd never willingly open?

He stood in the dark by his cheerless hearth and blamed the girl for spoiling his excitement, thought vengefully that Emma, asleep upstairs with the Atchison's bound girl, would put conscience to no such test.

Then other feelings began to seep into his thoughts. All the while he'd talked to her in that upstairs hall, in his man's vague way he'd been insistently aware of the soft new dress, but not in the least bit vague was his sense of how it fitted or what even the tucker couldn't hide.

He'd watched the candlelight on her face and been struck by a new realization. Why, she wasn't pretty at all! Her eyes were too far apart and slanted, and maybe long ago an Iroquois *had* sneaked into that French seigniory. Her skin wasn't pale white; her too-high cheekbones burned indelicately bright, excited. Her chin was too square. And her mouth, well, it had no thin bow shape at all; her lips were full and, rapt as she was in her listening, she licked them and made them shine and it wasn't seemly.

He shook his head, realized in confusion that of course she wasn't pretty; she was growing too vigorous, arresting, individual to be pretty. *I believe she'll be, instead, what they call beautiful.*

He tamped out his pipe, took his foot off the fender of his dead hearth.

Robb McIves, high-minded man of conscience, you didn't risk speaking up for the forgemen, did you?

I'm angry at Bernadette. I'm most of all angry at myself.

Trev, grinning, rambled toward her as she started to open her bedchamber door. His rumpled coat front stretched over a well-stocked stomach; she could just imagine what a scavenger of tables he'd been! He was sleepy; he looked like a dark, ruffled owl. But small and disordered, he still had an imperious air — the "Little King," the boys called him, but not to his face.

"Did he make you leave all the fun?" he asked shrewdly.

A sharp longing smote her for that tantalizing ballroom. Then she remembered it hadn't been so easy, being a belle; she hadn't been trained for it and hadn't really relished being launched like a wobbly rocket in front of strangers. "I don't know the dance figures, Trev."

"Well, never mind. Hopping around like that's a bore."

She waited, hand on knob.

"I guess they've offered Pastor McIves a chance at Uncle's New York church."

"Yes. How did you know?"

"Oh, I was hanging around the room when the men were talking about it. I think Uncle wants to get him out of Riga. Now Uncle's over being sick I think he's tired muddling around in his conscience. He says a man can lose his shirt that way, especially in a business panic. Uncle told the others McIves would do a first-class job prodding vapory females toward heaven while the men go about the job of making money and building the country up. He says if the Pastor gets too carried away with antislavery, the men down in New York will put him in his place. Besides, he says, it don't take many sermons writ up in the stylish newspapers to make a man's belly crave more."

"He makes it sound awful," she protested.

"No, Uncle don't," Trev denied. "He makes it sound the way it is. Of course, if McIves gets the job, I wouldn't let him be a sexton in any church I owned. I could own that church someday, you know. But then, if I did, I'd sell it. Who wants to own churches when there's railroads?"

With that, he ambled sleepily on.

She shut the door, passed in front of the long mirror — and paused, surprised.

A strange girl shone there, a girl who, in her new bought dress, looked, well, almost American.

How many years had she thought of herself as *colt, French, moose, injun?*

She smiled at the new girl in the mirror, smiled in relief.

Then, feet under her on the bed, she unpinned her braids, shook out her hair, thinking soberly of other things — Pastor and his church, the Ironmaster and Pastor, Glaudin and the forgemen . . .

🌿 23

Emilie Glaudin went away leaving Robb to rub his chin, outraged at this witch's brew he was suddenly dunked in.

He heaved up, sighing. If he were to go to Mount Riga this afternoon, Bernadette must stay with Emma; his just-cupped wife lay white and motionless in the bed upstairs.

Where was Bernadette? he wondered irritably, then remembered he'd let her go to watch the skaters on Wononscopomuc Lake. He'd ride past that way, send her home.

It was beginning to snow — innocent cotton flakes drifted down, obscuring a deadly intent. The weather better not keep him off that train to New York.

He mounted his horse, set out.

When Emilie had appeared at the door, he'd ushered her into his study, swept part of the sofa clean of papers. But she'd just stood rooted, saying, "My husband's gone, monsieur *le clerc*," and then she'd sat down on the papers he *hadn't* cleared.

"Charles gone? Well, where would the fellow be?"

"After the anchor-weighing, he went down to Hartford with some navy men to fetch back some things he needed."

"But he's only been delayed, Mrs. Glaudin; supplies have probably been held up."

"No, monsieur," her blue eyes were dark, "he's in danger. There are matters I can't tell you of."

"If there are matters you can't tell me of, then I can't advise you, can I?" he'd asked impatiently.

She'd sat locked in secret indecision; then anxiety had pushed all the shocking facts out of her.

Charles Glaudin and some of the forgemen, grown desperate for the out-of-work men from the destroyed forge, had finally talked of threatening to plug up the line from the bellows to the great furnace unless the Ironmaster promised to take the men at another forge.

"Unthinkable!" Robb had roared, leaping up. "Why, the great furnace would die!"

"Now, now," she'd reminded, "they only *talked* of it, monsieur."

But because Glaudin wasn't back when he said he would be, she feared that the matter had somehow leaked out and her husband had been impressed to get him out of the way.

"Impressed!" Robb had exclaimed, disbelieving. The Ironmaster setting a gang of hired cutthroats onto a good family man, lugging him on shipboard to serve three years? Impossible. Yet her face had grown more and more dogged the more he'd refuted her.

"It's been rumored of the Ironmaster before; he has powerful navy friends. Would you speak to the Ironmaster, see if he knows *anything* of Charles?"

He'd turned his hand against her. "Don't ask any favors of me. If this is what Charles would plan, I've no choice but to report it to the Ironmaster."

"Oh, no!" she'd cried. "Charles trusted you, had hopes of your help!" she'd gasped; then had broken down, crying dreadfully.

Her pleas had echoed off the shell of his resolve. "No matter," he'd answered, and she'd run from the house hysterically. Now here he was, catapulted into a huge moral

swamp he didn't have time for. And hunting for Bernadette
— he didn't have time for that, either.

But on the way to the pond Robb's shock blunted against
a surprising reaction. Concern for Charles's safety began to
stir in him; apart from the ugly question of informing on
Charles, Robb discovered he'd acquired a grudging admira-
tion for the doughty Bavouist artisan.

And the Ironmaster, his mentor? Would he, slipping back
into his unreconstructed nature, be capable of employing a
press gang for a clever, troublesome worker?

He came to the pond, drew up his horse, scanned its
whitening banks for Bernadette, saw there wasn't a soul
watching the handful of children playing on the ice.

Annoyance filled him. Where *was* the girl anyway?

A figure far out on the ice caught his attention, a woman
skating. Well, if a woman were going to demean herself by
skating, she'd better do it far off by herself, he thought
critically. Skating was beyond a woman's capacities —
imagine, if she fell down, what a spectacle that'd be!

But how well she skated, he observed, wondering how he
could get nearer to see who had so forgot herself. The
carefree movements of the sliding form evoked in him an
unexpected, strongly sexual response. The woman skimmed
happily in a great circle, reversed, skimmed the other way.
Her red scarf floated behind her, the skirts of her brown
cloak rippled in the snowy wind.

Red scarf? Brown coat?

He realized suddenly he was watching his ward, Bernadette!

Robb McIves's first instinct was to shout indignantly but
prudence stopped him; better not call further public attention to her.

He rode around the pond toward her, but as he rode, she

moved farther away from him. He wheeled, rode toward the other bank; she moved off, skating with a calm grace which filled him with furious amazement.

"Bernadette!" he stood up in the stirrups and shouted, finally too angry to be still.

She swung around abruptly and right before his eyes fell backwards on the ice. Then she sat up; after that he didn't see what she did, he was too busy scrambling from his horse to try to get out on the lake and pick her up.

At his first step on the ice he slipped, of course, went down on his knee, fuming, retreated back to the ground. He could see her face clearly at last. It was round-eyed — as usual when she'd done wrong.

"Take those things off. Where did you get them?"

"Trev lent them to me; they're his old wood ones," she replied, sitting down beside him, stooping over so he couldn't see her expression.

"Young women don't skate in Furnace Village."

"They do in Montreal."

"While you live under my roof you're not to skate, do you hear? You're to go home; Emma needs you. I have to go to Mount Riga. Charles Glaudin was plotting to stop up the bellows line and let the big furnace die. I'm going to tell the Ironmaster."

Her face shot up in dismay.

"Who told you?"

"His wife. I've no time to explain."

"But you mustn't go to Mount Riga!" she cried. "What'll happen to Charles?"

"He should have thought of that," he answered cruelly, starting back to his horse.

She scrambled after him, seized his arm.

"You mustn't tell!" She pressed his sleeve convulsively.

He swung up, eluding that grasp. "Bernadette, I've a duty."

"Where's Charles?"

"Still in New Haven."

"Emilie?"

"Home by now, I expect."

He rode away, already painfully sorry he'd said anything to her about Glaudin. That's what came of chasing after her around the pond; that's what came of her skating, eluding, defying him. How passionately her willfulness always roused him!

"I'm going to Emilie's!" she called suddenly in a high, defiant voice.

He reined in, swung around. "Bernadette, you go home. I command you."

"No!" was all she shouted, plunging into the leafless underbrush, moving along the tangled trail with fleet determination.

He started to dismount and go after her but stopped himself, aware once more how close the pond was, how many people lingered there. He couldn't capture her, drag her home before onlookers, even though he quivered to do that very thing. He'd settle with her later. After he'd gone to Pettee's, he'd go back to Emilie Glaudin's. What he needed was a place to be alone with her . . .

Yet several hours later, plodding to Glaudin's house in the twilight, he had no desire to struggle with Bernadette. His mood was leaden; what he'd done at the Ironmaster's lay heavy in him like a sour congestion.

The door opened; the smithy's wife peered out. Never had he been invited so grudgingly across a threshold.

Bernadette sat on the bench by the hearth, the baby asleep on her shoulder. He went to her, put his foot up on the seat beside her, stood, elbow on his knee, his chin in hand. He stared at the fire, let the seconds pass in emptiness . . .

She scowled at him, looking around the baby's profile with its drooping head and arm hung limply down. Behind them Emilie Glaudin waited.

"Shall we go?" he asked quietly at last.

Bernadette shook her head.

"You can't stay here, Bernadette. As long as you live in Furnace Village, I am charged with your right upbringing."

"I'm going to stay with Emilie until Charles comes home," she declared.

He sighed, took his foot down, turned to the waiting wife. "The Ironmaster disclaims all knowledge of why your husband's been detained, madam. I pressed him minutely; he says that he expects Charles back at any time and has no personal knowledge of anything which might have befallen him."

As to the rest of it? He wouldn't confess that; it must wait for some willingness inside himself.

"And you believe the Ironmaster?" Emilie asked scornfully.

"I have his solemn promise," he replied matter-of-factly. "I think you'll see he doesn't lie."

"God have mercy that I shall."

Robb went to the peg, took down Bernadette's coat, held it open for her. She didn't stir, only sat.

"Bernadette, this is childish. Emilie Glaudin can't keep you here, even when Charles returns. And if he should, by some evil chance, have met misfortune on the road, she'll be even less able to keep you."

To his surprise, Emilie Glaudin spoke up.

"Bernadette, what the Pastor says is true. I wish for you to stay with me, but it is not right. If the Ironmaster takes

214

vengeance, I will have no home tomorrow. Another mouth to feed, another burden to carry —"

"I'd help you."

"It would be impossible, *chérie*. Your uncle in Ohio, your cousin in Canterbury, they would not permit it."

Emilie came and sat by Bernadette, put her arm around her waist, spoke to her in French. Finally Bernadette rose, handed the mother her little one. Robb put Bernadette's coat around her, led her down the path to the horse, helped her mount. Grabbing up the reins, he started toward the trail for home.

Their trip in the falling light was silent. They passed the big furnace; its ruddy fire lit the sifting white snow. The wind was rising in the pines; there'd be a blizzard tomorrow.

It mustn't stop the cars from going to New York. The thought of New York was more than he could bear. Head lowered, dragging the rein, he walked the last frozen steps to his house.

They clopped into the shed; he fumbled for the lantern, scratched out a feeble light. She slid off the horse, slipped past him to the open door.

"Bernadette," he called.

She didn't answer, only turned and looked stilly back at him.

"I didn't tell the Ironmaster what Charles was planning," he said. "God forgive me, I didn't tell him."

She stood for a long moment, absorbing his news, then she made a queer choking noise and rushed toward him. He hardly had time to open his startled arms before she was pressing against him, her face turned up in a blind, adoring frenzy.

"I couldn't believe you'd tell," she murmured breathlessly. She pulled his face down and suddenly he felt soft kisses pressed in ardent succession on his lips and cheek, a child's kisses begat from a woman's heart.

"I love you," she whispered, then fled his stunned embrace.

She was gone.

He sat down against the stall, the lantern between his legs, put his head in his hands.

I'm terribly in love with Bernadette.

Feeling invaded him; he was glad to be off the legs he knew would tremble were he standing. A triumph not yet subdued by shame began to grow in him; before he could stop himself he prayed, *Dear God, thank you for letting me feel again.*

No longer because of Emma-guilt would he sense with overpowering desolation that he'd lost some central power to love. No longer would he feel barren, long to awaken by any instrument at all, savagely put longing down.

He still experienced his grievousness at deceiving his benefactor, the Ironmaster, but as he sat, her presence grew overpowering — her lifted face, her kisses of gratitude, her body against his.

He gave himself up to it.

New York City
January 23, 1838

Dear Bernadette,

It's a magnificent church. Weld and I stood under its towers and gaped like country fellows.

But the men who are building it are a deal different from Otis — these are close-mouthed city men of complicated coils, their human edges long ago honed hard by success.

216

Weld says that the pulpit smells of power. Make no mistake, I want it.

My candidate's sermon scandalized folk (don't speak of it to Emma). Long ago you asked me why a church drove out a drunkard at the very time he needed church worst. I've thought much on that so my lesson was that Christians have an inescapable concern for drunkards (they, too are children of God), drinking just may be more sickness than sinfulness and there is a great Christian healing tradition.

Duncan Pettee said it was a provocative sermon but Erskine disapproved — said we wouldn't pay off the church mortgage by filling the pews with puling soaks. But both liked *very much* the city papers quoting in detail my "revolutionary" message.

I hate this merchandising of myself.

Weld is the one clear marker in my landscape of obscurity. We walk back and forth to the city from his attic room where he lives with his black family. We split wood for his stove. We get up in the cold dark to do bone-jarring exercises in the park. We talk constantly of abolition and the National Antislavery office, what time, that is, we don't talk constantly of 'my' church!

There's one thing I've tried to get Theo to face, viz., the extraordinary lapse from his usual shrewd political sense in sending the Grimké sisters to New England, then, when they caused such a furor, not yanking them back to New York.

But I've never seen Theo like this — he looks at me like Samson struggling between Dagon's pillars and

217

won't say a word unless it be simpleton mutterings like 'Miss Angelina's been sick,' or 'Miss Sarah's a splendid writer.'

Well, to me Theo was a man without flaw but perhaps I must now recognize one — he can't bring himself to admit a mistake.

I hope by now you've gone next door to tell them to pen their dog. He's got a cruel streak and I won't have him badger our cow anymore. Oh yes, please run to Otis and tell him he and the elders should protest the new poling place at Lime Rock — it's in a room off the barroom.

I think of you every hour,

Robb wrote, looked at the truth, knew he must re-copy the letter, threw it on the table, thought of Weld, folded it into his pocket. Weld, he was sure, would view such a final sentence to Bernadette as shameful.

But Weld, too, had a letter, the one in his pocket right now, the one *he* secretly fingered as Robb talked. After he'd got it, he'd gone about in a sleepless dream; the dizzying sun rose, set, the blurred hours passed between.

He'd finally confessed his hopeless love to Angelina; astonishingly, a love-reply had come back — "I feel," she had written, "we are two bodies animated by one soul . . ."

He was thirty-five, strong, vital, but wholly promised to abolition. Now at last he had to face himself in all his tormented personal want. He spent four days longing for tears to relieve the immensity of his unbelieving joy before he could frame a coherent reply: "My heart aches for utterance, but oh, not the utterance of words! . . . I have so long wrestled with myself like a blind giant stifling by violence all the intensities of my nature that when at last they found vent . . . all the pent-up tides of my being so long

218

shut out from light and air broke forth at once and spurned control."

The plan was for him to go quietly to Brighton next month to be with her.

Sitting with Robb, but thinking only of Angelina, he felt nothing but panic at the prospect. In pain, in patience, he and Angelina had hammered out a true view of each other; at Brighton they'd make plans to marry. Brighton would come soon, he knew. He wished for it never, wished for it tomorrow, sooner than tomorrow; he prayed for courage.

He'd go to Brighton, but secretly, secretly. He insisted he must go to Angelina secretly; not yet could he own to anyone his weakness of need and love.

 24

ROBB CAME BACK from New York with the offer of the church. He told Otis, told Bernadette. He told everybody but Emma, the most essential person of all.

Days wore on, a week went by; he kept her gossiping callers at bay while he asked himself over and over what he would say.

He went back to the source of it all. Genesis told two stories; they spoke differently. In the second story, God said to the male, the female: be fruitful and multiply, fill the earth and subdue it. The primal urge of all creatures to repeat themselves with timeless persistence. But was it noble enough merely to beget? Who knew better than he, whose rebellious tears had glistened on the delicate skin of his

219

stillborn son, how precious true begetting was. But enough?

No, surely not enough.

It was the first Genesis story which really obsessed him as he went through his days. God saw that the man He'd created needed a companion more like him than the beasts. "It is not good that man should be alone; I will make him a helper fit for him."

"A *helper fit for him*." But how did faith define this fit helper? It didn't. That was the trouble.

He snapped shut the Bible. Did he dare count on the promise of the grand new church to make Emma well? She'd want to be well for such a success, but he was filled at last with hopeless certainty it was beyond her psychic powers.

He knew what he must do.

Like a sleepwalker, he dragged himself up the steps to her room.

She was slumped against her pillow, staring at the rain which ran down the window in importunate rivulets. He pulled up a chair, turned its back toward her, straddled it, arms crossed.

She looked toward him listlessly, trying to compose her face into a wifely smile.

"Emma, the Ironmaster's promised me the pulpit of a large church in New York City."

At first she didn't understand; then blankness gave way to an expression of pure satisfaction — a personal sort of satisfaction, he saw.

She sat bolt upright.

"Oh, Mr. McIves, how gratifying! I *knew* you were headed for great things! What a reward for us!"

He didn't miss that word *us*.

"There're matters we need to consider," he spoke somberly. "It'll be a large church — far larger, more demanding than the one here in Furnace Village. There'll be many

220

more duties, more for the pastor, more for the pastor's wife . . ."

Emma said nothing, waiting.

"The question is, after we've arrived in New York, would you consent to be treated by Dr. Thorndyke? I've always felt recovery was possible for you."

"Treatment with Dr. Thorndyke?" she repeated vaguely.

"Oh, Emma, Emma," he replied with worn pity, worn remorse. (How strangely forgetful she often was, though he and Bernadette had steadily denied her the opiate medicine.) "The doctor you wouldn't treat with in New York," he reminded.

"I didn't like him!" she exploded with a malevolent look.

He couldn't bear it; his bride, his once-lovely bride. But after his brief flash of compassion, weary decision renewed. His future was in her hands.

"I need you to be well, Emma. Remember how it was when we first came to Furnace Village and you were such a help to me? Everywhere I called, you went with me; all our church people were struck by how young and beautiful and pious you were, eager to serve them all . . ."

"Yes, yes!" she answered, her face lit by excitement. "I *was* eager, I *was* eager to serve every one of them. I was most of all eager to serve you."

"Emma, you did serve me. I loved you; I wanted to help you; I wanted to make a true wife of you. I yearned for us to have a true marriage."

"Yes, you leading and I following," she chanted.

"Emma, what happened to us?" he asked, anguished.

The excitement died from her face; her expression closed up as though shriveled.

"I was afraid of you," she whispered, the answer surprised out of her. "I was most afraid of you when those babies died. I don't want any more of those dead babies . . ."

221

It terrified him, the way she spoke of their sons as strangers to her flesh. It terrified him, the glimpses he had of her fears. If she'd ever loved him, how could she possibly have feared him? And if she'd feared him, how much more she must fear him now after all that he'd done — or not done? — to her. He must promise what would help to take that fear away, promise her what he'd refused her all these long bleak months . . .

He leaned over, shook her arm so that she'd be sure to hear exactly what he said. "Emma, what if I promise there'll be no more babies?" He kept looking fixedly at her, holding her arm, waiting out her incomprehension till a small light leaped into her eyes — a light which grew larger and larger. In that light, relief shone dim; but triumph shone strongest of all.

Every lingering trace of yearning for her died in him then. It died with such sickening finality he knew the second it went . . . how the rain beat on the windowpane, how she sucked in her breath quickly, how her thin arm jerked in the circle of his hand. What must compel him now was the permanent weight of Christian obligation — and, yes, his practical need for her to face his world with a semblance of health and capacity.

"I promise even if your health improves, we'll live as brother and sister," he added matter-of-factly, deadened past embarrassment.

"Brother and sister," she whispered. Then, "Brother and sister," she repeated emphatically. He clamped his teeth down hard on his pipestem when she said it twice.

"Emma, will you see Dr. Thorndyke?"

Long-absent dignity came into her demeanor; she reached and set her cap right, pulled the quilt up over her rumpled nightgown.

"When we get to New York perhaps I'll be so well I shan't

need Dr. Thorndyke," she replied coolly. "But if I shouldn't be, yes, I'll go to him."

"Very well," he told her, rising. "I'll make the final arrangements to accept the new charge." Leaving, he tried to beat down in himself a new and malignant litany: *I mustn't hate her. She can't help it. God enjoins me to love my wife.*

This was the last one he'd haul to her from Dr. Turner's; either she was drinking them straight or she had a pile hid away. How had he ever let her cadge off him like this?

Juggling the bottle with irritated abandon, Trev leaped the fence and went around to the back door. Yes, there was old Shatterbrain peeking from behind the window curtain. It was like she had the evil eye on him.

Now all she talked about was her and Pastor McIves moving to New York. You'd think New York was the only place and Philadelphia didn't count. Personally, he'd rather live in Philadelphia, where he was bound this summer. Everyone knew Philadelphia had a grand new waterworks; New York still used wells and pumps.

"You up there?" he called from the foot of the stairs.

"Why, Trev!" she declared in that sweety voice, as though surprised right out of her wits. "It's nice to see you."

She certainly looked better than she'd looked the first time he'd laid eyes on her; now she looked tidy, she wore her hair tucked under a neat cap, and she leaned on the wall with only one hand, not with her whole body. Still, even now she didn't look to him as if she could win a sack race.

"In another month we're going to go down to New York and find a house," she trilled. "It hardly seems possible it's coming so soon . . . time used to just drag by."

"Bernadette says you'll visit Philadelphia."

"Oh, yes," she answered casually, "Pastor McIves is going

223

to the general assembly meetings. While he attends them, I'll stay in Wilmington with friends. I'm not strong enough to be by myself in a strange city."

"Maybe you'll see the waterworks."

"Waterworks? In Philadelphia? Oh, I really don't think so. Bernadette's cousin Hester Fry will be traveling down with us; she's taking Bernadette back to her Uncle Marcus in Ohio."

Trev wasn't listening; he was too busy thinking that anyone who went to Philadelphia and didn't go see the waterworks had left their senses behind. He knew Bernadette wanted to see the waterworks; she'd said so when he'd told her all about them.

"Pastor McIves says we'll keep a carriage in New York and a pair of good horses — in time, of course. Our house'll be ever so much larger, we'll be able to keep a girl, not just someone like Bernadette we're helping out. And we'll get some better furniture, not these sticks the cabinetmaker whittled — store things, gilt and carved."

"Yes, ma'am," Trev replied when the steady flow of words wound down; his boredom was complete. "It's too bad Bernadette won't be living in New York with you."

"Oh, she's going to that woodsy college. I don't approve, but Pastor *will* have it, and Bernadette and her Uncle fall in with him. But then, if you teach a girl quadratic equations, she's bound to be odd."

He knew how hard Bernadette had worked in this house for her; the very way Shatterbrain spoke of Bernadette made his blood boil.

"Well, here it is."

He held the package out to her. She nodded casually as though she were royalty and he a serf; then, while he climbed the steps toward her, she said brightly, "There's really so much to do to get ourselves ready for the move. It's a wonder my strength comes back as well as it does, faced with so many tasks. But then, the Lord does show Himself in times like this." She had the bottle now but didn't look at it, just put it behind her, acted as if it weren't there.

He quickly clopped back down the stairs and was about to excuse himself when he heard the back door open. Before he had time to turn around, there was Bernadette.

Her face was a study, seeing him there, looking up, seeing Mrs. McIves standing above. "Trev, what are you doing here?" she asked.

"I was bringing Mrs. McIves more medicine," he answered before he remembered he'd promised not to mention it.

"Medicine? What medicine?"

"Now, Bernadette, it's a matter between Pettee Trevelyan and myself," Mrs. McIves spoke up sharply. "You needn't concern yourself at all."

Bernadette reached out and grabbed him; he didn't like her to take hold of him, shake him that way.

"What medicine, Trev? Where did it come from?"

"Dr. Turner," he answered sullenly. "I get it for her."

"How many times have you brought her medicine?"

He counted up quickly in his head; five, since that first time, he thought.

"Master Trevalyan, you mustn't stay," the voice from above shrilled. And then, to Bernadette, "Besides, Dr. Turner knows all about it . . ."

Bernadette looked up at the Pastor's wife; Trev couldn't believe how stern a look she could wear, thin-lipped, riled-up. She really *did* look like an injun.

"You promised not to ask for laudanum after we came home from New York. For months I've tried hard to keep you comfortable so you wouldn't need it —"

"Tried hard?" Mrs. McIves countered scornfully. "Tried hard while you sat down in that study and never came near me? When you and Mr. McIves went off together to the Ironmaster's and left me alone? Oh, I know how hard you've tried, missy, but it wasn't to keep me from pain. It was to make place and time to be alone with him, that's what the effort was."

Bernadette stared up, speechless.

"She's going to be a bad woman, Master Trevelyan," Mrs. McIves accused. "Her loose papist beginnings and lack of respectable family make her that way. She's after my husband, Master Trevelyan . . ."

"Trev, you mustn't believe her," Bernadette implored. "She isn't herself, hasn't been for a long time."

"She's forward, will doubtless turn scarlet, being foreign and poor and pretty and all . . . he's always been afraid she might, Mr. McIves has. I didn't want to take the medicine but I couldn't stand it. I paid for it with coins from my auntie. Now go away! Everyone go away!"

Unexpectedly, Emma McIves put her head on her arm, leaned against the wall and began to sob into the crook of her arm, "They shut me away because I didn't want to die. But you mustn't tell Pastor, Bernadette! I'm going to get well in New York. No, you mustn't tell him about the bottles! No, no!" she ended on a shriek.

He had to get out of this crazy place, with this crazy creature babbling those strange, awful things and Bernadette looking more unraveled than he'd ever seen her.

Bernadette grabbed his arm as he dashed past her. Her face was terrible-looking; he didn't want to look at it. "Trev, don't pay attention to her!"

He didn't stop to answer, just skinned as fast as he could through the kitchen and out the door into the fresh spring light.

He ran across the yard like a jack popped out of its box, dived through the lilac hedge and burst into the field beyond. He ran across that field, jumped the stile, ran the next pasture and came at last to the mountain road. Beside the road he threw up; ever after, he couldn't figure out why.

Bernadette forward with that beetling big man? He wouldn't believe it, it was the ugliest mad lie he'd ever heard.

But wait — think of the way McIves was with her, like he owned her. Certainly Uncle wasn't that way with *him* — let him run where he wanted, only knocking him on the head if he did something truly fierce. But girls — well, didn't they have to be looked after by fathers, by the men who wedded them, even by a guardian who taught them for a time?

Still, *he'd* never taken care of her and he knew in his bones she *liked* the way he was with her when they went roustabouting.

It was too confusing, how people were supposed to be with girls.

His wonder slid elsewhere. He couldn't remember any out-of-the-ordinary thing she'd ever said to him about Pastor McIves — only how she'd have to do this or that, or he'd be mad at her. Then he remembered something his Uncle had said. No, it wasn't exactly what Uncle had *said*; it was just a gesture when he mentioned the pair, a look on his face, a cock to his shaggy eyebrow . . .

"You'll see she'll turn out to be a bad woman," Shatterbrain had shouted and because of her words, deep in Trev there remained a raw sick feeling that made him want to keep on giving up everything he'd ever eaten. Finally he decided he'd never see Bernadette again, that was the truth of it. When she came to Mount Riga he'd go out the back door. That thinking he'd marry her someday was something a boy thought of, not the man he'd be.

He'd forget this afternoon, forget crazy females, forget the mistake he'd apparently made in bringing the medicine, forget everything but how fine it was going to be to live in

Philadelphia, with his other uncle, the one who had business interests in the South and would let him visit the Sea Islands plantations of Mr. Pierce Butler. Butler had the most niggers of any plantation-owner in the south, rice mills and levees, big boats that the niggers rowed; after the spring floods you could bag rattlesnakes.

They were going to send him to Princeton after Philadelphia.

Suddenly he wanted to leave Mount Riga this very afternoon.

He hated Mrs. Shatterbrain, hated Bernadette Savard, hated the Pastor worst of all — savagely wished he'd kicked the Pastor's shins that day he'd been caught in the shed.

Still and all, he'd always remember how Bernadette had stood there in the rain, singing that funny song about not drinking and looking like she'd rather be dead. He supposed he'd never find another girl who'd splash around on a raft with him, come to the top of a furnace, light a charcoal hearth, jump from a haymow, cadge rides on a sled; he *knew* he'd never find anyone else who'd want to collect names to free niggers.

She'd certainly been a funny girl: one minute teasy and bossy, the next minute wide-eyed and listening to him; one minute racing him like a boy, the next dressed in a yellow dress with silk puffballs over her ears, embarrassed she'd come down by mistake to where the gentlemen ate. Lately he'd been fascinated by her lips — they were full and soft and he kept wanting to kiss them. And then sometimes — it was very strange — he caught himself wanting to bite them.

All in all, he supposed it'd be a long time before he'd forget the way she was.

He felt a little better now, though for a time he'd been afraid he might cry. What kind of a man would a crying man be? Better get away from anything that could reduce Pettee Trevelyan to the boyness of tears.

Philadelphia, Pennsylvania. What a great place it'd be!

While Emma watched with hate-filled eyes, Bernadette searched the room, doggedly going through the drawers, looking under the beds, even feeling the ticks. She found three bottles, put these in her apron and carried them downstairs out behind the shed.

She poured the liquid on the ground, smashed the bottles on the stones, smashed the bits of glass to a powder. Smashed for herself, smashed for Robb, knowing she'd never tell him what kind of a wife he really had.

After that, she leaned against the shed and cried till only shivering was left. When she no longer shivered, she sat like a lump, hugging herself.

Nothing, she knew despairingly. *There's nothing I can say or do to make Trev trust me again.*

In a sense, Emma *had* spoken the truth. Only not in that ugly way; it wasn't the way she'd screamed it at Trev. Bernadette sat there, holding her head.

Finally she got to her feet; with such a wife, Robb needed her help.

I fought for Emma in ways he couldn't or wouldn't. When I finally understood what her fear was, I even liked her. Emma said she cared for me.

People like Emma, she knew at last, couldn't truly care for anyone. They could need them, they could ensnare them by charm or weight of authority. But love was loyalty; loyalty asked more permanence than mood-torn Emma was capable of.

Once Bernadette decided that, some of the bitterness ebbed from her.

229

She needed to go away. Go away with all of this locked up in her.

Yet that very night she nearly came unlocked.

There, in the memory-filled study, she was helping Robb sort out his books and papers. She put them carefully in the right barrels as he handed them to her — the Latin grammar they'd used, the beginner's Greek, the little volume of algebra. How much she owed him . . .

"Only the piles of papers left," she spoke, ruffling a stack of them, sighing, looking at the clock. "We might as well do them now. There isn't much time."

He handed her more bundles; she worked to put them into the leftover crannies.

"This may be hard to fit in" was all he said to her. Without thought, she took what he gave her.

It was the portrait she'd drawn of him — he'd kept it pressed in a book.

She looked down at it, looked up at him.

He sat there with a rugged, struggling tenderness shining from him. All he said was "Though once I was shocked by it, I'll never forget the girl who drew it, Bernadette."

Words were mere awkward interruptions to the clotted and tangled connection which shouted between them.

She fled the room, realized in the parlor there was no place to go — not back to him, not upstairs with Emma.

Only to Ohio could she go. In Ohio she'd sit beside Uncle Marcus in search of the tranquil child she'd once been; she'd climb the trees and run the trails. Would those places from a simpler life still be there?

Ohio must make her the gift of peace; she was nearly apart from Connecticut's battle.

230

🌿 25

IN THE KITCHEN Emma was describing the new carpet she'd have, as though nothing had ever occurred between her and Bernadette — Emma, the only complacent one of them all and she so voluble in her content.

Robb rushed in the door waving a letter, was hardly inside before exploding, "Weld's marrying Angelina Grimké! We're invited to the wedding in Philadelphia."

"Miss Grimké!" Bernadette exclaimed, setting the stove lid down with a clatter.

"Miss Grimké!" Emma echoed in horror, looking up from her fichu-mending. "Not the one who makes speeches to men?"

"*That* Miss Angelina Grimké," Robb verified dramatically. "How could Theodore Weld do such a thing?"

Stunned, Bernadette started to stir with the wood spoon right in the stove flames, saved herself, realized she didn't even know how to consider such a startling prospect. The dark pirate and her Angelina? When had it happened? And how? And love? What would love be between them?

She stirred, sloshed, food sizzled; she felt shaken, baffled, bereft, jealous.

"That freakish troublemaker, that stuck-up, domineering, opinionated woman!" Robb was doing his usual agitated circumnavigation of the kitchen.

A coal from her wood spoon dropped right in the broth; distractedly, she stirred it in. Robb was worried for Weld, of course; *she* was concerned for Angelina. Life changed mysteriously.

"Well, Bernadette, you're quiet on the subject," he finally challenged.

"I hope she'll be happy wed to him."

"*She* be happy wed to him! It's whether he can endure being married to *her!*" Robb shouted. "I'm certain she doesn't know the first thing about wifery and hasn't any intention of sacrificing herself to it."

"It's not just knowing the domestic arts," Emma chimed in censoriously, "it's knowing all the things that keep a husband content . . ."

"Hush, Emma!" he really bellowed. He wheeled to Bernadette. "Weld told me he'd never marry. Now right here he says he's had this intention ever since wintertime." Robb gave the letter a slap. "If only I'd known when I was in New York I might have reasoned with him. Miss Grimké! What a desperate mistake!"

Bernadette's racing spoon in the scorching pot was evidence of how upset his words were beginning to make her. "I don't know what she knows about housework, but Miss Grimké's loyal and brave. And she's a great Abolitionist, too. In five months she and Sarah spoke in seventy-five towns, to fifty thousand people; they even spoke to the Massachusetts legislature. And they started abolition societies, too, lots of them. And didn't speak just for slaves but for free speech and women."

"Tsk, tsk," Emma shook her head.

"You can't see her in her true light, she's bedazzled you," Robb charged bitterly. "I *never* approved your cousin's letting you go to hear her lecture in Pepperill. It wasn't fitting."

"Indeed it wasn't," Emma leaped in. "But really, I don't see why it concerns you, Mr. McIves. All you have to do is write saying you simply won't attend the wedding. I shan't be in Philadelphia, but if I were, nothing could drag me to it."

"My concern doesn't begin and end with the wedding ceremony, Emma," he answered with irony. "My concern's whether a very dear and honored friend is taking a step which will render him forever miserable."

"Oh, it surely couldn't do that to Brother Weld! He's dedicated heart and soul to his work, Mr. McIves. He'll always have that."

Bernadette could only guess what volcanic reply Robb McIves must have wanted to give Emma; she guessed it by the way he strode toward the door to escape.

Otis Atchison rapped at that instant, come by to show off his first grandchild.

"Weld's marrying Miss Grimké," Robb announced.

"Ye don't say! What a wedded life that'll be, both of them rushing about making speeches and no knowing which one gets into the britches in the morning."

"Sir!" Emma remonstrated.

"Beg pardon, ma'am," Otis apologized, "it slipped out. But that's a pretty pass for your friend Weld, ain't it?"

"Pretty indeed," Robb answered, then fell into a morose silence, absently responding to Otis's questions about when the man from the tannery should pick up the new hair trunk.

Spooning out the ruined stew after Otis left, Bernadette recalled how Angelina Grimké had called Weld the "Lion of the Tribe of Abolition," how her eyes had often lingered on him during the training of the Seventy. Remembered, too, how harsh and impassive Weld's face was when he'd greeted Miss Sarah, Miss Angelina. Clues, but conflicting?

Weld, she pondered, *do you truly love Angelina?*

While Bernadette was waiting to go with Pastor to meet

Hester's stagecoach, Trev slipped out from behind the bushes and made her jump a mile.

Every day the thought of him had haunted her and with it a guilty anxiety: would he talebear Emma's talk to the Ironmaster? Trev hated Robb McIves.

"Trev!" she exclaimed, overjoyed.

"I came for the dog," he muttered awkwardly; long ago he'd promised to take it.

"I was worried about that; we're leaving tomorrow."

Silence, painful and long. He hung his head, scraped his foot, wouldn't look at her.

"The Glaudins are clearing out."

"I know. I'm sorry."

"I am, too. Uncle isn't, though. Says good riddance, let Hopewell have Charles; says he's an agitator and the forges in Pennsylvania are welcome to him. I didn't know he was an agitator; he didn't look like one to me."

"Charles wanted better things for the workers. Your Uncle's wrong."

Trev shrugged. "No," he said flatly, "Uncle has to make money. Everyone does."

Silence.

"Trev," she finally commanded softly.

He forced himself to look up. His expression was curious, hostile, veiled. No trace of what used to be there.

"You believe what Mrs. McIves said, don't you?"

"Of course I don't." Yet she sensed skepticism under his bravado.

"Pastor McIves taught me, that's all. And I tried not to leave Mrs. McIves to herself."

"I know you were always having to race home for old Shatterbrain. If I'd believed her, I'd have told Uncle. I didn't, though."

234

"Emma isn't daft; she just gets queer ideas she can't get out of her head. You could smash Pastor's life, telling something like that."

"I wouldn't mind that," Trev replied bluntly, "but I just wouldn't be able to get it out of my mouth about you. Still, I'm bound for Philadelphia soon; I've got a lot more things on my mind than talebearing. I've got to visit all the furnaces, say goodbye to the top men. I want to take our raft apart so's nobody else can have it."

He began to look at her steadily now, as though trying to sum her up, settle her.

"Philadelphia'll be a fine place to live," Bernadette said wistfully.

"Hope so. Better than here, I expect."

"Maybe I'll come to Philadelphia someday, have my school there," she assured him with sudden archness, sick of his stare.

"Maybe."

What was the use standing any longer while he just said nothing?

"The dog's in the shed. You can take it."

"My other Uncle's Albert Trevelyan on Race Street. He's more related to me than Uncle Pettee is."

"Well, of course if I came to Philadelphia I don't know if I could find you."

"I'd find you," he said matter-of-factly. "That is, if I'm there. I may just stay down in Georgia at the Sea Islands. They sound ripping."

"But you'd be living in slave country, where slaves are!" she protested.

"I wouldn't mind."

"Trev, you *would* really mind, wouldn't you? You helped with the petition, remember? You can't forget *that*." She could see a yawning world of mistakes ahead of him without her. "What's to become of you without me?" she asked in panic.

Just then the back door banged and there was a crunching on the steps. Trev eased into the bushes like a slick dark shadow.

She nearly dived after him but Robb was calling her. "Hurry, Bernadette, we'll be late!"

She watched the leaves tremble on the bush where Trev was hiding.

"Trev?" she called just once, heartbroken, before she ran. But he didn't answer her.

Hidden from her, man or no man, Trev did answer. He cried.

 26

PHILADELPHIA, Friday, May 11, 1838.

Wide, airy streets, paved and clean, lit by stunning gas lamps. Red-brick and awning houses, some with marble steps and all with handsome doorways. Neat footpaths, green parks. The stately order of Mulberry, Arch, Chestnut; trim Independence Hall . . .

"It's different from New York, isn't it?" Robb noted dubiously.

"Tidier," Emma summarized.

"The houses aren't such a bright red," Bernadette added curiously.

"Well, they say," Hester smiled, "New York boasts money, Boston brains, and Philadelphia family."

"I'm not surprised," Emma pounced. "It has a look of breeding like Cincinnati. The shop windows aren't a hodgepodge, either. Oh, dear, perhaps we *ought* to be coming here, Mr. McIves. It's clearly more genteel."

"New York's where my new charge is," he answered sternly.

On Spruce Street they found the Saverys' Abolitionist home; Robb left immediately to take Emma down to her friends in Wilmington.

"You must stand in nicely for me at the wedding" was Emma's sweet goodbye advice to Bernadette.

She would stand in for no Emma McIves, Bernadette vowed, pulling on her mitts; she would go to Angelina Grimké's wedding as herself.

She and Robb walked to 3 Belmont Row — she too expectant to notice how she affected him as she tripped along, proudly yet shyly wearing Mrs. Pettee's gold ball dress with its pious-impious tucker, managing with an unconsciously nonchalant air to carry her shabby shawl. After her hard work braiding, she'd have been dismayed to know how he felt about the soft, unruly wisps of hair around her forehead and the nape of her neck.

He seized her hand, pulled it through his arm; she never broke step.

They stopped before a black door with a shiny brass knocker, decided it was where Brother Weld, as Robb put it, was "throwing his happiness away."

It was the home of Anna Frost, Angelina's sister, and it was teeming; a festive din rose from people crowding the hall, dining room, parlor — fifty at least, Bernadette guessed. But the one face she wanted to assess most of all was missing. At

237

her questioning look, Robb said the bride would doubtless not appear till the last minute.

Everywhere were familiar faces. Whittier bounded up full of excited joshing, complaining he was about to be betrayed in the celibacy pact he'd made with Weld, quoting a line from a poem he'd written about it: ". . . scoffing at love and then sub rosa wooing."

"How are his friends taking it?" Robb inquired.

"Generally well," Whittier confided, "though Lewis Tappan hurt Weld by commending him for his moral courage in marrying a woman like Angelina, and some Abolitionist whose name I don't know wrote him that nature recoiled at the idea of a man of high feeling marrying such a creature."

"What does Mr. Garrison think of *her* marrying *him?*" Bernadette asked.

"A trifle anxious, I'm told, Miss Bernadette. He's afraid that once wed to a minister, she'll give up her Garrisonian views, take to church orthodoxy, and give up public speaking."

"Wouldn't hurt her," Robb noted dryly.

Garrison's expression as he moved toward them was benign; his look said that, despite his qualms, he'd somehow personally arranged the romance.

"Well," the New Englander greeted them, "how do you like honoring the most mobbed man and the most notorious woman in America?" His glasses flashed; he gave Bernadette a teasing smile as he added, "What a collection, since *I'm* often called the worst man in America, young lady!"

"Who're the blacks?" Robb asked.

"Speak low," Garrison warned. "The sister, Mrs. Frost, has had a hard time accepting them; things are still tense. Those two over there are two former Grimké house slaves — one's a minister who'll take part in the service."

238

"Minister? It won't be a Quaker service?" Robb turned to Friend Whittier.

The poet's swarthy face clouded. "No, and undoubtedly Angelina'll be ostracized for marrying outside our sect. I even have to step outside until the ceremony's completed."

Only Whittier's engaging way plugged Robb's snort. "Well, then, what church's form *will* they use?" he snapped.

"None," Garrison responded happily. "They 've made up one of their own. Oh, it'll be legal — Sarah Grimké's made sure of that . . ."

Bernadette could tell that the loose-form, stiff-necked Quakers and the gloating nonsectarians were beginning to gravel Robb equally, could just hear him saying afterwards that the whole ceremony was another muddled example of Weld's shocking flight from reality.

As she moved with him among the other guests, she overheard snatches of conversation: Theodore had found a little house at Fort Lee, in Jersey, with a view of the Hudson; he, Angelina, and Sarah would live there simply, their domestic work reduced to a minimum — though Angelina was determined to prove a female lecturer could learn to bake bread! . . .

"Thoda's had the worst time finding plain furniture, says everything's bedizened, gewgawed, gilded . . ."

"He'll stay on at the Antislavery office . . ."

One remark caused a special tingling in her: "They're planning to begin a huge study, the three of them — a book called *Slavery As It Is*, based on the South's own testimony. Weld says they'll comb thousands of southern newspapers; it'll be a great exposé . . ."

Angelina's last letter to Bernadette had said only that with things as pressed as they were, there was no time for *Slavery As It Is*. "Meantime, I want you to make other plans for yourself, safer, more suitable ones . . ."

Bernadette now had more reason than ever to pray for a quiet few moments with Angelina!

Suddenly there was a hush.

Theodore Weld entered the room.

Bernadette was amazed: the once-rumpled, rough-hewn leader wore a new brown coat, a high white cravat faultlessly tied, a light waistcoat, and — wonder of wonders! — fawn pantaloons! If it hadn't been for the bristly hair and blue jaw, she would have thought she was looking at a city popinjay. Still, the expression, at least, was familiar — serious, intense.

Angelina Grimké rustled in, took her place by Weld — tall, spare, more matron than bride. Bernadette stared in fascination at that serene and angular profile, with its high bright color and fine, clear eyes.

The first ominous sign of Quaker blight was a silent waiting upon the Lord through which, beside her, Robb shifted impatiently, his very body telling her he protested this leaderless travesty of sacrament.

At last Weld spoke. He and Angelina, he began, would speak from their hearts as the Lord gave them leading. He promised to renounce all rights to his bride's person save such as the influence of love might give him. In defiance of the law, he accepted no control of her property. "We acknowledge only that authority which love gives to us over each other . . ."

He loves her, Bernadette realized, overwhelmed. *Theodore Weld does love Angelina Grimké!*

In Robb's mind, memory. The words which he and Emma had said? ". . . which holy estate . . . be entered into . . . in the fear of God . . . I charge you . . . as he will answer at the dreadful day of judgment . . . that if either know impediment . . . ye do now confess it . . ."

"The authority of love," Weld had said.

240

Angelina promised to honor Weld, prefer him above herself, love him fervently, with a pure heart.

Robb remembered Emma's dutifully murmur: "I will obey . . ."

Then the guests were asked to kneel. Angelina and Weld led the prayer; very simply, they asked for increased usefulness, for unbroken faith in God.

A Negro minister prayed; a white brother followed. Sarah Grimké gave a touching thanksgiving — for Sarah, what a giving up!

Garrison, obviously enjoying his important role, read the marriage certificate and concluded the service by circulating among the guests so that all could sign it.

Bernadette signed, passed the quill to Robb, little suspecting how her smile pierced him.

Hugging Angelina, being hugged, Bernadette knew now was no time to ask selfish questions of the bride.

Her own part in *Slavery As It Is?*

Later.

Later they'd agree by letter.

Well-wishers clotted the dining room door to watch the Welds cut the wedding cake.

"The wedding cake was baked by a Negro confectioner and made with free sugar sent north from a mill that didn't use slave labor," Whittier explained to them. The Welds, he added, would be free-produce people, trying to buy only those materials and foods non-slave-produced.

Standing in the crowd, Bernadette sensed that abruptly Robb's mind, long molded in a skeptical shape, couldn't stand polite talk any longer.

He excused them to Mrs. Frost; they were soon back on the quiet street.

Bernadette floated to the Savery's on wings.

But he?

He sat on his empty bed. What had Weld said? "We marry, Angelina . . . together to do and dare, together to toil and testify and suffer . . . to live a life of faith . . . rejoicing always to bear another's burdens, looking not each on his own things but each on the things of the other, in honor preferring one another . . ."

He'd felt so sorry for Weld.

Tuesday, May 15, 1838.

For three days, grand dedication exercises had been planned for Philadelphia Hall, the immense memorial to free speech on Sixth Avenue which had just been built by Abolitionists and other reformers who couldn't find places to meet safe from mobs.

Working-class men and women — a lot of women — had bought twenty-dollar shares in order to construct the beautiful hall at the staggering cost of forty thousand dollars. The hall, it was hoped, could house in peace the societies, conventions, and lectures banned by Philadelphia's less hospitable meeting places.

The pillared wooden hall — so new it smelled wonderful, Bernadette sniffed — stood three stories high, with shops and committee rooms on the first floor and a huge hall and gallery on the second and third.

The Antislavery Convention of American Women.

She was by now so used to meetings she settled down to this one with plenty of room to spare for her own thoughts.

What was Robb doing this afternoon? she wondered, always aware of his life, his living . . ."

He'd a whole lot rather be here at Philadelphia Hall with her and Hester than where he was, she knew. But as a minister, he had to attend the general assembly sessions. He'd told them what was going on in that landscape of hate: savage dissension, that's what.

242

The Act of Union between the Presbyterian and Congregational churches, cemented in uneasy alliance for thirty years, seemed to be ending at last. The main cause was the festering argument between New and Old Lights, but stirred into this heated theological sauce were abolition and the determination of some New Light synods to push the slavery issue. It was no accident that the antislavery synods were all ones Weld had visited, Robb had noted.

She knew that yesterday Robb had been in the thick of the fray, rising with other Abolitionist pastors to speak against men like Witherspoon of South Carolina, who claimed abolition would lead to murder, rapine, and every vile crime an ignorant slave could commit; such alarms were sweeping Old Lights south and north.

In a few days she would no longer be aware what made Robb weary, gave him pleasure, what he felt, wanted, thought, needed; yet she couldn't imagine such a time . . .

Up on the platform, the Quaker Lucretia Mott was leading a discussion of the petition campaign; the women decided that for each antislavery petition rejected by Congress they'd send five new ones.

Bernadette didn't know exactly when the trouble began; she'd heard some undertones in the street for quite a while before taking any notice of them.

What ripped her attention away from the meeting and out to the street below however, was a sudden shout: "Niggers up there with white women!"

Then began an irregular thumping and knocking, like the sound of people pounding on doors.

Oh, no, she groaned inwardly. Wasn't Philadelphia Hall where they could be safe? Was there no place to be safe?

Listening, Bernadette concluded, No, there was no safe place after all.

By midafternoon, every woman there had accepted the

243

ugly fact that abolition was once more under mob attack.

At three o'clock Robb slid into the seat beside her and Hester. "I heard there was trouble," he whispered. "On my way, I passed a bunch of hooligans reading a poster someone had just slapped up. Said there was a female convention here to urge immediate slave emancipation. Said it was every citizen's duty to come right over."

Judging by the racket, Philadelphia wasn't lacking in dutiful citizens, Bernadette surmised.

"As I came in off the street, I heard a fellow yelling that at Weld's wedding there'd been six black groomsmen for six white bridesmaids."

Bernadette couldn't help snickering into her glove, thinking of Weld's plain wedding. Twelve attendants of any color? How funny!

On the way home, Hester and Robb got into a monumental argument whether Bernadette should be allowed to go to the evening session of the women's convention.

"It's dangerous!" he shouted.

"No more dangerous than a lot of other places she's been taken," Hester retorted.

"I'm going," Bernadette said quietly, squeezing her way into the shouting.

"Well, of course, she's not in my care anymore; if she were, believe me, there'd be other choices made. And I've got no choice," Robb concluded furiously, "but to abandon the assembly and escort you to Philadelphia Hall tonight."

The way he went up the Savery steps, it was a good thing he wasn't a swearing man — he'd have left a blue trail behind. Emma'd always claimed it was undignified for him to take steps two at a time, but she, Bernadette, somehow she had never been able to resist chasing right after him.

Robb's warnings were confirmed that night.

244

Hester and Bernadette had to push their way through a great noisy throng to enter the hall; three thousand other reformers had to do the same.

William Lloyd Garrison delivered the Keynote speech for the women's convention; as he finished, there was a commotion, and a shouting crowd, fists raised, broke into the upstairs.

Part of the audience started to rise, but Maria Chapman, she whom Robb had called an unsubdued versifier, commenced to speak; the intruders retreated back to the street.

During Mrs. Chapman's speech, bricks hit the outside walls; there was a persistent stamping of feet, chanting, clamoring, booing.

Angelina Weld came to the speaker's stand next. She'd been married two days; she wore her wedding dress.

A ragged sigh escaped Bernadette. *Let her be allowed to speak*, she prayed.

The moment Angelina started to talk, a brick crashed through the window and fell on the stage at her feet. She went on, however, and before she finished, two more windows were broken, half a dozen more bricks fell. The din outside grew deafening.

Unflinching, Weld's bride challenged those both inside and out: "Every man and woman present may do something by showing that we fear not a mob. . . . We may talk of occupying neutral ground but there is no such thing as neutral ground. He that is not for us is against us, and he that gathereth not with us, scattereth abroad."

She can be angry, willful, foolhardy, Bernadette recognized.

But found Angelina Weld no less wonderful.

27

THE NEXT MORNING, as he moved about the church assembly, Robb kept track of the rumors circulating in the city about beleaguered Philadelphia Hall. The mayor, Robb heard, had requested that the antislavery women keep blacks from attending their evening session; that was, the official said, what had infuriated the mob yesterday and endangered the safety of all.

Soon Robb heard that when the mayor's request was read to the women by Lucretia Mott, they refused to exclude blacks from their evening session.

By early afternoon, his self-discipline eroded by anxiety, Pastor Robb McIves left the wrangling church assembly to see for himself what was going on.

As his hack turned onto Sixth Street, the roar grew louder; soon he could distinguish separate noises — screams, catcalls.

The new hall rose up before him, its few unbroken windows glinting in the sun. Masses of people milled the street. Robb jumped from the hack, plunged toward an entrance, grasped the heavy latch, pushed inside, fought his way upstairs, stood searching for Bernadette among the somber gray bonnets and dark shawled backs which lined the benches.

He couldn't spot her; his attention turned to the platform where as usual a Quaker woman was talking. He shrugged in nervous distaste, his aversion to platform females rising in him, his mind tired of words, words, words. Why couldn't women, at least, spare a troubled world torrents of talk? He

246

felt an inward shaking, knew it to be an invisible motion which bespoke too many pressures — the world's, his own.

Where *was* Bernadette? What kind of bonnet did she wear, anyway?

Swore softly at himself for never being able to remember.

Suddenly pandemonium erupted; even the inexorable speaker stopped midsentence.

The outburst broke through the lower entries of Philadelphia Hall and rose toward them. There were screaming voices right on the other side of the door behind him. He struggled briefly to keep the door closed, was shoved aside, knocked up against the last row of seats by a knot of street people.

Women's faces swiveled in apprehension; without the mysteries of bonnet crowns, he found Bernadette.

The speaker was calling, "Ladies, ladies! This time we shall have to recess. As you leave the building we ask that a white woman take the arm of a colored sister . . ."

Something finally broke loose inside Robb, some tight-lashed anchor of restraint. Rage that Bernadette was here with these irresponsible women, fear that she'd be hurt — above all, a dreadful wash of jealousy that she wasn't any longer his own to command.

She's mine. Simply, he said the words to himself; he saw nothing in them to agonize over. While women got up from their seats, he shoved his way toward her.

"She's not walking out with any black woman; I'm taking her home," he told Hester.

For once, the Fry woman was sensible.

"My thanks, Robb. I must go to the Motts'."

Negro and white women were pairing up at the exits; two-by-two, they began to struggle down steps jammed with troublemakers. His arm around Bernadette, Robb pushed his way through women and rioters alike. He was torn by relief at sight of the front door, then instantly apprehensive. What would greet them as they came out on the street?

An angry sea of faces, derisive faces formed in a menacing circle about the door.

He plunged ahead, his hand a circle of iron on her wrist.

With a fervid prayer of relief, he spied a hack pulled up down the block; they headed for it.

"White women coming out with black!" he heard the hysteric call.

"Black men? I can't see."

"I think so; what'd you expect? . . ."

Fear for Bernadette leaped in his throat as he passed the last group of street folk. No more walking — head down, they ran.

They were only a few yards away from the hack when stones began to thud all about them. He heard her startled gasp.

He yanked the hack door open, shoved her in, shouted to the driver, "Spruce Street! Get moving!"

"This hack's hired — " But the cabman had no sooner begun to utter the protest when he saw the ruffians chasing them. He yelled in fear, cracked his whip; the horse leaped from the curb.

The men gave chase for a while; then, defeated by traffic and eager to get back to the fray, they pelted away.

Robb turned to Bernadette. She was holding a hand to her cheek. He jerked it away; below the eye, on the cheekbone, a red welt was forming.

"Where else?"

She put her hand up to her right shoulder, said nothing.

His feelings were too disordered to bear. He wanted to slap her for her defiant folly; he wanted terribly to kiss her.

He flung himself out of the hack, tossed up a coin, led the girl to the Saverys' doorstep.

They went in the front hall; he noted dimly the absence of threatening sounds in the calm, shuttered house, the still street.

He threw off his cloak and beaver, turned to Bernadette.

She stood there, dazed, her hands across her folded shawl, looking at him as though he were the only person in the world.

It was then he saw the spot of blood seeping through the cloth underneath her crossed right arm.

"You're bleeding!" he exclaimed.

She looked down, seemed even more stunned than he.

He reached and took away her shawl. "You need camphor, towels, water." He led the way to the kitchen, to the dry sink where the water basin stood.

She followed him, simply waited.

He turned.

To help her he must touch her, must manage to get at her shoulder.

He pulled the huck towel from the bar.

A door slammed; there were quick footsteps in the hall. "Bernadette?"

"Here," he called hoarsely.

Hester's chiseled expression dissolved in relief; then, at the sight of bloody cloth, congealed again in anxiety.

"Dear child, what happened?"

Automatically, Hester took the water basin from Robb, reached for Bernadette's high, round collar, undid the buttons — not ripping as he, in his shaking anguish, his fear of himself, would surely have done.

Over Hester's head Bernadette looked at him steadily. He looked steadily back.

Touch me, her eyes pleaded. *Why couldn't we ever have touched each other?*

My darling, everything in him cried, *why couldn't we? Why couldn't we?*

Then, without another word, he went out of the kitchen.

He fled, saw nothing, saw no one, lived within himself.

After a time he slowed down, began to wander aimlessly.

And so he came back to Philadelphia Hall; it rose in the half-dark. The mob was still there; soon he was jostled and closed in on all sides, trapped and helpless among the excited throng.

While he watched, a man with a blazing torch ran forth, disappeared inside one of the front doors. Dumbly, he fell backward with the others; there was a keening, a shouting, then an awful silence when the first flames roared up.

Upstairs at a window a black gnomelike figure leaped past, a hot fountain rising up in its wake.

Robb tried to break loose then of the maddening human fetters, tried to rush inside the door. Fiends were setting the fires — he'd stop them. No, he yearned to be in that hall, to burn in the flames.

Everywhere fires were growing — from single pyre to scarlet sheet, from sporadic crackling to continuous roaring.

Suddenly the horror of his impulse invaded him, brought back his reason. What was he doing here? Why, they'd set Philadelphia Hall on fire! Where were the fire-fighters, where were the city police? If no one came to help, it'd burn down completely.

In a wakening frenzy he got out of the crowd, rushed through the noisy darkness.

Duty was what there was. He must do his duty.

250

"Police?" he grabbed a passerby.

"They've been here. Mayor, too. I think they went away. Firemen, too."

Fire-fighters, police, mayor — all had apparently abandoned the hall. He walked away, sickened but sane.

Duty was what there was. A man must make his way in God's ungentle world; must decide, then must live with what duty he'd chosen . . .

Oh, what this day had brought!

Job had said, "Let the day perish."

Robb, turning his face up to the ruddy night sky from the blasted hall, saw that Job's wish had come true.

Philadelphia Hall, memorial to the need of the oppressed for safety, was burned to the ground on the night of Thursday, May 17, 1838.

At eight o'clock, with the street still packed, the public lamps in the neighborhood went out. With darkness an ally, the mob broke down the doors. By the time the mayor and the police arrived, fires had already been kindled; pipes had even been ripped from walls and explosive illumination gas recklessly played on the roaring fires.

The police withdrew completely.

When the firemen arrived, they ignored the hall and spent their efforts protecting nearby buildings.

At ten o'clock, the roof caved in. At eleven, the interior was gone.

Shortly afterwards, two thousand onlookers, themselves in danger, cheered wildly as the front of the hall collapsed.

To save his life, friends spirited Garrison out of town. And a gang attacking the home of James and Lucretia Mott was led off by an unknown Abolitionist.

251

Friday morning, in the borrowed schoolroom of Sarah Pugh, the women Abolitionists reconvened. The Grimké sisters were elected vice-presidents of the convention.

The same morning Robb took Hester and Bernadette to Leach's railway terminal to escape the mob-torn city. The talk between him and Hester was wholly practical.

He didn't talk to Bernadette at all.

When the engine bell clanged, he looked at her at last.

"Goodbye," he said — didn't ask that she write him, didn't express the hope they would meet again.

"Goodbye," she answered softly, trying to read him.

He wouldn't let her: never had he really let her.

She wheeled, climbed into the car; through the window he followed that beautiful woman-gesture of hand to hair as she took off her bonnet.

He certainly couldn't stay to watch *that* train pull out.

His heart dead inside him, he strode away.

 28

SHE AND HESTER rode Leach's railroad west; the wild Appalachian country flowed past at four miles an hour.

Dragging valises, they climbed on a canal barge on the third day. On the afternoon of the seventh day they reached Hollidaysburg at the foot of the Alleghenies where they toted their luggage onto a brigade of little cars.

Powerful engines — each equivalent to sixty horses — pulled them up five great inclined planes to the summit of the vast Appalachian barrier. To the west, over the mountains, a summer storm raged.

The next noon they reached Johnstown.

Dragging valises again, they boarded a canalboat which slid and locked along the Conemaugh to raw young Pittsburgh.

"Lord help us, Bernadette," Hester sighed, hoisting her valise onto the rope berth of the Ohio River packet, "Cincinnati's next. I hope I last."

Bernadette had finally, for all time, deserted the hot, squalling women's cabin for weather-swept deck. The great Ohio twisted and bent, then broadened serenely. Log cabins scarred the unbroken forest; birds rose, wings beating. The trip evoked long ago memories of childhood journeys along the St. Lawrence.

But this river was a blur to Bernadette; its sights, sounds, scents were only background to the voyage of her own thoughts.

Her feelings for Robb in chaos, she kept coming back to the way he'd left her. In his stony silence, no tenderness, no promises.

Goodbye. She kept whispering it over and over, trying to make herself understand it.

But try as she would, either by feeling or reason, in pain and in terror, she couldn't envision a world without him.

The packet rounded a bend and there was Cincinnati. Hester, she thought, wasn't the only one who'd barely made it.

There at the boat landing waved Uncle Marcus!

"He has a beard," she murmured.

"His face is broader," his daughter Hester replied. "He looks a little stooped, yet not so much older."

"He looks good," Bernadette breathed.

Home to Uncle Marcus, his bearlike hug, the reliable affection of his glance.

The woodsmen, planters, German peasants, the waterfront dancing and fiddling places, the wide streets farther up the

253

low hills filled with spanking barouches and lined with clapboard houses — she didn't absorb any of it.

"You've growed into a right handsome, polite girl, lovey," Uncle Marcus teased, obviously pleasured by her. "Hester, you and McIves done well."

At first it was better; she was home. Home was no place to be lonely.

But little by little she began to learn she couldn't sweep her life clear of memory.

Even with Uncle Marcus, even with Hester, even with talk about the future — talk of Oberlin, for instance . . .

After she'd been at the farm several weeks, Uncle Marcus said casually, "Oh, by the way, long ago I laid something aside for you. He gave it to me to give to you before he had any idea he'd ever see you again."

He went ponderously into the dining room with his old man's step, came back with a card, handed it to her, watched innocently.

She recognized who it was instantly.

She held in her hand a black paper silhouette some simple itinerate country artist had cut of Robb McIves and mounted on a little card.

Stupified, she looked at the forehead, nose, lips, chin of a perfect stranger. Robb, black and blank.

Her stricken eyes must have spoken to Uncle Marcus.

"Well, I know," he murmured. " 'Tis not much of a likeness, is it? But what's it matter anyway? You know what he looks like; you've lived with him."

"Yes," she stammered. "It doesn't matter."

But somehow it mattered a lot; somehow it came to be a symbol, not of their separateness, but of what she couldn't solve between them — what was lost in his untelling darkness.

She began to carry the card with her everywhere, hid it in pockets of jackets and skirts, in aprons.

She was carrying the silhouette one noon when she finished helping Aunt Leah stuff pillows with new feathers. When Aunt Leah went off to sew up the ticking, Bernadette wandered across the farmyard, walked aimlessly into the woods.

Hoping for places of past joy, always hoping for places where this new memory wouldn't chase her.

She'd walked here a lot since she'd been back; Trev would have loved to explore here.

The stifling heat pressed down on her. She found a huge fallen log, leaned against it, took the snip-out from her pocket, studied Robb's blankness, looked up, unseeing.

Slowly saw . . . a wooded loneliness.

Let herself feel the great silent trees footed in dead forest debris. No animal, no bird, not even an insect visible for company. Not even wind; the leaves hung stilly. Not even sound, none at all. No color, either: browns, blacks, murkish greens — way up, a white sky.

Realized she'd always been terrified of the no-oneness here.

Could hardly breathe, let alone run away.

I'm lonely for him; lonely beyond telling.

She was a lonely child again, hunting a space, a home.

Of all the painful things she'd felt, being an orphan was worst.

("*From time to time, everyone in their life's an orphan,*" Miss Sarah had said to Miss Angelina. "*In the spirit,*" Miss Angelina had smiled back.)

Good bye; he'd said; not even "Write me."

Suddenly it came — not a soft sound to break the spell, certainly not a poetic one: the sharp, workaday tattoo of an invisible flicker against a tree tunk.

255

She put her face in her hands, listened to that rude symbol of life and energy.

I have to begin to live alone.

I'm separate from him.

But being afraid of the loneliness of that, trying not to feel it, running away from it, only made it worse.

She took a first struggling breath; it felt like the first breath she'd drawn in Ohio.

She felt that in those last few seconds she'd explored to the ends of *I am alone* — not fought it, not fled it.

Loneliness could tell you who you were, and knowing, you were released.

Loneliness was risk, could ravage, waited for change times.

But loneliness was natural. It was real and alive. It was part of the orphan in each of us.

You grew whole from knowing it was there.

She got up, touched the tree trunk, felt it. A dark, shiny beetle crawled between her fingers, scuttled blindly out again.

The wind set up a sudden sighing, leaves rattling.

She started to run up the trail, paused, hovered, glanced back at the great, hot, shut-in grove.

Here she'd drawn a first breath in the infinite spaces of the world.

Here for a healing instant she'd found a psychic turf, a hearth for herself.

Loneliness, her wondering heart said.

Then, *Loneliness, yes.*

That night, with the lamp wavering and an owl softly hoo-ing in the buckeye tree, her pen sped across the page. No indecision in that racing.

"Dear Angelina Weld," she wrote, "You've never really answered for sure about my drawing for *Slavery As It Is.* I'll

256

be seventeen after next winter at Oberlin and Ohio's close to Kentucky. I hope you can use what I draw for your book. But even if you can't I mean to draw it anyway . . ."